For Mom
who let a boy's imagination run free

CRUMBLING EMPIRE

EMPIRE OF THE PEAKS BOOK 3

ADAM J. MANGUM

ROCKET CROSSING

ISBN: 978-1-945359-15-6

ALSO BY ADAM J. MANGUM

The Empire of the Peaks

Assassins & Rebels

Peak Crosser

Wayward Flight

Crumbling Empire

The Sycorax Series

Caliban's World

Seeds and Masters

Claribel and Caliban

GUILT AND FAILURE

Zandia's eyes snapped open, her mind grappling with facts that seemed too slippery. Where was she? She breathed in and smelled trees, a distant hearth. She was in the woods outside of Thandar's farm. She looked around, but even her blessed eyes saw little more than darkness. She moved, but it was slow, groggy, like when she'd been sick as a child and her entire body had felt caught in a web.

She stood suddenly, the facts snapping together into clarity. The girls. Trillia Magistrate had taken the girls!

Zandia had tried to stop her, but Trillia and her giant had drugged her, and she must have been unconscious for a bit. How long had she been out?

Zandia reached out with her mind to sense the time, though nothing came back. At her neck, blood had congealed around the brastilia spike. She growled and yanked it out.

At once, the world erupted in her senses. Four hours since she'd been drugged. She'd slept too long. Where were the girls?

Mayfran. She sent the thought out to her not-Shindar and could feel his mind.

Zandia, came his panicked reply. *I've been trying to reach out to you for hours! I couldn't even feel you.*

She told him the entire tale as succinctly as she could, including her desire to deprive Trillia and Mabhif of their limbs. For once, he did not try to quell her murderous rage.

If the Dundraz wanted the girls, why didn't they take them when they took Calla? he asked.

She's not Dundraz, Zandia thought back. *Maybe it's that other group you've heard about. Maybe it's the Empire.*

Zandia sensed his agreement through their bond. *You've got to make sure Calla's parents are okay, and go get the girls.*

Calla's parents. Zandia looked over at the house, which was dark now, the lamps inside burnt out. She'd failed her nieces; she could not fail the parents of her brother's wife. She tucked the small, bloody brastilia spike into her pocket and ran toward the house.

She closed her eyes. Thankfully the second sight came and she could see Calla's parents through the walls of the house, their glows still red with life. Zandia opened her eyes as she reached the front door and burst through, stopping when she reached the kitchen.

Thandar and Caladria lay on the floor, their shallow breaths verifying what her second sight had seen. Zandia searched the pantry and saw an open bag of herbs. She smelled the contents to confirm it was what she needed. She took a small handful and, kneeling next to Caladria, cradled the woman's head in one hand and crushed the herbs in the other, bringing it close to her face.

Caladria's eyes shot open. Upon seeing Zandia in the slight moonlight, she flinched, then her muscles relaxed. "Oh, Zandia! You're alive."

"As are you." Zandia managed a small smile, taking care not to show too much of her wicked teeth.

"Where are the girls?" Caladria asked, her voice cracking with emotion.

"I don't know. It's been several hours since Trillia left with them. She may have already fled the valley."

Caladria held back a sob, tears falling in a stream. "Go get them," she said. "I'll wake Thandar. Go find our girls."

Zandia helped Caladria into a sitting position, and after she was sure the woman wouldn't fall right back over, she sprinted from the house toward the town. Instinctively, she reached for her missing hatnuthri. Even without her brastilia short swords, she was deadly, but against something like Mabhif, Trillia's half-giant, she needed more, so she changed her destination and ran to Zornan's house.

Zornan's house was quiet, with the air of a place no one had lived in or even had been in for days. She found the crawlspace underneath the stairs. With one swift kick, she knocked the lock from its hinge. Very little moonlight shone through the windows of the sitting room, so she closed her eyes, opening herself up to the second sight, and the brastilia weapons gave off their familiar green glow. Three hatrindi and two hatari (both in short form) caught her vision, though she'd wished for a pair of hatnuthri. She'd trained with all weapons, of course, and excelled in each, but hatnuthri were as comfortable as her own hands.

She picked up a hatari and opened her eyes, commanding the weapon into full length and weighing it with a twirl. This was the best choice. A hatrindi was not long enough; she would need to keep her distance from Mabhif's massive paws. If she fell into his grip again, she likely wouldn't escape alive.

Shrinking the hatari to make it easier to run with, she sprinted from Zornan's house and down the dark streets of the town. Usually, she would have worried about stealth, but not tonight. She ran as fast as she could, still feeling a little sluggish from whatever that accursed woman had given her. Hopefully, she was enough of herself to do what needed to be done.

Zandia came to a stop across the street from what she believed to be the Magistrate's home — the largest in town with three stories when everything else was two. When she opened her second sight, the soft green glow of brastilia permeated through, evidence of a rich person. Yes, this was the Magistrate's home.

She scanned the structure and saw only one orange glow: a living person in a second-floor room. Only one, though, and it wasn't a giant or a child, but a regular-sized adult. Zandia cursed under her breath. Who could it be? The person looked like they were lying down. Not Trillia; the Magistrate wouldn't nap with a Baldra chasing her. Zandia considered ignoring the house and circling toward the tunnel entrance, but perhaps Trillia and her giant were there, concealed by some unknown magic, like the spike that had blocked some of her abilities. Or maybe the person there would know where Trillia was.

Zandia crossed the street, running toward the space below the second-floor window next to where the orange glow had been. She reached top speed and jumped, hoping her dulled abilities wouldn't stop her. She climbed into the air, growing the hatari with a thought, pointing it toward the oncoming window. The glass shattered, and Zandia's extended leg finished the job. She landed and rolled, her weapon pointed toward where the glow would be.

But nothing moved. She closed her eyes, and the orange glow appeared as a shape on the floor. The glow dimmed ever so slightly. Dead, and for some time. She hadn't been able to tell that from across the street, maybe because of her addled mind. Zandia stood, then stuck the hatari into her belt after shrinking it. In the darkness, even her blessed eyes could see nothing, so she knelt next to the body and felt the dead person's face. Old, but too much fat for Trillia. It didn't take long to find the cause of death — the person's neck had been snapped, just like a giant might kill someone.

Sensing it close by, Zandia brought to life a glow globe in the corner of the room, keeping it dim. She only needed a little light. On the floor lay an older woman dressed in modest night clothes. A servant, or perhaps a neighbor who'd looked in at the wrong time? But why kill this woman and leave Thandar and Caladria alive?

She scanned the small room; it was certainly a servant's bedroom. The bed was unmade, recently slept in. They had come back to kill her. She'd known too much. Caladria and Thandar knew little. Still, even with her befuddled mind, Zandia knew something was off. If Trillia was some terrible monster, why leave Calla's parents alive? They would tell the story to whomever asked, and a dead servant would dump further suspicion at the Magistrate's feet.

Knowing she was missing too many rocks to fill in this wall, Zandia jumped from the house. She had to assume they were gone now, and she had to hope they hadn't left the valley yet, though her hope grew dim. This had been planned. The servant had been killed before they went to gather Windsa and Caldry, her brother's daughters. She would have readied transportation.

Zandia landed on the street. A house opposite had a light in the window where a woman stood, mouth agape at seeing Zandia. Too late for Zandia to pull up her hood; the woman had likely seen Zandia's ghostly features in the moonlight. No matter. She ran toward the tunnel.

When she reached the edge of the woods near the tunnel entrance, two Enforcers stood there, glow globes burning around them, and off to the side, stood a plain-clothed guard as if he wasn't sure of his place. Zandia paused, then stepped into the light.

"Demon's claws," the guard mumbled, not even reaching for the sword on his hip.

"Stay out of this fight," Zandia said to the man, who stood still, clearly following her advice.

The Enforcers attacked, but they were slow, and Zandia quickly disarmed one with a strike to his hand. She ducked away from the other, picking up the first one's dropped hatrindi, blocking two strikes with her hatari, when the second Enforcer lunged again. She faked a parry, then dodged, spinning the hatrindi and decapitating him with a fierce stroke.

She turned to the other Enforcer on his knees holding his bleeding hand. "Where did the Magistrate go?"

"Rot on the Fire Moon."

"She wouldn't have told you anyway." Zandia plunged the hatrindi into his chest, sinking it to the hilt. She didn't bother pulling it out and let him flop to the ground, his life seeping from him.

She turned to the guard, who quivered down onto his knees, mumbling pleas to spare his life so he could care for his children.

"I'm not going to hurt you," Zandia said. She'd tried to remove all malice from her voice, though she wasn't sure she'd succeeded. His eyes said she probably had not. "How did the Magistrate leave?"

"Using a private ferry." The man had barely choked out his reply.

"When?"

"Hours ago."

"Where to?"

He shook his head.

"Where to!?" This time, she infused the question with a growl.

The man sunk to the ground, sobbing. "I don't know. I didn't see them leave. Please, moons above, help me, believe me!"

She's gone. Mayfran's voice came into her mind.

Yes. I'm going to find a sled and follow her. Zandia turned from the man and walked into the tunnel.

Follow her where? Fallindra is a central location. She could have gone in any of three directions, and then from there, in a dozen more.

So, what do you suggest? she snapped. *Do nothing?*

No. Mayfran paused, and Zandia could sense his unease. It calmed her. She wasn't alone in this. *But we need to assure the safety of Calla's parents. They may be in danger. I'm sending men to Fallindra. Wait for them, and they will escort Calla's parents to safety.*

Zandia backed out of the tunnel and walked past the guard, who hadn't moved from his prostrate position.

For the first time in years, she felt guilt well up. At first, it was hard to recognize regret's close cousin. But no, this was stronger than that.

That quivering man deserved none of this; he was a guard doing his duty. She looked over at the Enforcers' corpses. They had also been doing their duty, and in her rage, she hadn't realized she knew one of them; he'd been there when she'd arrived at the farmhouse. Maybe they had been evil associates of Trillia, or maybe, like many Enforcers, they were simply bullies, or worse, rapists and thieves. But maybe they hadn't been, and she'd cut through them as if their lives hadn't mattered, as if she were still under the dark compulsion of the ruthless Dundraz. She turned away.

It's not your fault, Mayfran soothed, sensing her deep remorse. *You are unlearning what you learned; it takes time.*

Those men will still be dead. That guard will carry me into his nightmares for the rest of his life.

Focus, Zandia. His words struck her like a blow, and the guilt faded. An order, inadvertent or not. She was glad to give up ownership of her decisions; she didn't do well making them herself. *Wait for my men to come, and then you can go find Trillia, or return to the valley, or go hunt your father. But make sure Calla's parents are safe.*

Unsure if compulsion or something else fueled her, Zandia sprinted into the woods back toward Thandar's farm, which she reached a few minutes later, her full strength nearly restored. Lamps lit the house like it was just after moons rise.

Caladria stood in the kitchen, boiling water for tea, and Thandar sat at the table. They both looked up when she entered. The old farmer flinched, afraid of her as always, but Caladria's eyes held no fear, only hope that Zandia would now have to dash away.

"Trillia is gone," she said, unable to meet their eyes. "The girls are gone on a ferry to moons-know-where, and it's my fault, I failed those little girls . . ."

Zandia fell to her knees, sobbing for the first time as an adult. She had once been a girl in need of rescue and everyone had failed her: her brothers, her mother — no one had been there to save her from the terrors. And now, she'd failed Windsa and Caldry in the same way.

A moment before Zandia thought she might collapse, Caladria

wrapped her arms around her. "Hush, girl. We all failed them." And Caladria shook with sobs of her own.

How long before Thandar climbed onto the floor and wrapped his arms around both women, Zandia could not tell. No one spoke as they all cried.

2

THE REBELS

Travel to the Thick was slow and plodding, and Jayzca spent most of the time between worlds or with Chage in the Otherworld. She groaned, feeling grumpy as they traveled, muttering about Chage and her father and someone named Cha-something. The sarcastic girl Mizcarnon had met in Mazz had been replaced by an unpleasant, frustrated one.

Mizcarnon's feelings mirrored the girl's. They traveled toward rebels, which gave Mizcarnon some hope, but the road was not easy, and Mizcarnon was not fully recovered from his wounds, so each step brought discomfort. Their guide was Jix, a massive man who offered no conversation because he could not; his tongue had been removed by Nansartan soldiers. With Jayzca sulking and rarely in their world, and a mute guide, Mizcarnon could do nothing but fly in his own dark thoughts.

They traveled with a single doofa, staying off the main road just west of the White Mountain and its smaller twin, the Black Mountain. Four days into the journey, they were safely out of range of the Nansartan army camp. Since Shin'Ra, Mizcarnon's captor, was dead, it was likely the Nansartans did not fully understand what had happened in their camp. But one thing would be clear: the Mazzdu had someone who could summon a Hol'Feel'Koo, and that would bring the eyes of the conqueror Nansart.

Mizcarnon wished he could talk with Jix, not just to fill up the time. Jix was a Croxshinese rebel, and Mizcarnon wanted to know more about the resistance before walking into the secluded camp. Were there lots of rebels? Had they been successful in any way? Was there any tactic or path that had slowed or wounded the invaders? Mizcarnon had already voiced some of these questions, hoping he and Jix could communicate through gestures and yes-or-no answers. But Jix had made no attempt to answer any questions unrelated to their current journey.

On the fourth day, Jayzca walked with them, having left the Otherworld behind for a time. She'd been even more sullen than before.

"Is everything all right?" Mizcarnon asked.

Her face tightened, and a crease appeared on her brow. "No," she said, though she would say no more about her disagreement with Chage or her other worries.

On the morning of the fifth day, Jix pointed across a deep river. On their side, it was forested with broad, tall trees and some undergrowth. Across the river stood the Thick. The air had grown heavier as they traveled. Now it hung like a curtain, thick and wet. The jungle across the river had shorter trees with broader leaves and a dense undergrowth dotted with colorful flowers. But the biggest difference was the noise: a mixture of animals, buzzing insects, and the din of the slow-moving river; it drowned out even the sound of Mizcarnon's own breath.

After pointing across the river, Jix sat down next to the doofa to eat some dried fruit.

"How are we going to cross?" Mizcarnon asked.

Jix answered by pointing back across the river, then moving his flat hand slowly back toward himself.

"I think he's trying to tell us a boat will come for us," Jayzca said.

Mizcarnon peered out across the river. Had they already been seen by Jix's rebel friends? The Thick was so dense, they could easily have spotters at the river's edge observing the forest with little chance of detection.

Mizcarnon wanted a mrakaro, wanted to take to the air to get a better view of the Thick, and he wondered if he'd made the right choice in following Jix instead of returning to find the wild giant flyers living on the White Mountain. But in the end, he'd decided to trust Dina, the rebel who'd helped them after their escep, and Jix. With a silent guide and a sullen girl on the banks of a deep river, however, he questioned the wisdom of his decision.

As the day drifted toward afternoon, they waited there silently, eating dried fruit. Humidity had made the air oppressive, their clothes wet with a mixture of water and their own sweat. Mizcarnon considered himself a patient man, though the stress of this frayed his usually calm nerves.

As the heavy sun hung over the Thick, a noise from across the river startled Mizcarnon and Jayzca. Jix sat still, unaffected by the sudden bellows.

Mizcarnon stood and looked across the river, yet he saw nothing. The sound came a second time — a horn of some kind, high and strong. When the call rent the air a third time, he finally saw some movement.

To the south and to the north, about twenty yards in each direction, men emerged carrying large rafts. All of them were armed, swords hanging from their sides, many with bows strapped across their chests. Without looking at Mizcarnon and Jayzca, they set their boats down and paddled across the river to the forested side.

As the first two rafts approached, a third raft emerged from the

Thick directly across from Mizcarnon — a smaller craft, carried by six men. After they'd placed it into the river and four men had taken rowing positions, a woman emerged from a jungle, small in both height and fame. Her face looked young, although Mizcarnon had never been a very good judge of those things. She wore a dark red shirt and brown leather pants, their cleanliness contrasting with the mud- and sweat-covered clothing of the men surrounding her. She wore short swords on each hip.

After the woman stepped on board, the four rowers guided the flat raft across the river, with two other men flanking her, bows in hand but arrows still in their quivers.

Jix finally stood, eyes showing nothing; his silence stretched beyond words.

Mizcarnon looked over at Jayzca, but she was gone, inevitably watching the scene from between the worlds. Had the Croxshinese rebels seen her disappear? What would they make of that? On his first visit to Croxshine, he'd never even heard of Mazzdu magic, and he suspected that most Croxshinese knew little beyond superstitious rumors.

The men rowing did so deliberately, maintaining a straight, slow course across the broad river. The woman remained standing, impossibly still, her face set as stone. But under her glare, Mizcarnon refused to flinch or look away. He'd spoken face to face with the Emperor, had successfully stared down High Counselor Lanthia. He would not shrink under the eyes of this woman, regardless of who she was.

The woman's raft hit the shore just feet from where Mizcarnon stood next to Jix. A rustling in the trees came to his right and to his left, but he did not look. The other rafts had disembarked and had taken up flanking positions.

The woman regarded him for some time before she finally spoke in a familiar Croxshinese accent, an accent from the city of Damdi. "Who are you? And why has Jix brought you to our camp?"

During their march from Kalsrah, Mizcarnon had considered a dozen cover stories but had decided on the truth instead. He had to trust someone or he'd never get home. "My name is Mizcarnon Peak Crosser, and I come from the Empire of the Peaks, a great land across the northern sea."

The woman's eyes widened. "Yet you speak our language."

"This is not my first visit to your land. I came here four years ago, and before that, I was tutored by a Croxshinese man."

"Why have you come to Croxshine?" she asked, using the name of the fallen kingdom.

"To better understand the threat the Nansartans might pose to our Empire. When Jix and his companions indicated they knew of an active rebellion, I thought we might be able to help one another."

The woman snorted. "Help one another? Are you offering aid to our small rebellion?"

"No. I have no aid to offer, except maybe my knowledge of their weapons and magic."

"You have the powers they have?" She turned her head slightly to the side.

Mizcarnon nodded. "I am a Peak Crosser, and as such, I have certain blessings."

"What blessings?"

"I am stronger than all but the strongest men. I can fly on the back of a giant flyer without getting sick. I can speak to other blessed through our minds. And I can use and work our brastilia weapons." He briefly considered using his hatari to verify his claim, but dismissed the display as too aggressive.

"Can you bless others with such power?" she asked.

"No. We have Priestesses called Bendathdrans, and they are the only ones who possess the power to bless."

The woman shook her head. "No, your Priestesses aren't the only ones. Our conqueror knows how to bestow these blessings." She walked forward to stand before Mizcarnon. She was short, with long, black hair pulled up behind her head. "I am Kirna, one of the leaders of our camp. If you fight Nansart, then you are very welcome."

Across the broad Three Mountain River sat the rebel camp, nestled deep in the Thick, to the west and south of the bend where the river turned. It was more a small town than a village. They'd carved something out of this un-tamable land, with some farming and a few crude buildings, and most of the camp's inhabitants looked like the men who'd accompanied Kirna at the river: dirty, armed, and stoic. But others lived in the camp, too, including children chasing each other with sticks and adults sewing clothing or working metal. Like Kirna, most of the women were armed, and some even walked with the male soldiers as equals.

Mizcarnon had thought it possible Kirna was not a leader but a scout sent to ascertain Mizcarnon's worthiness. Her position among the rebels became clear, though, as they walked through the camp — both men and women bowed their heads toward her, and she acknowledged them in return with a nod.

As they reached what appeared to be the camp's center, Mizcarnon noticed a collection of small buildings at its northern edge, a section that contrasted the rest of the camp in its silence and lack of people.

"What is that?" Mizcarnon asked, pointing to the isolated buildings.

"That," Kirna answered without breaking stride or looking at him, "is where our sick recover." Her eyes went down and her voice went soft. "We have a lot of sick."

They walked up to a large tent with heavy leather draped over a large frame. The door flap lay open, tied back.

Kirna stopped short of the doorway to look up at Mizcarnon. "What of the girl?"

For a moment, he couldn't think of whom she meant. But of course, she'd seen Jayzca on the shore before she disappeared. What did the rest of Croxshine know or believe about the Mazzdu? Was Jayzca standing next to him between worlds, watching and listening?

Before Mizcarnon could respond, Jayzca appeared in front of him, dark eyes on Kirna.

"I am here," she said, as if her sudden appearance was nothing remarkable.

Kirna stepped back, her stony confidence shattered if only briefly. She regarded the small Mazzdu girl. "What are you?"

"I am Mazzdu," Jayzca replied. "And I hate Nansart as much as anyone in this camp. Do your plans include erasing the Nansartans from our lands?"

Kirna smiled, like one did at an overeager child, and Mizcarnon hoped Jayzca did not take offense at the patronizing glance.

"Of course," the Croxshinese rebel said.

"Then, when it is appropriate, we will talk more." And Jayzca disappeared as quickly as she'd come.

Kirna turned to Mizcarnon. "Does she do that often?" she asked.

"Too often," Mizcarnon replied, smiling at the space where Jayzca had stood. Was she still there? Would she be amused or annoyed by the Peak Crosser's flippant response?

Kirna smiled as well, then walked into the tent. Mizcarnon followed. Jix, who had trailed them through the camp, bowed and strode away with the four soldiers who'd marched with them.

Though several standing oil lamps were spread throughout the tent, none burned, and the only light came from the door. The space was nearly filled with people all dressed similarly to Kirna: dark red tops and leather pants, although a few wore scraps of metal armor. Like the soldiers, their weapons varied from swords to knives to staffs to scimitars, similar to the Mazzdu. The weapons also varied in quality, from the most well-designed and polished, to quick metalsmith work done in the haste of wartime.

"This is your command center." Mizcarnon eyed the maps lying on wobbly tables and those tacked against the leather walls. Conversation filled the space, though most had hushed, all gazes falling on the outsider.

"Yes." Kirna turned to address the crowd. "This is Mizcarnon Peak Crosser of the Empire of the Peaks."

Some responded with knowing nods, others with narrowed eyes.

A small man approached whose eyes and face were younger than Kirna's. Mizcarnon looked around; most of those in the room were young, only a handful beyond their third decade.

"General Ornuo," the man said, addressing Kirna.

"I've told you, Nuno, I prefer less formality," she chided with no bite in her words.

"Of course, General," Nuno replied, not recognizing his own irony. "We are ready for war council; we've been waiting on you." The small man slipped away.

"You didn't tell me you were a general," Mizcarnon said.

"I'm the highest ranking officer we have left," she replied. The grief in her voice was nearly as thick as the moisture in the air. "Come. You should hear our council, and then we can show you all we know about our enemy."

3

NEW VISIONS

C alla sat in her chair, hands tugging at her skirt, face pulled into a harsh scowl when she didn't think about smoothing it. For the past hour, she'd been trying to read, but she couldn't concentrate on the text. Somewhere out there, Zornan searched tirelessly, possibly trading the man she'd fallen in love with for a more vicious version, all in the hope of bringing her home.

Though she couldn't control it completely, Calla could bring on the visions after some focused concentration. Well, not every time she tried, but most times. She'd seen Crisdan talking with a mustachioed man in Kandrinal, and she'd seen Zornan settling into an inn in the same city. How had fate brought her husband and the High Investigator to the same place?

Most times, though, the visions were nothing more than watching Zornan eat or Crisdan talking with his Enforcer companion. Now that she could somewhat control it, she saw everything from the vital to the innocuous, unlike before, when the visions had only been powerful moments.

So, she tried to read, but she couldn't focus. What if she missed something important? It didn't matter, partly; she'd been unable to communicate with either of them so she couldn't affect the events, just observe them. Completely different from mindspeak or the bond between a Shindar and her Baldra.

She set the book down to consider Crisdan's mental conversation with Trillia. They were tracking Calla, as well, hunting for a Dundraz spy in Kandrinal, possibly the opulent Magistrate Calla had observed. She'd also felt some of Crisdan's emotions. His heart burned to find her. Yes, Trillia commanded him, but Crisdan wanted to find her, wanted to rescue her, and the thought of his fervent search thrilled her.

A wave of guilt struck. Did she still have feelings buried somewhere deep in her heart for the Investigator? Why were the visions limited to these two men? Her husband made sense — if the moons were going to bless her with the ability to see through someone else's eyes, then seeing through her husband seemed good and right. But seeing through the eyes of a man she'd nearly cheated on her husband with, a man who had kissed her when she'd been at her most vulnerable? She remembered the kiss with shame, but she'd rejected him, which proved her love for Zornan, didn't it? Crisdan had become different, though, and now Calla understood why. Trillia had conquered his will. The last time she'd seen Crisdan, he'd seemed different, remorseful for the kiss, and the anger she'd harbored against him had begun to fade. He'd not been acting entirely of his own accord.

Calla shook her head and closed her eyes, the hot fire of shame burning in her bosom. Here she was thinking about Crisdan, when she should have been focusing on Zornan. Didn't really matter whether or not Crisdan's will had been his own; Calla should not have led him on to the point where cementing their relationship through touch would have been a potential next step. Zornan deserved better, and Calla knew she was better than that.

But her mind would not leave Crisdan and Trillia. That woman! Calla had trusted her, done what the Magistrate had told her to do. Calla had let a monster become part of their lives. What other horrible things was that woman capable of?

Another vision arrived unbidden, light filtering into a small room. The view was low, like Calla was kneeling. But it wasn't her own eyes she saw through; it was the eyes of someone else. Whose? Zornan's?

Someone sobbed nearby, and the view turned. Caldry, sweet little Caldry, lay on a mattress on the floor in the near-darkness. A small hand reached out and stroked Caldry's short, dark hair.

"Shhhh," came a soft, little voice. Windsa. She saw through Windsa's eyes! Calla forced her own eyes to stay shut, forced the vision to remain. Why was Caldry crying? The room was not familiar — not her home nor her parents' home. Where were her children?

A door opened, and Windsa turned to a small figure who stood silhouetted with sunshine at its back. A larger silhouette appeared behind the first, blocking out almost all the doorway's light.

"I told you to keep your sister quiet," a voice said, its menace altogether both foreign and familiar. Trillia spoke, though she was not the kind, intelligent woman Calla knew, but the terrible, cruel woman from Calla's visions.

"She's scared," Windsa replied, unable to keep the fear from her own quivering voice. Tears leaked from Calla's closed eyes.

Trillia stepped away from the doorway, her face now half-revealed in the bright light, and her gaze softened and became almost tender. Calla wanted to scream at her, scream that she didn't get to show kindness when she was . . . What *was* she doing? Had she taken the children? What had happened in Fallindra?

"Our father will find you." Caldry looked up, her face stained by tears and snot, her short, dark hair matted against her head. "I've watched him practice fight. He's even better than your giant. He'll find us and free us."

Trillia smiled, that same smile that had always made Calla want to smile back, almost as if she had to smile back. But in her room in the capital, Calla didn't smile, and neither did Caldry.

"Your father will try," the Magistrate replied. "He's tenacious, but he's a fool. A well-meaning fool. They are the worst kind."

Caldry moved so fast it was a blur, leaping from the ground to tackle Trillia. Windsa gasped, stepping forward, but then she stopped as Trillia's giant lifted the smaller girl up into the air like Caldry was a tiny stick and not a little person. Caldry shook violently, swiping as vehemently as she could, but the giant's arms were too long, and when she scratched his hand, he didn't even flinch. He tossed her back to the ground, then stood between Calla's youngest and the Magistrate.

"Juthrana," Trillia cursed, standing. Blood trickled down her cheek, oozing from a scratch of about two or three inches long between her nose and her cheekbone. "This stone didn't roll very far from the peak." Calla feared Trillia might be angry, might lash back, yet her eyes held no anger, just surprise.

"Someday, you will understand all this," the woman continued. "Someday, you will understand I did this for your good. Your father is a good man, but a naive one, and dangerous. Your mother . . ." She trailed off, her eyes fixed on the light behind her. "By the light of all three moons, I hope she will forgive me."

Then the vision faded, and Calla screamed. She slid from her chair to the floor and curled into a ball, trying to bring the vision back, trying to see again through Windsa's eyes. Nothing came but darkness and sorrow, and she sobbed. Her sweet girls were caught up in these snares, held by a woman as despicable as any under the moons. Thinking of the Magistrate brought on a wave of nausea and disgust. She remained curled up on the cold floor, crying out for her children.

Sometime later, strong arms lifted her into her bed. Calla didn't bother opening her eyes. She'd been frantically screaming and crying, and she had no doubt Leanda's guards thought she'd lost her mind. But she didn't care. She was trapped with no escape, and her girls were trapped as well. Calla shuddered and curled into her oversized pillows.

Oh Zornan! Don't come for me, Zor! Go for the girls. Find our girls! Did he even know they were in danger? Away from Fallindra searching for Calla, Zornan likely didn't know.

The darkness of her mind's eye suddenly dissipated, and Calla instinctively knew she'd found Zornan's mind. He sat in a common room of an inn or a tavern, eating tuber stew, his favorite meal. Mairie sat across from him, eating some kind of flatbread dipped into a thick, grainy sauce. As Zornan's eyes turned, Maeltha came into view, and a pang of jealousy struck Calla again. The Peak Crosser woman was beautiful, with smooth skin and short, curly hair. Many years ago, Zornan had loved her when they'd been Peak Crosser initiates. Now, Calla searched his current feelings and found nothing of that left. He did not even like her. Maybe some attraction still lingered in his heart, but nothing else.

"This isn't going to work," Mairie said through a bite.

"It will, if we stick to the plan." Zornan's voice thrilled her, as it often did when they'd been apart.

Both women grimaced. Apparently, they didn't like the plan.

Where were they? Calla wondered, and in that moment, she knew: they were still in Kandrinal. Were all these threads so tightly woven together?

"Calla?" Leanda's soft voice drifted into Calla's mind, and her eyes opened, the vision gone. Calla looked up. The older woman stood next to the bed. "The guards said you've been screaming. What's wrong?"

Calla sat up, smoothed out her dress, then reached up to wipe the tears from her face, but found it already dry. "Nothing is wrong."

The woman offered a quizzical look but said nothing more. She held out a book. "I brought you something new to read. It's an obscure text from only a hundred years after the formation of the Empire. Fascinating insight about Emperor Gussa, the first Emperor. This historian theorizes that Gussa had many of the abilities of the High Trade."

Calla refused to take the book from Leanda's outstretched hand. "I don't feel like reading, Leanda. I feel like going home." She wanted to scream at the older woman about keeping her captive, about her children having been taken by someone who might be part of the mooncursed Dundraz or whoever held her. But she choked back her words. Her visions would remain hers and hers only.

Then panic gripped her, and she caught a short breath. She'd already told two people about what she thought were dreams: her mother and Trillia. Did the Magistrate know what power Calla held?

The older woman frowned, placing the book on the table with the rest of Calla's collection. "You are my guest, Calla, as much as it doesn't feel like that. You should make the best of it. I told you before—"

"A guest?" Calla stood and faced Leanda. "Guests can come and go as they please and aren't confined to a single room."

"I see you don't believe what I told you last time. I realize you and your husband are game pieces being moved against your will, but I assure you, I'm not the enemy."

Calla turned on the woman. "And maybe you don't understand my meaning. Maybe your intentions are as noble as you say they are, but I will not assuage your conscience by telling you I feel safe under the Empire's care. If this is how the Empire treats loyal citizens, then maybe the Kuthraz or the Dundraz should finish their revolutions and pluck you fools from power." Calla drew in a deep breath, bringing her tirade to an end.

"I can see you are not feeling well today," Leanda said, her voice as flat as it had ever been. "I will leave you. Sad parting, Lady Calla."

Calla did not return the parting as Leanda turned and left the room.

4
THE SAME TARGET

Zornan, Maeltha, and Mairie stood across the street from a one-story building where Maeltha used to meet her Dundraz contact. The building was one of the smallest on the street — only one story where most were three, and half as narrow. Spiraled columns sat on top of wide stairs, traffic in and out was sparse, and it was completely made of brastilia, at least on the outside, an impossible expense not even used at the Imperial palace. Zornan had never seen a building like it.

"What is it?" Mairie asked, mirroring Zornan's thoughts.

"A private club," Maeltha responded, "for Kandrinal's elite."

"So, we just wait out here until your contact shows himself?"

Zornan asked. He'd only seen one person enter the building since they arrived.

The former Peak Crosser shook her head. "The elite come through another door. Only whores and criminals walk in the front."

"Then you should have no trouble walking right in," Mairie quipped, earning Maeltha's most withering glare.

Zornan ignored the latest example of their constant bickering and began walking again, trying to act as casual as he could, but feeling very conspicuous. "But we've circled the building three times. That's the only door, and there are no windows."

"Their entrance is secret. I don't know how they get in. I told you this plan was terrible."

"What does your contact look like?" Mairie asked.

"Short, fat, blond hair. Curly, painted mustache."

"You just described almost every man in this moon-forsaken city," Zornan replied.

"Yes, and to make it worse, once inside the club, the city's elite wear robes to hide their station. So, he could be a merchant, High Trade, low trade, government — I have no idea. I never saw him outside a private room."

Zornan stopped as they finished a loop around to the back of the strange building. Its construction made sense; the brastilia likely kept High Trade abilities at bay, like his room in Doorie. But how did its patrons enter?

By tunnel, most likely. But it could lead in from anywhere, its entrance hidden in a residence, a store, or a government building. Tracking it could take weeks, or even months.

Zornan closed his eyes, his head hurting from the frustration. The light did not blink away, though, but glowed green. At first, he thought it was just the glow one sees after closing one's eyes to bright light. Yet the color pulsed a vibrant green in the exact shape of the building. And not just its shape, but its every detail.

"Mother of moons," Zornan grumbled.

"When did you start cursing?" Mairie responded.

He opened his eyes, and the green glow disappeared. "Have you heard of second sight?"

"I have it, Zornan." Mairie titled her head. "Are you all right?"

"Can you see brastilia?"

She shook her head. "Only people in the dark, and light or heat."

"My sister said she can sense brastilia, and steel with it." Again, Zornan closed his eyes and the building glowed green. Then he gasped. He could see the tunnel below the street. "Grab my arms," he commanded, and when each woman took an arm, he moved along the green path glowing beneath his feet. A few steps later, the women held him back, but the path continued. He opened his eyes to face a three-story, brick building.

He pulled free from their arms, "Follow me," and circled around the block. At the next corner, he closed his eyes again. The glowing green tunnel extended past the next block. He opened his eyes, dodging other people, and walked another block, the two women struggling to keep up with him through the crowd. On the next corner, he closed his eyes. This time, the green pathway stopped, and he opened his eyes.

"There." He motioned with his head when the women reached him. "That's the entrance to the club."

A nondescript building stood in front of them, with signs for a tailor and a baker on the first floor. Traffic in and out of both was heavy, including those dressed in fine clothes or High Trade apparel.

"So, now we just watch this place until Maeltha's contact walks up?" Mairie asked.

"No," Zornan said. "That might take weeks, and we don't have the time. Maeltha's going to go into the club and get a meeting with her contact. Then we'll follow him after he comes out."

* * *

LATER THAT AFTERNOON, Zornan watched the entrance to the elite club. Many had come and gone in the last few minutes, and anyone of them could have been their target; several men matching Maeltha's description of her contact had already come and gone just in the brief time they'd been there.

After Zornan had described his plan, both women had finally agreed on something: they hated it.

"It's been three years, Zor," Maeltha had said, "and your dramatic entrances and exits from Dagtarna and Manmandoo are likely common knowledge. They'll know I'm a traitor, and the Dundraz don't like traitors."

"Funny," Mairie had retorted, "I hate traitors, too."

But Zornan had prevailed, telling Maeltha she had to do it, and they'd returned to the inn where they'd left their stuff. They'd purchased new clothing for all of them: nice dresses for Maeltha and Mairie, and a merchant's suit for Zornan. They needed to blend in better, and Maeltha needed to be properly dressed to enter the club.

When Maeltha entered, Zornan's connection to her disappeared. As Maeltha had indicated and Zornan had feared, the building's walls acted like the prison walls in Doorie, blocking out mindspeak.

"She's going to run," Mairie breathed, her posture screaming annoyance.

"Maybe," Zornan said flatly. "But this is our best chance — maybe our only chance — to question someone from the Dundraz."

Mairie's posture loosened a little.

"Wait here for her to come out," Zornan said before leaving the sullen woman behind. "I'll keep an eye on the other entrance."

So, Zornan waited. Mairie would escort Maeltha here as soon as the meeting had ended, and then Maeltha could point out her contact.

But as the time dragged on, Zornan began to worry. Had Maeltha betrayed them again? Very possible. Zornan did not know if Maeltha had ever been the friend he'd believed her to be during their days at the Peak Crosser Academy. Maybe the years had changed her from the kind, young woman he'd known, or maybe she'd always been duplicitous and he'd just been too naive to tell.

He also wished he could mindspeak with Mairie, but her Bendath-dran mother had not blessed her with that ability. Zornan looked up toward the sun. Nearly two hours. Mairie was likely crawling out of her skin. Hopefully, the impulsive woman wouldn't just burst into the club, waving her hatnuthri to get answers.

Just as Zornan considered running back to where Mairie watched the club, the two women hurried up to him.

"That took long enough," Zornan said as they approached.

"He kept me waiting almost all that time," Maeltha said. "I thought an assassin might be the one to come, not him."

"Would they do that in a club like that?" Zornan questioned.

Maeltha shrugged, eyes on the entrance.

"How did your conversation go?" Mairie asked.

"Not good. He seemed nervous and annoyed. I asked if they wanted my help, and he said no. He asked why I had been gone so long. Told him I went back to work for Mazthain, and now that the gangster was dead, I was looking for work again. He's usually very flirtatious and calm, but this time, he didn't give me a second look." Under a glare from Mairie, Maeltha bristled. "Our relationship wasn't like that, you judgmental little—"

"Keep your eyes on that building," Zornan said. "Go on."

"He didn't give me an assignment," Maeltha continued. "He said to come back in a week and he'd let me know."

What had made the contact nervous? Maeltha's appearance? Something else?

As Zornan turned over the possibilities, Maeltha's voice entered his mind. *There. He's leaving the tailor.*

Immediately, Zornan saw the man — red-painted mustache, double chin, bright blond hair. But Zornan's stomach sank when he saw what the man wore: the purple robes of a Magistrate.

"Stay here," he said to the women, and he followed the Magistrate down the street. After several blocks, the man turned down a residential street to enter a large, two-story home. Zornan sent the location to Maeltha's mind, and they joined him a few minutes later.

Another man walked down the street, and as he passed, Zornan spoke to him. "Greeting, fine sir."

"Welcome greeting, merchant." This man also wore merchant clothes. "Do we know each other?"

"No," Zornan said. "My name is Nagtorn. I'm a merchant from Rinderel who's looking to start operations here. This seems like a fine street, and I was wondering if you lived close by."

The man beamed with pride, his gold-painted mustache rising with a smile. "It is the best residential area in the entire city. My house is there on the end." He pointed to a smaller but well-built home.

"Do any High Trade live close by? I find streets safer when a Magistrate or an Investigator is near."

"Why, yes." The man continued his smile, and he turned to point to the house Maeltha's contact had just entered. "That's the home of Laran, the head Magistrate of Kandrinal."

They exchanged a few more pleasantries, then said their partings.

"A moon-blasted Magistrate," Zornan said. "Just our luck. How are we going to question a moon-blasted Magistrate?"

"Easy," Mairie said. "We break in tonight and scare him into talking."

Maeltha rolled her eyes. "Brilliant. I'm sure he won't have guards and Enforcers."

"In case you hadn't noticed" — Mairie stepped closer to the former Peak Crosser — "I don't really worry too much about guards and Enforcers."

"Stop it," Zornan said, feeling like he was separating his girls during a petty playtime fight. "Maeltha, you don't get a vote. You lost that voice when you whacked me on the head on Doorie." Then he turned to Mairie. "So, we come back tonight and do it your way. If that man knows the Dundraz, then he will tell us how to find them."

Crisdan reached the street near Laran Magistrate's house, where Stargarn awaited him. He'd been called urgently by the Enforcer and had come at a near run from the tavern. He'd been forbidden by Trillia to get drunk, but the command had not forbidden drinking up to that point, a futile attempt to drown his terrible existence.

"What was so urgent?" Crisdan said, annoyed.

"It's gotten even better since I called you," the Enforcer replied, his face more arrogant than usual. "Look over there, but stay behind me so you aren't seen." Then, with his mind, he added: *In front of the house with the statue of a mrakaro on its front porch, across from the Magistrate's house.*

Crisdan looked, and his eyes widened. Zornan Peak Crosser and two women. One was unmistakably the Destroyer girl, Mairie, daughter of Stethdel and confederate to the Kuthraz. The other was just as tall as the Destroyer girl, with dark skin and short, black hair. He was unsure of her identity, but she matched the description of the former Peak Crosser-turned-criminal, Maeltha. Zornan had been betrayed by that very woman three years before.

"Walk with me," Crisdan commanded, and he turned up the street, out of view of Zornan and his fugitive pair. Stargarn followed.

Once out of sight, he turned on the Enforcer. "Next time," he said, "don't be so dramatic. They could have seen me — Zornan would have recognized me. Just use mindspeak and tell me what under the Peaks is happening."

"I apologize for the dramatic flair," Stargarn replied, though his smug face and faint smile indicated he wasn't sorry at all, "but I was right about Zornan. Look who he's with."

Crisdan sighed and switched to mindspeak. Though no one was close by, he needed to be safe. *Stargarn, he was desperate. He's trying to find Calla. And this confirms what we feared: Laran is Dundraz.*

Confusion finally cracked the arrogant face. *How is that?*

Why else would Zornan be standing across the street from the home of the very man I questioned?

Doesn't mean Zornan is innocent, the Enforcer thought back, sulking.

Idiot Enforcer playing Investigator. Crisdan wanted to cuff the man.

From the corner of his eye, Crisdan saw Zornan and his companions head in the opposite direction.

Follow them, Crisdan commanded. *I need to figure out what to do next.*

Stargarn frowned and made to object, but then turned and followed Zornan instead.

Crisdan reached out to Trillia's mind. *Trillia, we have a problem.* He related to her the arrival of Zornan, Mairie, and Maeltha.

Then I need to activate my contingency plan. I need you to keep your muscle-bound partner away from Laran's house tonight. And leave Zornan alone.

How am I going to justify that? A known confederate to the Kuthraz and a known criminal walk free, and a suspected Dundraz Magistrate left unmonitored. Stargarn will have a thousand questions and objections.

That's not my concern, Trillia shot back. *You're the High Investigator. You figure it out.* She closed her mind to his.

Crisdan cursed under his breath. He couldn't ignore her command to divert Stargarn, but the Enforcer wouldn't like it. And, truth be told, neither did Crisdan.

5

A NIGHT IN KANDRINAL

Kandrinal's residential district was quieter than Zornan had expected. He'd not spent a lot of time here, and wasn't familiar with the city's rhythm. Many of the Empire's largest cities buzzed with night activities, but Kandrinal remained eerily quiet.

As she was the most accomplished spy among them, Mairie led Zornan and Maeltha through the streets, but Zornan worried about their raising an alarm at any minute. None of them had ever sneaked into someone's house in the middle of the night, and somehow, the city's immense stillness amplified the likelihood they'd be discovered.

They stopped in the shadows of two glow globes burning near Laran Magistrate's home.

"What now?" Mairie whispered.

Zornan didn't know. The house was large, and even though they could force themselves in through a window, would it be close to the Magistrate's chambers? How long could they stumble through without a servant or the Magistrate hearing? Zornan began to doubt the viability of a plan he'd been so enthusiastic about a few hours before.

He pushed aside his doubt. This would work. He closed his eyes, opening his mind to the second sight. If Zandia could see people in the dark and through walls, then maybe he could, as well.

At first, only the now-familiar green glow of brastilia came. He could see the cubes in Mairie's sleeves, her hidden hatnuthri, and when he looked at Laran's home, a faint green glow sparkled throughout, all brastilia accents in his lavish house.

Then the colors shifted, erupting into bright reds and oranges. Zornan almost opened his eyes to banish the brightness, but he kept them closed, and after a few moments, the illumination dimmed to two orange shapes walking in front of them near the house. He opened his eyes to the wall surrounding the house. Guards on patrol.

"I think I can figure this out," Zornan whispered.

"How?" Maeltha demanded. "That house has probably twenty rooms. It might take us all night to find the right one."

Zornan closed his eyes again to focus on the house. In the middle of the night, most of the orange glows were horizontal and unmoving. Two orange glows moved briskly. More guards, perhaps.

Then he saw a large, orange glow lying down in a room that, judging by what he'd seen of the house, would have a window toward the back on the second story. In there, the most concentrated green glows of brastilia surrounded the sleeping person. The most ornate room would be a good place to start.

"I think his bedroom faces the courtyard in the back," Zornan said. "We can climb the wall over there, then scale the house."

"All right," Mairie responded.

"Are you two insane?" Maeltha whispered. "That wall is more than ten feet high, and surely guards are awake and patrolling."

"I bet I can throw you over," Mairie said, earning another glare.

"You can stay here," Zornan replied, and both women stared in shock. Looking over at Mairie, he said, "She'll slow us down. You and I can clear that wall, no problem."

"But she won't be here when we come back."

Zornan looked at Maeltha. "I won't ask for your promise, because I know you'll trade that easily. But please, stay here. We could still use your help."

"Stay with her," Mairie said. "I can handle this on my own."

"Handle questioning him? No, I want to talk to this snake, and it might be more dangerous than we think."

Zornan wasn't quite sure in the dim light, but he thought he saw Mairie roll her eyes.

"The girl is right, for once," Maeltha said plainly. "I won't be here when you get back."

At this, Zornan hung his head. Why had he expected anything more from her? "Then goodbye, Maeltha."

Zornan stalked away toward the wall, and Mairie followed. He didn't look back.

When they reached the wall, Zornan looked up. Ten feet felt like twenty. Fallindra had no walls of the like, so he'd never been trained to do this. He closed his eyes and opened the second sight. The guards' orange glows passed right on the other side of the wall. He looked up at the sleeping, orange blob across the courtyard. It still lay motionless. After the guards turned the corner, he opened his eyes.

"Now," he whispered.

Mairie crouched, then jumped and, sailing through the air, she landed on the top of the wall. A heartbeat later, she stepped off and disappeared over the other side. Zornan mirrored Mairie's crouch, then jumped, pushing with all the strength his legs could give him.

He shot into the air but did not land on the top of the wall; instead, his feet cleared the wall by two or three feet and, after clearing it, Zornan flailed his arms, as if it might help him steer in the air. It didn't, probably succeeding in only making him look like a wounded hatchling.

As he fell, he closed his eyes, turning slightly to see Mairie's orange glow crouched against the wall's interior. His feet hit soft grass, and he rolled onto his back. In his own ears, the thump sounded too loud, but he felt certain he'd made little noise. As soon as he stood, Mairie sidled up next to him.

Zornan looked up at the second-floor window where hopefully Laran Magistrate slept, its panes visible in the dim moons' light. They could both make the jump, but the ledge wouldn't be enough to land on; Zornan was more likely to crash through the window than he was to land deftly on the narrow ledge.

He looked over at Mairie, who inclined her head toward him in the dim light. She seemed calm, at ease, and, without a word, she began to climb the stone house. The mortared seams didn't look deep enough to be good finger holds, but Mairie moved smoothly across the vertical surface. Only when she reached the window ledge and stood safely there did he realize he'd been holding his breath.

Another heartbeat later, Zornan began to climb. All his hours of training in his field, slicing imaginary villains with his brastilia weapons, seemed useless. Now he needed to jump fifteen in the air and scale brick walls.

Pushing his doubts aside, he focused on climbing, finding it easier than he'd thought it would be, able to keep both a grip and his balance. He focused intently on the task; they didn't have a lot of time before the guards circled around again. But his attention had been so intense, he didn't realize he'd reached the window ledge until he saw Mairie standing next to him, her mess of hair silhouetted in the moonlight. Zornan stepped onto the ledge next to her. Now, they had to get through the window.

Mairie pushed and, thankfully, the window came open, swinging inward, unlocked. Even in Kandrinal, even at a Magistrate's house, no one worried about a second-story window. Zornan slipped into the room behind her, landing on the floor, and he closed the window behind him.

Moonlight through the window illuminated enough to see details, and none were good. The large, ornate bed was empty, its covers rumpled like someone had gotten out in a hurry. The bedroom door was open. Laran Magistrate was gone.

Mairie cursed quietly beside him, and he pushed her with a motion of his hand. Zornan closed his eyes to see the sleeping orange shapes he'd seen before, along with two other shapes moving quickly, a third shape carried between them. He couldn't make sense of it.

"I think someone got him before we did," Zornan whispered, and Mairie cursed again in response.

A sudden shuffling coming from the other side of the bed shifted their attention, and Mairie's hatnuthri grew from her hands as Zornan pulled his hatari from its back holster, growing it to full size with a thought. He nodded, and Mairie rounded the bed one way, Zornan the other.

They reached the opposite side at the same time, weapons raised.

"Please don't kill me," squealed a man lying on the floor. Even in the dim light, Zornan knew it wasn't Laran; his skin was darker than a Kandrinian, and he was half the size of the obese Magistrate. He was old, thin, and dressed in bed clothes.

"Keep your voice down," Mairie declared in a menacing whisper, the ominous hiss of her voice sending a chill down even Zornan's back.

"Please," the man said, pulling himself into a fetal position.

"Where is Laran?" Zornan asked, not even trying to match Mairie's commanding tone.

"They took him," the man whimpered.

"Who took him?" Zornan questioned.

"It's my fault. I told them everything. I led them here. Oh, Circlarl, forgive me. I thought they'd help him. Oh, dear moons above . . ."

"Who took him?" Mairie's repeated question came with more than a hint of threat.

"They said they were Sons of Circlarl."

Sons of Circlarl, a religious sect common in the southern Empire known for their moral zeal. They forbade any frivolities and followed a strict code of ethics, viewing all as a reflection of Circlarl's pure white or Dithdee's corrupted blue, with no room for shades in-between.

"Laran is a good man, but he needed repentance," he continued, "a reminder of where he came from and of his duties."

"Who were they?" Zornan said, letting his hatari shrink.

"The man I met with was dark. Maybe from the Ice Mountains, maybe from Crazdar."

Zornan shook his head. People from there shared little in the way of physical characteristics, except for darker skin.

"How did they get in here? Where are they taking him?" Mairie pressed.

"I let them in, Circlarl help me; I showed them where to come. Oh, moons above . . ."

A shout interrupted the man's feeble pleadings, and Zornan turned his head toward it. One of the guards had raised the alarm.

Get out of there, Zornan, Maeltha's voice came unbidden to his mind.

What's happening?

Two men just left the house carrying something. The guards are screaming and raising the alarm.

They're carrying Laran Magistrate. Follow them.

Maeltha agreed, and their bond broke.

"We need to get out of here," Zornan said to Mairie.

She pointed her hatnuthri at the sniveling servant. "What about him?"

"Let him be," he replied.

She nodded, and they pulled open wide both sections of the window. Subtlety would only slow them down now. Zornan holstered his weapon and followed Mairie's powerful leap out the window. A few moments later, they jumped the wall, both clearing it this time. Zornan landed roughly, but Mairie caught his arm to steady him, and they moved away at a brisk pace, opposite the entrance where the guards continued to raise the alarm.

6

A LOSING VICTORY

Crisdan stood in Laran Magistrate's sitting room, the same room he'd been in the day before, but this time, the quiet silence of the wealthy had been replaced by the noisy chaos of an investigation.

"Here is the servant, High Investigator," an Enforcer said, dragging a small, olive-skinned man into the sitting room. The man slumped, defeated and broken, and the Enforcer had to pull him upright. "Tell the High Investigator what you told me."

The man oozed guilt and fear, and his voice trembled. "I don't believe I'm worthy to even speak to a moon-blessed sort like a High Investigator."

Crisdan noticed the three moon tattoo on the base of the man's neck. *Great. A Son of Circlarl.*

"Speak, man," Crisdan said. "We don't have time for any nonsense."

The servant still wouldn't meet his eyes. "The men who took my master, I helped them," he said, flinching at his own words. "The dark one — no offense, your grace — he told me he was a Son of Circlarl, and that he wanted to call my master to repentance. Did you know Laran was raised by believers before he entered the High Trades?"

"How did you help them?"

"I told them all of his comings and goings. I told them where to find him at all times. I've served my master for ten years. Servants know so much about their masters; it's our calling."

Calling. They did not have time for this brand of stupidity.

Crisdan tried to calm his frayed nerves. For most of his life, he'd dealt with events like this with an analytical reserve. But peace eluded him now, his emotions churning like a storm-tossed sea.

"Who was this dark-skinned man?" Crisdan asked.

"He never gave me a name."

Crisdan's eyes widened. "You betrayed your master to someone who didn't even give you his name?"

Again the servant flinched. "Not a betrayal — an awakening, or so I thought. The man had the mark of the Circlarl." He touched his own tattoo. "I trusted another Son."

"Tell him about the others," the Enforcer said, shaking the man's arm.

"Yes, besides the men who took my master, two others came into his chambers."

"Others?"

Stargarn walked into the room to stand a few feet behind his fellow Enforcer and the sniveling servant.

"Yes," the servant continued. "Two people: a man and a woman. They both jumped through the window, looking for the Magistrate. But he was gone. Oh, moons above, he was gone!" He started to whimper.

"What did they look like?" Crisdan pressed.

"It was dark, great Investigator," he said, eyes downcast. "The man was tall, I think, but I was lying on the floor. She was tall, too, with hair like a prairie cat and a voice like the Daughter of the Fire Moon."

"Hold him in the library," Crisdan said to the Enforcer gripping the servant's arm, and he dismissed them with a nod.

"So, the Destroyer girl and the Peak Crosser were involved," Stargarn said while the other Enforcer pulled the servant from the room.

"In his disappearance? I don't think so. You heard the man: they came after he'd already been taken."

"Still, we should find them."

"Indeed." Crisdan looked out the window to the street where a small crowd had gathered. The alarm Laran's guards had raised early that morning had awoken half the neighborhood. Crisdan had tried to control the news, but most of Kandrinal would certainly know by sunset that their lead Magistrate had been abducted. What a disaster. In a few days, Crisdan would need to return to Bristrinia to report to the High Magistrates and his fellow High Investigators. In most cases, his status protected him from formal inquiry, but the other High Investigators, and especially the High Magistrates, would likely see Laran's kidnapping as a catastrophe.

I'm going to file a report. Stargarn's deep voice broke through Crisdan's mind. *You made me follow a Magistrate, and then you had me stop. You had the Destroyer girl, a known associate of the Kuthraz, in your sights, and we let her go. And after you had me stop watching Laran Magistrate, he goes missing.*

What are you implying? Crisdan shot back.

I'm not implying anything. But you're not telling me everything, either. And your behavior since we arrived in Kandrinal has been strange.

Crisdan turned on the Enforcer. *Are you threatening me?*

Stargarn sighed. *No, Crisdan, I am your friend. We've known each other for years.*

Strange. Crisdan had never considered the Enforcer a friend.

The questions I'm raising, Stargarn continued, *will be raised by my superiors, and I would hate for the narrative to spin out of your control.*

So it wasn't a threat, but it wasn't harmless.

What do you want, Stargarn? Crisdan asked.

I want to know what's going on, came his reply. *I want to know why we came here to question a Magistrate, and why you let Zornan and the girl go free.*

Crisdan took a deep breath. By law, he needn't tell Stargarn any of those things. The other man was an Enforcer — muscle to be directed by Magistrates and Investigators. Even though the Council of Enforcers liked to fancy themselves as leaders of influence in the High Trades, they did not control information, and information was power. Crisdan didn't need to share anything with him, and Stargarn's report could easily be dismissed. Investigators hated it when Enforcers criticized how they did their jobs.

But Crisdan needed allies. Ever since Trillia had pulled him into her vicious web, he'd been slow to trust anyone, fearing duplicity in almost every interaction. But Crisdan had never sensed duplicity in Stargarn. In fact, Crisdan now felt frustration and simple curiosity flowing from the Enforcer, not anger, hatred, or betrayal. In this twisted ocean Trillia had spun him in, he'd need some help navigating the tides.

Crisdan spoke into Stargarn's mind the tip he'd received about Laran, leaving out the source, then layered the truth with a few convenient lies. *I pulled you off Laran Magistrate because if he was a prominent Dundraz, I feared he'd have guards watching him and you might get spotted. And not tracking Zornan was probably a mistake; I trust the man, but maybe his grief and anger have driven him onto illegal roads.*

Stargarn nodded, curiosity and now pride burning inside him. The arrogant man loved being right about something, even if Crisdan had only said so to stroke the man's ego.

So, what now?

Take a few Enforcers and try to find Zornan and the girl. A goose chase that would keep Stargarn occupied. And if they found Zornan and Mairie, it might be helpful to the case, although Crisdan doubted that. The Peak Crosser's luck was likely just as bad as Crisdan's. Yes, Zornan and his friends had located a Dundraz contact, just as he had.

But Laran Magistrate was gone now, along with his connection to the Dundraz.

Stargarn nodded and left, while Crisdan slumped into one of Laran's oversized chairs. An empty pit grew deep in his gut. Trillia had commanded them to stop watching Laran, so his abduction or disappearance was likely her contingency plan. Despite the fact that Laran Magistrate was exactly where Trillia wanted him to be, Crisdan couldn't fight the sense that he'd somehow lost.

7

A FEVER

After two days in the rebel camp hidden deep within the Thick, Mizcarnon felt he knew what he needed to about the Croxshinese rebels. Six months before, they had been based outside of Fazdi, a city in the foothills of the Three Mountains and deep in the Thick. But the Nansartans had surprised them, inexplicably coming down from the mountains with a surprise attack. Afterward, the intent had been clear: to cripple the rebel leadership. The Nansartan warriors had targeted the officers, killing what sickness, hunger, and desertion had not already stolen, and more than eight hundred had perished in just one day, with the survivors forced to push east into the unsettled Thick until they arrived at their present camp.

Kirna had explained they'd been there for five months, and in that time, they hadn't made a single offensive maneuver. Fortunately, the Nansartans had left them alone. Either they hadn't found the camp, or maybe they didn't view the rebels as a viable threat anymore. Mizcarnon believed the latter.

The rebels continued to dwindle because of disease, hunger, and desertion, and the morning after Mizcarnon arrived, a dozen deserters were brought before Kirna for discipline. The eleven men and one woman were pathetic, with rags hanging from their slight frames and eyes that held hopelessness. Most looked as though they didn't care if Kirna sentenced them to death. She had spared them, though, bringing relief to some and disappointment to others.

Nearly a third of the camp dwelt in the section Mizcarnon had noticed that first day — a quarantine for a disease they called Thick Fever. The symptoms were drastic: burning fevers, painful boils, and delusions. Close to a third of those infected died or went mad, their minds never fully recovering. Survivors seemed to be immune. Mizcarnon worried nearly as much about contracting Thick Fever and bringing it back across the ocean as he did about the Nansartans' growing power.

"Try not to worry," Kirna had told him. She had contracted the disease a year before but had survived after three weeks of painful recovery. "Contraction of the disease seems random. Not everyone gets it, and we don't know how it is passed."

Their lack of knowledge brought Mizcarnon little comfort.

On the third day, Mizcarnon stood just outside the camp, watching the slow activity. Some of the soldiers and officers held their heads high, pride intact, at least on the surface. Most of the others shared the despair he'd seen in the deserters — a march of the living, walking inexorably toward death. Mizcarnon imagined the rich valleys of the Empire torn asunder by the Nansartan hordes, of this despair and destruction overshadowing his people. Was this inevitable? Could his Empire, smaller in population than the fallen Kingdom of Croxshine, beat back the hurricane winds of Nansart?

That the Nansartans had sprung from the mountains to devastate the rebel camp worried Mizcarnon to no end. It echoed reports similar to those during his initial visit when Nansartans had first invaded Croxshine and the island kingdom of Shur. The rebels spoke of mrakaros, cosows, and miotop diving from the skies, then foot soldiers seemingly springing from the ground itself.

Mizcarnon suspected how the Nansartans had done it. Their emperor knew the blessings of the High Trades — apparently, all of them. What if he had created an army of Tunnelers? Or what if his soldiers, blessed in strength and endurance, held the same blessings as Tunnelers? What if the Nansartans moved via tunnel and sprung an entire army out of the ground beneath their enemies' feet?

He tried to dismiss the theory as fancy, but facts overran his objections. Tunneling took time, limited by the number of blessed who worked on it. But what if you had dozens or hundreds with that blessing? How fast could you tunnel over from western Croxshine into the Thick and to the Three Mountains? Months? Weeks? Mizcarnon knew little of the mechanics of tunneling, so he could not be sure. The Empire of the Peaks had never employed Tunnelers as a weapon or for speed.

Was it even possible they had tunneled from Boothdrinka, under an ocean to Croxshine and Shur? Ludicrous. Yet, what else explained their sudden appearance? And according to maps, the leagues between Boothdrinka and Croxshine were only marginally more than the distance between Croxshine's northern shore and the Empire's southern edge. The Nansartans might already be working their way to his homeland, maybe lying in wait at their doorstep.

Mizcarnon had to leave, had to return to warn his people, to warn the Emperor. The Nansartans might not come by boat or by giant flyer. They might pop out from the ground, like burrowing rodents, catching his people unawares and unprepared.

Mizcarnon walked back into the camp, looking for Jayzca. Time to leave, time to find a way back to the Peaks; he knew all he needed to know. As much as he might have wanted to help the rebels here, he was a sole Peak Crosser scout without his mrakaro; he could do nothing for them. But he carried with him information that could be the difference between his own people being prepared for a Nansartan invasion or being caught unawares like the Croxshinese had been.

A sudden dizziness stopped him. Mizcarnon closed his eyes, trying to banish the feeling, but when he opened his eyes again, the huts and tents moved despite his feet staying still. He tried to walk, but his knees buckled and his vision spun, blurred. He sweated even more than usual. *No! Not now. I must leave.* Yet as he took another step, he collapsed, face hitting the packed dirt before he could even brace himself.

Mizcarnon tried to stand, but his body refused. Through the blurriness, he saw two people running over, one, he thought, might be Kirna.

"What is wrong with him?" came Jayzca's lyrical voice, though he couldn't see her. Maybe she spoke from the Otherworld? Could she do that?

"It's the Fever," Kirna replied.

"What can you do for him?"

Mizcarnon already knew: Wait to see if he survived. If he died, the knowledge of the Empire's peril would die with him.

Jayzca stood over Mizcarnon, tucked between worlds and safely away from the vicious Thick Fever. Four days ago, the Peak Crosser had collapsed, and his condition had only grown worse. He thrashed in bed, tied down by heavy ropes. He'd originally been tied down with thin cords like other patients, but his Peak Crosser strength had proven difficult for the survivors who administered to him. In addition to the pustules covering his entire body, rope burns now cut across his chest, thighs, and ankles.

Survivors dressed in black came twice a day to force-feed the patients and clean up the mess.

Mizcarnon slept restlessly most of the time, thrashing against the ropes, while in other moments, his eyes would pop open, frantic, and moving rapidly. He would call out, lamenting the Nansartans conquering the Empire of the Peaks, though most of his words were gibberish, the language of a fevered mind.

Jayzca watched him, helpless. Even with all her power through the Otherworld, a fever had stopped her plans and ruined Mizcarnon's goals. She'd seen the camp's survivors — all were scarred from the disease. Mizcarnon's entire body, including his face and hands, were covered by pus-leaking sores. If he survived he would forevermore carry the effects of the disease.

"There is nothing we can do for him," Chage said, standing next to her. "He will likely not survive this. We should return you to your people."

Her people. Chage's father had carried Jayzca's message to her own father, and Doos Mazratac's response had not been pleasant. He'd ordered her, through Cha'Farsa, to return home immediately, the command coming from both her father and her Doos, the one called her lead her people. But Jayzca had refused; she'd already defied Father in leaving, and she would not crawl back until she'd defeated Nansart or figured out how to.

Had she made the right choice? Was her father's path not one of cowardice, but of wisdom? She wanted to stomp her feet and scream. A little girl shouldn't have to carry the full burden of her people. But the bond was hers, and only she could do this. Father could commune with Cha'Farsa and other Hol'Feel'Koo, though only mentally, not physically. That burdensome curse had fallen only on her.

She knelt beside Mizcarnon, fighting the urge to enter her world and take his hand. What a brave man. He had sacrificed everything to protect his people, to right the wrongs of Nansart. No, she hadn't been wrong in following him, and the White Goddess had not yet blessed them with success, though she tried their resolve and patience.

Jayzca stood and looked at Chage. "Your medicine is far advanced from our world."

He nodded, eyes still on the sick Peak Crosser. "I wish we could bring him one of our healers; I have no doubt they could help him." Chage's eyes held intense sadness. Despite his reluctance to walk this path with Jayzca, he, too, had grown to respect and like Mizcarnon.

"We can't bring your healers here," Jayzca said, "but we could bring Mizcarnon to them."

Chage's eyes widened, and he turned to her. "That is not done, Jayzca. You know the laws."

"Laws?" She huffed. "Laws that allow good men like Mizcarnon to perish? Can't you feel the will of the White Goddess, Chage? Don't you believe Mizcarnon is meant to help us defeat Nansarta?"

"The White Goddess does not watch over our world," he murmured.

"But what of your god of health?"

"Juk'Jan'Fo?" Chage exhaled deeply. "He taught us to heal the sick, to bring relief to the suffering. He guided us with his sister, Juk'-Coz'Sin, to heal our greatest threats."

Jayzca knew the stories, but she wanted Chage to repeat them. "And what would Juk'Coz'Sin want us to do? Would he want us to help Mizcarnon?"

"His desires are below his father's, below the laws handed to us from Juk'Nun'San'Lux. Humans cannot pass into our world unless chosen by Juk'Nun'San'Lux himself, as you have been since birth. There is no other way."

"But it is possible?"

"Yes, but I've never seen it done, and it's dangerous. The journey might kill him."

"If we do nothing, he will die." Jayzca turned back to Mizcarnon, then walked into her world.

The sensations that did not penetrate through the barrier between worlds suddenly hit her senses. The healing tent smelled of urine, feces, sweat, and blood. Jayzca gagged, but kept her stomach, hearing Chage in the back of her mind, urging her to return to the Otherworld. She ignored him, held Mizcarnon's hand, and closed her eyes. She'd never brought another human into the Otherworld, never defied the laws of the Hol'Feel'Koo. Already she'd likely earned exile from her own people, and this action might mean she'd be banished by the Hol'Feel'Koo, as well, and as a result, they could sever her bond with Chage. Tears fell as she considered this possibility — that her connection to Chage might evaporate, leaving her truly alone.

But this had to be done. Mizcarnon and his people were the only hope in defeating the Nansartans. If Mizcarnon died, their hopes of stopping Nansart might die with him.

She closed her eyes and moved herself into the Otherworld, trying to bring Mizcarnon with her.

8

TRUE VILLAINS

C alla sat at her table, reading the book Leanda had brought, though she couldn't focus on it. Her mind kept drifting to Trillia, to the girls, to Zornan, to Crisdan; everything in her world swirled and churned, and she could do nothing but sit in her fancy jail reading history.

The visions had stopped. She still didn't know how her ability worked and she'd yet to figure out how to control it, but even at night, her mind remained devoid of visions. She'd tried to summon Windsa the most, hoping for more of her girls, but everything had stopped, filling her with fear instead.

Calla closed the book, leaned back in her chair, and rubbed her eyes. Since she was a child, all she had ever wanted to be was a mother. Trillia had once told her that's because she'd only been presented with that example. But in her heart, Calla knew it was only part of the truth. She'd wanted children, wanted the same love between her and a child that she'd shared with her parents. Trillia was an old High Tradeswoman, and Calla believed the Magistrate brushing aside a desire for children was simply an old woman justifying for her own childless state.

When Zornan had come into her life, Calla had loved him almost instantly. At first, he'd been mostly a mystery — a Peak Crosser, strong and handsome. But after she'd gotten to know him, she'd found a quiet, gentle, strong man hidden behind the shroud of his High Trade, and within months, she'd known she wanted to spend her life with him.

But there had been one huge problem: most High Trades were forbidden to have children. And even those who could (like Peak Crossers and Tunnelers) had to receive a special exemption from the Grand Council of the High Trades, after a sponsorship by the leaders of their own High Trade. When Calla had decided to marry Zornan, it had been with this knowledge.

On the day of their wedding, however, Zornan had presented her with an official letter from the Peak Crosser Council, giving them permission to have two children. She'd been ecstatic getting married, but this news had doubled her joy.

A knock on the door interrupted her thoughts, and Leanda stepped into the room.

"Good morning," Leanda said.

"Is it?" Calla closed the book, trying to push out of her mind her growing anxiety. "I wouldn't know."

The Shindar sat at the table next to her. "Come now, Calla. I realize this is an uncivil situation, but there's no need be uncivilized."

Easy for her to say. She's not the prisoner.

"I was thinking of writing a book about the history of Fallindra," Calla said instead, "but there's one massive hole, at least in the more modern era. What do you know of Trillia Magistrate?" She struggled to keep her growing disdain for the woman from her voice.

Leanda shrugged. "Not much. A reclusive Magistrate."

"Have you ever met her?"

"Twice, I believe." The woman paused to consider it. "I am older, so we were not initiates together. And Shindar and Magistrates don't get together often." Leanda smiled like she'd just said something particularly funny, though Calla didn't get the joke.

"Anyway," the Shindar continued, "I would have thought you'd know more about her than I would. Weren't you close to the woman?"

"I thought so," Calla replied. "She'd been in Fallindra almost my entire life, and though we've spent much time together the last few years, she never speaks of herself. I was also curious how High Tradesmen outside of our valley viewed her."

Leanda shrugged again. "Little, actually. Trillia Magistrate is a recluse; she's completely isolated herself over the past thirty years. The only notable thing I know about her was when she expelled the Investigator and Enforcers who'd been stationed in Fallindra. It was controversial, but most of us share a disdain for Enforcers, so it wasn't a surprise."

"Us?"

"Other High Trade." She glanced back at the closed door, then her expression turned sour. "Enforcers are bullies, ignorant brutes. Necessary, but ugly still."

"What happened to get them kicked out?"

The older women raised an eyebrow. "You don't know?"

Calla shook her head. "No. No one talks about it. My parents are farmers and not particularly connected to the social fabric. I've heard rumors, but . . ."

"It was an ugly affair. Rape, promises of marriage, theft. The two Enforcers were executed, and the Investigator was stripped of his abilities. He died shortly after." Disgust laced Leanda's words. So she was disgusted by them, yet not by keeping a slave assassin bound to her will?

"Do you need parchment and ink to begin your book?"

"Probably not," Calla replied. "I best wait until I'm free again."

Leanda forced a smile that only made it halfway up her face. "Calla, I came here with something more to discuss." She paused, her gaze turning hard. She glanced back at the door, and then leaned forward, her next words coming in a soft whisper. "I am going to get you out of here. I don't know how, and I don't know when. But you are not safe."

Her words struck Calla, and Calla desperately wanted to believe the woman, wanted to seize the swelling hope. But she pushed it back. A trick. Leanda pretended to be her friend, pretended to be good. But the woman was an assassin in league with those trying to destroy Zornan. And even though Calla did not yet know how Trillia fit into this terrible puzzle, Leanda was no better than that villain.

"I don't believe you," Calla replied, her voice soft but not a whisper.

Leanda leaned back. "I know. You have no reason to. But it will happen just the same." Her gaze softened, and she patted Calla's shoulder before standing up.

Calla looked at the woman: refined, strong, with a face that held her age well, retaining much of her youthful beauty. The tenderness in her eyes reminded Calla of her mother, while the fierce lines of the Shindar's face reminded her of Trillia.

"Are my children in danger?" The words had come out in a rush, and tears came unbidden, hot and stinging.

Leanda's gaze turned sad, deeply sad, but then she smiled past it. "I don't think so."

"You kidnapped me to get leverage on Zornan," she said, anger trouncing her grief. "So, why not the children?"

"The Empire does not kidnap children," Leanda replied.

Calla scoffed. "Zornan was taken at the age of twelve."

"A decision made by his parents." Anger replaced tenderness in the woman's eyes. "And Zornan has received a better life than he likely would have."

Calla fidgeted with her hands. The woman was not wrong in that.

"The Empire will not take or harm your children," Leanda assured.

"But the Empire isn't the only force at work here, is it?"

Leanda's own hands, which she'd balled into fists, now relaxed by her sides. "No, I am afraid not." She looked at Calla, her stare probing like an Investigator. "What do you know?"

"Know?" Calla motioned around the room. "I know nothing. I'm locked in a hole somewhere in the Empire, scared and alone. I'm a wife worried for her husband and a mother worried for her children." Then she fell into her own lap, crying.

Leanda stepped closer, like she might console her, but she stopped short. "I am truly sorry, Calla, even if you don't believe I am. I will make this right, I promise."

The door closed behind the older woman, and Calla remained sitting, with her growing grief and fear as her only companions.

9

A VOICE FROM THE PAST

Two days since they'd taken the girls, and Zandia was getting anxious. As Trillia's trail grew colder, so did Zandia's guilt as she watched Calla's mourning parents. Thandar sulked all day, while Caladria busied herself with domestic chores, moving slowly, her expression vacant and constantly on the verge of tears. They could do nothing to bring Calla or their grandchildren home, and their hopelessness shadowed their every moment.

On the third day, two men arrived, and through a quick mental conversation, Zandia confirmed they were, indeed, those whom Mayfran had intended to come. Zandia wouldn't hand over Calla's parents to be taken by the Dundraz, the Empire, or whomever Trillia had affiliated herself with.

These men are going to escort Thandar and Caladria to Fallen Mountain, Mayfran assured her. *We can guard them there. And you all need to leave Fallindra. A full squad of Enforcers, soldiers, and three Investigators are coming to find out why the Enforcers stationed there haven't communicated in days.*

A pang of guilt rose up at the mention of her latest kill. *What about the girls?*

Mayfran's doubt and frustration came through. *I don't know. If Trillia isn't Dundraz, what is she? The woman's been in that valley for decades. Where would she go?*

We need to let Zornan know about the girls.

I don't think so, Mayfran replied. *We need him focused on finding Calla. This news could break him.*

Zandia's anger swelled. *He deserves to know what's happened. And what does "we need" mean? Does Zornan's path favor some Kuthraz intrigue?*

I just meant he has an onerous task and needs focus. What would you tell him? That the girls are gone, and we don't know who took them?

Her anger hit a fever pitch. *You're lying to me, Mayfran . . .*

I'm not lying to you.

Fine. Obscuring the truth, then.

Mayfran did not reply, which confirmed Zandia's belief that Mayfran knew something, or that the Kuthraz were planning something. She watched Calla's parents gather a few things in preparation for the journey. These people were now woven into the fragile fabric of rebellion.

I need you to not tell Zornan, Mayfran finally said, his words walking the edge of a command.

Zandia couldn't contain her anger. *Or what? You'll compel me to do it?* The bitter taste of his last command still lingered in her mind. Calming her had been good at the time, but in the days since, her anger had grown over him forcing her emotions.

I told you I'd never do that, he replied. Was he really that ignorant of his previous command, or did he not know how much power he held over her? *It's in Zornan's best interest to remain focused on his current path.*

And the Kuthraz's best interest, she thought to herself.

Fine, she thought back to him. *But I don't like it.*

Will you accompany Thandar and Caladria to Fallen Mountain?

No, she shot back. What would she do, then? Try to trace Trillia's steps? Join Zornan's quest to find Calla? Finish her quest to kill her father? The thought of the last task refocused her anger — away from Mayfran, the Kuthraz, and Trillia.

You are welcome at Fallen Mountain when you need to return. This thought came wrapped in kindness and concern, nearly as distasteful as a command.

* * *

ZANDIA SAT in the tunnel just outside Fallindra, eating some dried meat Caladria had given her for the journey.

"I'd feel better if you came," Caladria had said when Zandia had told her that she would not accompany them to Fallen Mountain, and Zandia believed she'd meant it. But Zandia would not give in, even to the older woman's plea. Her free will had been muted for years, so making her own choices was invigorating, even if she wasn't sure if she was making good ones.

Now, as she sat in the near darkness of the tunnel, she wondered where she might go. Back to the Bowels? No, her father's trail had gone cold. Even if she could find some of his old associates and pry information from them, over the years, Zortranc had learned to erase his path well.

She wanted to reach out to Zornan, to commune with someone not connected to the Kuthraz or to their moon-cursed rebellion, but he wasn't really disconnected, was he? He traveled with Mairie, and it was clear from her mindspeak with Mayfran, whatever road Zornan traveled served their purposes as well as Zornan's own.

Who else would she talk to, though, if not her brother or Mayfran? She had no other friends. Even when Talalah Shindar had controlled her, Zandia had had more friends. She'd despised Dres'Dargpa, but found some kinship in their constant bickering, and if she'd ever had a real friend since the day her parents had sold her, it had been with Nin'Kindo, the other Baldra chained to Talalah Shindar.

Nin'Kindo. Since the day Talalah had died, she had wanted to reach out to him. But she'd resisted the temptation; he was either dead or had been driven to madness by the severing of his bond with Talalah. Or perhaps the Dundraz had found him and reconnected him to a new master, just as Mairie's mother, Kisthana, had done to connect Zandia to Mayfran.

Besides, even if he was still alive, Zandia wasn't sure she could connect to Nin'Kindo. When they had been connected through the same Shindar, they could mindspeak, no matter what the distance. Now, that mutual connection was dead, so Zandia doubted they could still speak across such vast distances.

Nin'Kindo had been a friend in the most unlikely of circumstances. They had shared nearly everything with each other — their pasts, their fears, their yearning for freedom. And for the thousandth time since their bond had been severed, Zandia's heart ached at its emptiness.

Nin'Kindo. She pushed the thought outward, desperately wanting him to respond. She thought his name over and over, hoping their connection somehow lingered. What would she find if she reached him? A Dundraz agent compelled to fight against her? The deranged thoughts of a mad Baldra, a constant piercing pain having driven out all rational thought?

She wasn't sure how long she'd been repeating Nin'Kindo's name, when a reply came back — *Tha'Strukra!* — in the familiar refrain of Nin'Kindo's mental embrace. *Tha'Strukra, you are alive!*

Joy and relief overwhelmed her. *Nin'Kindo! You're alive! What happened to you?*

I wandered for weeks in small valleys outside Junnindra, making my way toward Crazdar. Then they found me.

Who found you?

New masters, kinder masters.

57

Zandia paused in her thoughts. New masters? Who? The Dundraz? No matter what their bond, Zandia could put the entirety of the Kuthraz at risk.

I've missed you, Nin'Kindo, she spoke, pushing aside her doubts and worries to bask in the warmth of his mental embrace.

I have missed you too, Tha'Strukra.

Tha'Strukra. She thought little of her old Baldra name in the past three years. Mayfran, Zornan, everyone now called her Zandia, her name before her blessing day.

I'm called Zandia, was her reply.

Zandia. His mind lingered on the word. *I like that. I guess you can call me Dirik. My new masters still call me Nin'Kindo, though; the name fits me.*

Still no mention of the identity of his new masters. Of course, she hadn't mentioned her affiliation with the Kuthraz, so they were both clinging to their secrets.

We should meet. Dirik's request both thrilled and scared her. If he'd been bound by the Dundraz again, or even the Empire, then any strengthening of their connection could have dangerous consequences for everyone.

I've been trying to reach you for months, he continued after she didn't respond to his request. *I have some news for you. Why was your mind sealed to me?*

Because I thought you were dead, she said. *And I thought if I tried to find you, only to discover nothing but madness or death, I would . . .* Emotion overwhelmed her before she could finish her thought.

I found your father, he continued again. *I know where he is right now.*

Had Zandia been standing, her knees might have buckled. *You found Zortranc? How?*

The moons' fortune. He has worked some with my new masters, but they don't care for him. Recently, our paths have crossed several times, and I know where he is. I wanted to kill him when I saw him, torture him for all he did to you. Dirik's anger flared hot like a furnace, warming her inside like it had so often done.

Where are you? she asked.

Nabfryn, headed north.

I am in Fallindra, she thought back, trying to keep hope for their reunion from taking over her heart.

Then we should meet on my way to Rinderel. Your father is close to there. We could find him together. The thought burned as bright as the fire moon on a cloudless night. *Meet me in the eastern Empire tunnel just north of Nabfryn.*

I'll be there in two days, if you can wait for me. She stood, finishing off her dried meat, the thought of finding Zortranc nearly as motivating as reuniting with Nin'Kindo. No, Dirik. She would think of him as Dirik.

I will wait for you, came his thought, wrapped in an enthusiasm equal to hers.

10

HEALED

M izcarnon opened his eyes to memories filled with feverish dreams of all kinds — sometimes he woke to Nansartans torturing the Emperor; sometimes to Jayzca chained to a brastilia table while a Bendathdran priestesses twirled habindhis overhead, breaking the girl's connection to the Otherworld and handing her over to the Nansartan emperor; and most often to a vision of him flying into a burnt and vacant Bristrinia.

This dream, however, seemed different, peaceful. Soft light enveloped him as he lay on a soft bed. A ceiling of light blue stone sat high above.

Above him appeared a figure with a face like Chage, dark green skin bunched around a large snout. It spoke unknown words, but somehow Mizcarnon knew them. Not in his ears, but in his mind.

Rest, little one. You are healing. You will survive.

The words brought him peace; the first dream with any hope. Would he heal? Would he survive to warn his people? Mizcarnon gripped to that hope as he drifted back into sleep.

* * *

THE NEXT TIME HE AWOKE, it did not feel like a fever dream. It felt foreign, yet real. He sat up in the soft bed and peeled back the thin blanket, only to quickly replace it when he found he was naked underneath.

The same room as in his last dream — light blue stone marked the walls and tall ceilings, while smooth, yellow stone tiled the floor. No windows, yet a warm breeze passed through, and an open doorway revealed little but a massive hallway made of the same blue and yellow stone.

"Welcome back."

Jayzca stood beside his bed, and Mizcarnon pulled the thin blanket up to his neck.

"Where am I?" His voice came out rough, strained.

"The Otherworld." The girl's dark eyes held a sadness, and maybe regret. When had he gained the ability to discern those indiscernible eyes?

"I'm dreaming."

"No. You are awake. The Hol'Feel'Koo healers cured you of the Thick Fever."

Healed? Was that even possible? He looked at his uncovered arms. The open sores had been replaced by raised, dark pink scars. Mizcarnon brushed one hand across the other arm, feeling them. Then he touched his face. Scars dotted his freshly shaven cheeks and chin.

"They could do nothing for the scars," Jayzca said. "The sores were already too advanced."

"How did I come here?" It was one of a thousand questions dancing in his surprisingly lucid mind.

"I brought you here, against the will of the Hol'Feel'Koo." She dropped her gaze to the tiled floor.

"You are in trouble."

She nodded. "Chage and I are to be banished. Father and Cha'-Fal'Kanrruu'Farsa agreed, and now we must leave the home continent of Croxshine and of the Hol'Feel'Koo." Tears dripped from her eyes, and she convulsed with a sob.

Mizcarnon wanted to comfort the girl, but his nakedness forbade him. "I am sorry, Jayzca. You did not need to do that for me."

She looked up, wiping away the tears with the back of her hand, and in that moment, she looked every bit the child she was. "I just wanted to help you and my people. I can't imagine being alone . . ." Her words were lost in another sob.

"You won't be alone," Mizcarnon comforted. "I will do what you did for me. I must leave this continent soon, anyway. I will return to the Empire and warn my people. You can come with me."

Jayzca stepped toward the bed and buried her next sob into his covered knees, while Mizcarnon clutched the blanket to his chest with one hand, stroking Jayzca's white hair with his other. The girl had not abandoned him; in fact, she had saved him and maybe the entire Empire. Duty demanded he watch out for her, bring her into his family.

Jayzca pulled away. "I'll be right back," she said, disappearing into nothing, and for the first time, it wasn't strange to see her do that.

She appeared a moment later with a bundle of gray Peak Crosser clothing, his hatari balanced on top. "These were Beeldrat's. You are taller, so he helped me make some alterations. They won't be a perfect fit, but they will work."

Mizcarnon smiled as she lay the clothes onto his bed and stepped back.

"Turn around, Jayzca," he said.

"You outsiders are so weird." All the same, she turned around.

Mizcarnon pulled the sheet away and dressed as quickly as his stiff body would allow.

After he had finished tucking his hatari into the holster on his back, she turned back around and said, "There's more you need to know."

"We can discuss it as we go," he replied.

She smiled hesitantly, like his smallest sister had often done when she had bad news.

"What is it, Jayzca?"

"Bringing you here had some effects." Her words had come out quietly.

"If we're going to be together now, Jayzca, you have to be frank with me. Dancing should be reserved for a hall."

"Best if you see it for yourself." She grabbed his hand and pulled him to the corner of the room, where a tall piece of polished glass reflected the blue hues.

Mizcarnon saw his own reflection. The Peak Crosser clothing hung loosely on his too-thin body, the effects of his sickness. His gaze started at his feet and moved up his torso, and he barely recognized the skinny figure before him. Then he halted as his eyes met themselves in the mirror.

He gasped and stepped back. His eyes were completely black, like Jayzca's.

He reached up and almost touched his now inhuman eyes. "What happened to me? Part of the healing?"

"No. It happened when I brought you here. You bonded a Hol'Feel'Koo. You should be able to walk between worlds now, as well."

Mizcarnon lowered his hands as his recently revived mind tried to grasp the implications of what he saw. What was he now? Was he still human? Mazzdu? No, his hair had remained blond, and his skin had retained its normal color. He was himself, but for the eyes.

"Oh, Jayzca, you know you're not supposed to be in here."

Mizcarnon turned to face the figure he'd seen in his dream. The Hol'Feel'Koo looked similar yet different from the brief glimpses he'd had of Chage. It was slighter, shorter, and lacked the tusks jutting out underneath its snout. Just like in the dream — which maybe hadn't been a dream — the Hol'Feel'Koo's words were foreign to his ears, but rang true in his mind.

"I'm sorry, Jo, but I needed to see him."

The one Jayzca called Jo stretched her mouth in what might have been a smile. "Off with you, before Cha'Farsa sees you."

Jayzca returned the smile and disappeared.

"I'm glad to see you up," Jo replied. "I'm Jo'Rul'Scoo, your healer."

She held a small cup out to him. Mizcarnon reached for it, but it ended up much larger than it had appeared, too big for him to grab with one hand as the Hol'Feel'Koo had.

"Drink it," Jo instructed. "Your body is almost rid of the infection, and we need to ensure it won't return."

Mizcarnon drank the thick brown liquid, which tasted bitter, but not terrible, and burnt slightly as it went down.

Jo's large eyes, which remained fixed on his face, looked entirely human, with dark green around a black pupil.

"Are my scars that bad?" he asked, conscious of the healer's intense stare.

"It's not that." Jo took the empty cup. "I've never met a human before, besides Jayzca, and I only first met her a few weeks ago."

"How long have I been here?" he asked.

Jo turned to leave. "You should rest."

"Please." Mizcarnon placed a hand on Jo's arm. "What's happening to me?"

Jo turned and snorted. "You mean about your eyes? I know nothing of the bond. I'm just a healer, not a priest like Cha'Farsa. You were unconscious for nearly two weeks after you arrived."

Two weeks. Hopefully the delay didn't mean doom for the Empire.

"I can tell you, however, that you have bonded a Hol'Feel'Koo," Jo continued, "and that you're like Jayzca now. But I assume you already knew that."

Mizcarnon nodded. "Who did I bond with?"

Jo's mouth stretched again into a flat Hol'Feel'Koo smile. "Me."

THE OTHERWORLD

Mizcarnon sat on the edge of his bed, mind whirling. His body had healed wonderfully, and after three additional days in Jo's care, he felt strong. During his sickness, he'd lost more than weight; his muscles had weakened, his reflexes slowed. Jo assured him all he had would return in time, but Mizcarnon soon grew impatient with a body that hardly seemed like his. Especially the eyes.

Mizcarnon looked up at Cha'Fal'Kanruu'Farsa, leader of the Hol'Feel'Koo in this part of the Otherworld, and Chage's father. He'd also banished Jayzca.

"I'm sorry you don't understand our ways and laws." The

Hol'Feel'Koo leader spoke in a guttural tongue that sounded like incomprehensible grunts in Mizcarnon's ears.

But in his mind, Mizcarnon heard Cha'Farsa's words in the Imperial tongue, like a new kind of mindspeak. No one understood Mizcarnon's ability — Jayzca had learned their language as a child — and when he spoke to the Hol'Feel'Koo, they in turn heard his words in their minds. Unprecedented. Cha'Farsa believed his blessing someone interacted with the bond, making it unusual.

"I love Jayzca like a granddaughter," continued the old, wizened Hol'Feel'Koo, "but I cannot make exceptions. Bringing you here was dangerous."

"But your god," Mizcarnon replied. "The one who rules over the Otherworlds . . ."

"Juk'Nun'San'Lux," Cha'Farsa supplied.

"Yes. He granted me power, bonded me with Jo'Rul'Scoo. It must be his will."

The old Hol'Feel'Koo looked down at the floor. Even seated, he still was taller than Mizcarnon standing. "The gods work how they will, Mizcarnon Peak Crosser. But Jayzca must be punished."

"I will take her with me to my lands, then."

Cha'Farsa blew out his lips, spit spraying; a gesture akin to a human sigh.

"Our world is very different in those lands. The Hol'Feel'Koo there are not like us; they are more primitive and highly superstitious. We don't have many dealings with them. If Cha'Ganeer or Jo appears in their lands, it could end in violence. They are as unpredictable and emotional as their own god, Juk'Stan'Kiez, who is the god of storms and chaos. In their land, there is no order."

"Life is risk, Cha'Farsa."

The old Hol'Feel'Koo's throat enlarged, and he chortled out a laugh. "You are wiser than any human I've met, including any among the Mazzdu."

"You honor me too much, revered one."

"Cha'Geneer and Jayzca of the Mazzdu will need you to guide them. They are but children."

Mizcarnon held back a smile. Chage, a child who stood over eleven feet tall.

"Since he has decided to stay by her side," said Cha'Farsa, gaze drifting to the ceiling, "I fear for his safety. The journey you take is a dangerous one, and I want my son to feel safe." Cha'Farsa's throat expanded outward in a rapid series of movements, a Hol'Feel'Koo gesture for sadness.

Mizcarnon stood, newly darkened eyes meeting the deep green ones of the Hol'Feel'Koo leader. "I promise nothing lightly, Cha'-Fal'Kanruu'Farsa, and I make this promise to you: I will help them as I can."

Cha'Farsa nodded. "You're the only hope I have for them."

"And what of Jo'Rul'Scoo?" Mizcarnon hoped his newly-bonded partner would accompany them, though he did not feel it proper to ask. Jayzca had said Jo could remain with her people, if she so desired.

"She is in the temple, contemplating her fate. She asked me to decide for her, but I have refused. She is a gifted healer, and our unforgiving world can always use gifted healers, yet I feel you and your friends will need help from her. Plus, she's very fond of you — infatuated, I might say in other circumstances."

Mizcarnon tried to suppress a blush and the turning of his stomach. He was grateful for all she'd done, to be sure, but he could never think of a creature like her in that way.

Cha'Farsa laughed again. "Do not worry, Mizcarnon Peak Crosser. It was only a joke. You, as a human, wouldn't survive even one night of lovemaking with a Hol'Feel'Koo."

The old Hol'Feel'Koo laughed again, and this time, Mizcarnon could not quell his embarrassment.

MIZCARNON FOUND Jo in the temple adjacent to the healing center. Hol'Feel'Koo architecture amazed him. He'd been so awed his first time in the Imperial Palace, though that now seemed pedestrian when compared with handiwork of the race of the Otherworld.

The Hol'Feel'Koo city of Ria'Fin sat near Mazz in his world, though with a different topography. Whereas Mazz sat on an ancient mountain, Ria'Fin had been built on a virgin mountain not half as tall. Much of the continent, including this northern shore, Cha'Farsa had explained, was still volcanic, and the distant earth fire burned to the south, transforming a beautiful sunset into something magnificent.

The Hol'Feel'Koo had built using the liquid fire that came from the earth. They would drill down and bring the magma to the surface to pour it into massive molds made of some composite rock they called jinran. The forms gave the buildings a natural feel, as if the gods themselves had made the city like a potter might mold clay. The result? Impossible arches, waving walls, and surfaces both thick and thin. And none of the buildings were old; the Hol'Feel'Koo world changed too often for that, forcing constant construction and rebirth of their buildings.

In Ria'Fin, the temple was by far the most fascinating building, its outside stone smooth and irregular, appearing as though polished by years of running water. Inside was entirely different. Walls arched into a thirty-foot ceiling, though they did not meet in a straight beam of wood like in the human world. There was a beam of sorts, but it weaved across the ceiling like a snake. And while the insides of other buildings were covered in colorful tile, the temple remained the stark black of the volcanic rock.

The temple had no chairs or seating of any kind, just a smooth, black floor polished so finely, Mizcarnon could see his dark reflection. A circular pattern dominated the center of the room, its geometry mirroring the sections of a half-cut orange. Jo'Rul'Scoo knelt in the middle, facing Mizcarnon, though she did not look up; her eyes were closed tightly as if she feared to open them. Deep breaths expanded her chest like a bellows.

When he first met her, he hadn't known she was female; the gender differences among the Hol'Feel'Koo confused him. Females were smaller, though not always. Males had upward-jutting tusks in their lower jaws, and while females had tusks, they had them removed in their first or second decade. All Hol'Feel'Koo walked around naked, their thick fur their only protection. That did not help with gender identification; gender organs were concealed under skin and fur.

"I came here to find solitude." Jo's voice was higher than the males', more melodic. She did not open her eyes.

"I did not mean to disturb you. I will leave."

But before he could turn around, her bright blue eyes snapped open. "I think I won't have much solitude in the years to come; I shouldn't pine for it."

She stood, towering several feet above him. Everything about the Hol'Feel'Koo was oversized — massive hands, broad shoulders, feet that could easily crush a man. Yet despite her size, Jo moved more like a trained dancer than a giant-like Shantierd.

"Cha'Farsa said you were still thinking about whether to come with us," Mizcarnon said.

"Do I really have a choice?" Jo looked up at the temple's high ceiling as if imploring her gods. "I am neither an adventurer nor a warrior. I trained for years to become a healer, and now I will leave everything I've known to follow some human to lands long forgotten by the gods."

Her soft, sad voice brought Mizcarnon shame. How could he ask this of her? How selfish could he be? How would he feel if someone forced him to forsake his Peak Crosser calling, to never take wing again into the sky?

He knew the answer — had the moon-blessed Emperor asked that of him, he would indeed give up being a Peak Crosser. He would do whatever duty called him to do.

"My world needs me," Mizcarnon said, knowing this was an insufficient explanation.

"But I won't be in your world, unless you control me there. I will be in my world, not here among my people, but among a wild race who might see me as a threat."

Mizcarnon glanced up at the ceiling, then back to Jo. "Do you believe in the will of your gods?"

"I worship Juk'Jan'Fo, master of healing and life. I have ignored the other gods, trusting in her will for me." Jo moved her gaze around the concentric shape at her feet. "Do I believe in their power? Do I believe in their graces? Yes. But not even the gods agree on everything, Mizcarnon Peak Crosser. And on your world, you talk to moons, lifeless rocks in the heavens. Which god should I follow? Which will can guide me?"

Mizcarnon offered no reply. He'd never been a particularly religious man; too much religious devotion in the Empire was a conflict of duty. Yes, Mizcarnon believed the gods existed, the three moons watching over their fallen world. But he never prayed, never paid homage. The gods had done their work; now, it was time for humanity to do its own.

"Forget the gods, then." Mizcarnon looked heavenward again. "I'm sorry if that's an irreverent thought in this place."

"Some of my kind would be greatly offended by your words," she replied, adding with a toothy grin, "but I'm not most of my kind."

Mizcarnon returned the smile. Talking with Jo was never dull.

"I must return to my people," Mizcarnon said after a few moments of silence. "They need to be warned about the Nansartans, that the invasion is coming. My duty is to them."

"Duty." The word echoed through the temple. "My duty has always been here, healing the sick and the wounded. But maybe I'm meant for a different path."

Jo placed a massive hand on Mizcarnon's shoulder, like a mother might a child. "I will come help you. But before we leave, I need a promise from you."

"Of course."

Jo examined Mizcarnon's face. "You will only bring me to your world with my permission, and if violence is part of how you wish to use me, you will first get my blessing before you act. I'm not naive enough to believe we can do what you want without a fight, but I will not be used against my will."

Mizcarnon thought back to the devastation Jayzca had caused to the Nansartan camp using Chage, and he cringed to think he had that much power.

"You have my word and honor, Jo'Rul'Scoo."

"Good." She stepped past him. "Then let's be on our way."

REVELATIONS

The day after their failed kidnap attempt of Laran Magistrate, Zornan and Mairie met up with Maeltha outside Kandrinal beneath the hot afternoon sun, the air thick with the moisture that always seemed more potent near the ocean. Despite Maeltha staying behind and warning them the night before, Mairie still feared an ambush.

"You can't trust her, Zornan," Mairie had said.

"I don't trust her. But she could have left, and she didn't."

"Then it's part of something that serves her. Not you, not us. Her."

Zornan had simply nodded. No, he couldn't trust his one-time friend, but allies were in short supply.

Maeltha stood exactly where she said she would be – at the bend in the road. Nightgrip and Moonie circled overhead, tiny enough in the air to appear as though they might be their smaller cousins.

We stand ready to help, Moonie thought to Zornan. The mrakaro was bored of hiding in the foothills.

We may need that today, Zornan replied. He had no idea what they'd face, but a couple of giant flyers at their disposal could be helpful for battle or, if it came down to it, a quick escape.

Maeltha stood there, sweat beading on her forehead and drenching her clothes. She'd been running since the early morning hours, ever since she'd witnessed Laran's abduction.

"They're in a fisherman's house outside Kandrinal, on a hill over-looking the ocean," Maeltha said, her voice punctuated with deep breaths.

"Who are they?"

She shook her head. "Two men, big like Enforcers. And a third man greeted them. Looks Crazdarian. I don't recognize any of them."

"Dundraz trying to extract him and make it look like an abduction?" Mairie said. Zornan had not considered this.

Maeltha shrugged. "Could be. Or Kuthraz, or the Empire, or someone else entirely. He's a corrupt Magistrate involved in a dangerous rebellion. He's probably got a list of enemies longer than mine."

Mairie scoffed at that.

"Let's go pay them a visit," Zornan said. "We need Laran to tell us where we can find the Dundraz."

"We don't know what we're walking into," Maeltha replied. "A lot is going on, most of which is covered in fog. We could run into some-thing big and not see it."

"Not that she gets a vote, but I don't like it either," Mairie said. "They capture a prominent Magistrate using just two or three men? The countryside is going to be crawling with Investigators and Enforcers within a day. Hiding in a shack twenty miles from the abduction place is stupid. There must be more."

"Doesn't matter," Zornan said. He breathed in deeply. He couldn't waste time with a discussion. "We have a Destroyer, whatever the moon I am, a Peak Crosser, and two giant flyers. Unless they have two dozen Enforcers buried under that house, we can handle it."

Mairie wrinkled her nose but held her tongue. Maeltha rolled her eyes.

"Then, how do we proceed?" Maeltha asked.

Moonie, come, Zornan thought to Two Moons. *Bring Nightgrip with you.*

The road was empty, which was good, since two giant flyers landing on a lonely road might seem strange to other passersby. The mrakaro and the cosow landed just off the road in a patch of short grass.

"Mairie," Zornan continued, "bring your bow. You'll stay behind us and provide cover. Be close enough to be seen but far enough away that only a Baldra could hit you." Mairie took her bow and quiver from Nightgrip's saddle. "Maeltha, you're with me." Zornan pulled the Peak Crosser's hatari from Moonie's saddle and tossed it to her. "Can we count on you to fight with us?"

Maeltha's eyes widened as she snatched the weapon from the air. "I've made a promise to never betray you again, Zor. That promise probably means less to you than words from the Emperor's slippery tongue, but I mean it." Her gaze held something Zornan hadn't seen since they were initiates: hope. Hope for what?

They rounded the next hill and approached the lonely fisherman's house, which stood on a crest overlooking the never-ending ocean. Built of weathered wood, it had been painted once, the only evidence against the ravages of the ocean air a few paint flecks in crevices, and it couldn't have been larger than Zornan's sitting room back in Fallindra, with one door and one window visible on the ocean-facing side. The sun dipped toward the ocean, the day growing long.

"It will be hard to get a good sightline of the front door." Mairie lifted her bow, then pulled out an arrow and nocked it, pointing the weapon at the ground.

"How's your shot from the back of a cosow?" Maeltha asked.

Mairie nodded. "Yes, that could work. I'd be moving, but the wind is light, and I could see everything I needed to."

They shared a brief nod, then turned their gazes from one another, ashamed by their agreement.

"How should we approach, Zor?" Maeltha asked.

"Like invited guests." He left his hatari in its sheath.

Mairie shook her great head of hair. "That's not your best idea, Zornan."

"But certainly not my worst."

Nightgrip returned to the ground, and Mairie mounted the cosow.

She should be riding me, Moonie shot at Zornan, *not that furry flying rodent.*

Easy now, Moonie. Cosows glide better, and we'll need you if we get outnumbered.

Of course you will, Moonie replied, exuding pride. *Cosows are nearly useless in combat, especially on the ground. Though* Zornan had seen very little combat, he didn't think that was true, yet he decided to let that thought remain in his mind, unhatched.

Mairie and the cosow launched upwards, joining Moonie in circling the hill hundreds of feet in the air.

Zornan walked toward the small house, and Maeltha matched his pace. They approached the dwelling at an angle, straight toward one of its front corners. They could see the front door and its window, though not as clearly as Zornan would have liked, but he felt more secure seeing Nightgrip's shadow near the front of the house. Mairie was in position.

The front door came open, and Zornan stopped, resisting the urge to pull out his hatari; Mairie would unleash one of her arrows if whoever was in that house came out looking for a fight.

"Greeting, Zornan Peak Crosser." A man walked into the daylight, voice and face unmistakable: Cradris, the strange man who'd saved Mairie, Ballin, and Liven from the Dundraz in the forests of Bastarna.

"Welcome greeting, Cradris."

"I warned you to stay out of this storm, yet here you are again. And you bring the girl." He glanced up at the circling cosow.

Zornan did not look away from the mysterious Crazdarian. "You kidnapped Laran Magistrate."

"Most certainly," said Cradris, speaking like a farmer who had only pulled weeds from his field. "The man is a Dundraz agent. Penetrating their group is very difficult, as you know."

"I need to speak with him."

"I'd suggest again that you stay uninvolved, but I assume you'll continue to ignore me."

"Do you know what the Dundraz have done to my wife?" Zornan had practically barked the words, anger cresting.

"They kidnapped her."

"When we spoke in Bastarna," Zornan barked again, "you knew something. You knew the Dundraz meant to harm my family."

"We had heard whispers," Cradris replied, eyes serious, "but if we had known they would be so bold, we would have stopped them. The Dundraz are clearly desperate; they fear your Kuthraz friends, and they fear the softening heart of Emperor Tothdarin. Plus, they fear an enemy far across the sea." He looked south toward Kandrinal, then back at Zornan. "Fear can make people do stupid things."

Zornan took in a deep breath, eyes and face pinched in anger, knowing the man spoke of the Kuthraz and of Zornan. "Stop talking in riddles, man. I need to find where they're keeping Calla, and I'm going to make Laran tell me."

"And what will you do if you find her? They know you're coming, Peak Crosser. They will be prepared for you and the Destroyer. They might not realize how dangerous you are, but their caution will be enough to trap you. Then, if you don't reveal the Kuthraz to them, they will threaten to kill Calla. You will reveal them, and an army will descend upon your rebel friends like a host of dung ants. And then they will kill you and your wife. Your wife is gone, Zornan Peak Crosser, and you should—"

"Don't tell me what I should do!" His shout silenced the Crazdarian. "I will tell you what I'm going to do. I will rip apart every piece of the Dundraz, crush them until they are no more so there will be no one to pursue us, no one to haunt us. And I will kill the moon-blessed Emperor himself, if I find this twisted conspiracy rises to his throne. I will gut you like a mule deer if I find out that, despite your protestations, you are aligned with those animals. Now let me speak with Laran, or may the moons show mercy for what I will do next." Zornan's heart pounded in his chest, blood coursing through him in a rapid flow.

Cradris did not flinch but nodded as if he expected Zornan's outburst. "You have been awakened to the reality around, Peak Crosser. That is good. I hope you can live with the journey you're about to walk through and the part you'll play." He motioned toward the house. "Come. Speak with Laran. But once you have the information you need, I would ask that we keep him. I have need of some information you care little about."

Zornan and Maeltha followed Cradris, stopping only when Nightgrip landed close behind them.

"What are you doing, Zornan?" Mairie questioned.

"Going inside to question the Magistrate."

Mairie jumped off the cosow, landing between Zornan and the house. "I heard your little tirade, Zornan, as did most of the coast. I know the darkness you speak of; I feel it almost every day. Don't let it consume you."

Zornan closed his eyes, trying to calm himself. But the fire of his anger remained. "If this darkness is what's required to get Calla back" — he opened his eyes — "then I will use it."

Mairie stepped aside. "You may not like yourself after all this is done."

Zornan stepped inside the small house leaving Maeltha and Mairie outside.

Two large men loomed over Laran, who looked just like the man Zornan had seen pompously prowling the streets of Kandrinal. His rich nightclothes lay in a heap next to him, and he sat in his own filth, the stench assaulting Zornan's keen senses as he entered. His curled Kandrinal mustache hung limply over his lips, the red-painted tips now a faded pink. Zornan looked around the small, one-room house whose bare floors were mere dirt. It smelled like sweat, urine, and mold.

"Who are you?" Laran said, and one of the large men kicked him in the stomach. The fat man wheezed as he clutched his large belly.

"Answer only what is asked you." Cradris stood at Zornan's side. "Cooperate, or my friends here will be free to play as they wish."

Zornan flinched as the other man kicked Laran in the back, and the Magistrate cried out in pain.

"I'll see you all hung from your toenails, you vile—" The first man again kicked Laran in the belly, and his curse disappeared in a pained huff.

"This man has a few simple questions, dear Magistrate, and you will answer them." Cradris' voice remained low and calm.

"You'll kill me," Laran hissed.

"No, opulent Magistrate, I have no intention of killing you. We do not kill needlessly."

"Don't feed me that rotten fish," Laran replied. "You Kuthraz are not any less ruthless than us, no matter how you fancy yourselves."

"I am not Kuthraz," Cradris replied. "I represent the interest of Nansart."

Though Zornan did not know the name, recognition lit Laran's face. "So you are here, hiding in the Empire."

"Not for much longer."

Zornan looked at Cradris. What was the meaning of Nansart? And why would Laran Magistrate be more willing to bow to that than to the Kuthraz?

"You are coming to take the Empire," Laran said in a near whisper.

"A new era dawns, Laran Magistrate," Cradris responded. "And you are an opportunist. You placed your bet with the Dundraz because you saw the Empire's weakness and rot in a way most don't; you anticipated a winner. But the Dundraz will not win. We will win. Time for you to change your bet."

Laran's stare shifted between the men looming above him, to Cradris, and then to Zornan.

"What do you want to know?" Laran sat up, wincing.

Cradris looked at Zornan and nodded.

"I want to know where my wife, Calla, is."

Laran laughed, then stopped short in a flinch like a kick might come. None did, though Zornan had considered it.

"You are Zornan Peak Crosser." Laran seemed almost amused. "My friends would like to find you very much."

"Where is my wife?" Zornan demanded.

"In Bristrinia," he replied. "But unless you fancy another brastilia prison room, I wouldn't rush toward the capital. After all, I want to look out for the best interests of my new friends." He smiled like a crooked merchant selling an impotent potion.

"Where in the capital?" Cradris questioned. "And what resistance might Zornan encounter?"

"I don't know the defenses exactly, nor the location. I am part of the group, but not in its inner circle. I've heard the place called 'the basement,' and it is in the capital, close to the palace for sure. I would fancy a guess there's at least fifteen Enforcers there all preparing for the Destroyer girl to come along. We . . . they . . . want her, too." At that, he smiled wickedly.

"Who holds Calla?" Zornan asked. "Who is the mastermind behind all this?"

Laran hesitated, frowning. "If she ever discovers I told you . . ." He shuddered.

"She won't," Cradris replied. "And even if she does, you have our protection now. But I can't protect you if you don't help us. Answer the Peak Crosser's question."

Laran sighed, which forced another wince. "This would be easier if you hadn't broken half my ribs." He struggled to his feet with the assistance of one of the large men. "The Peak Crosser's wife is held by our leader, none other than the High Counselor herself, Lanthia, the moon-blessed advisor to Emperor Tothdarin."

The revelation slammed into Zornan's psyche, threatening to overwhelm it. The Dundraz conspiracy stretched into the throne room of the Emperor! She could command dozens, maybe hundreds, of Enforcers, soldiers, Baldra. Besides the Emperor, she might be the

Empire's most powerful person, and Laran Magistrate had given her up because of some fear Zornan did not understand.

"Moons above," Cradris said. "Lanthia. I'll be tied and thrown into a prairie cat pit. She plays the part of love-crossed Counselor, weak and feeble, yet she's the predator. Amazing, indeed."

Doubt filled Zornan. "I can't storm the prison of the moon-blasted Counselor to the Emperor." The revelation of the Dundraz's leader left Zornan weak and hopeless.

"Let's step outside, Peak Crosser." Cradris left the room, and Zornan followed. The Crazdarian closed the door behind them, and they stood on the small porch with the ocean's waves crashing in the distance, a constant rhythm mostly foreign to Zornan's senses. Moonie, Nightgrip, Maeltha, and Mairie stood twenty feet off, postures tense.

Are you all right? Moonie asked.

Zornan tried to mask his dread, mustering a weak reply, *I will be.*

"Not feeling so brash now, eh, Peak Crosser?"

"The moon-blasted Counselor to the Emperor," Zornan repeated.

"Indeed. This is unwelcome information for us both."

"I can't do this alone."

"No, you cannot. Even you and the Destroyer aren't enough. By the Emperor's foolish bones, that woman might control the whole Empire, Tothdarin dancing to her seductive tune. This changes everything." Cradris looked over at Mairie, then back to Zornan. "But you have friends, and with this revelation, your Kuthraz friends will help, assuming the Magistrate isn't lying to us."

"You think he's lying?"

"No, I'm almost certain he speaks the truth. But even I can be fooled. The indulgent bastard might have more wits than I give him credit for."

"Who is Nansart, and why would Laran fear him so?"

Cradris frowned. "You don't want the burden of this. But since you seem so inclined toward self-destruction anyway, Nansart is my master, and he's conquered Boothdrinka and Croxshine."

Zornan had heard the names of these kingdoms across the ocean, but he knew little more. "And he comes for the Empire," Zornan said.

Cradris smiled. "You've seen the rot of the Empire closer than most, Peak Crosser. The Emperor is weak and failing, the Dundraz are cruel and violent, and the Kuthraz are so wrapped up in their own intrigue, they can no longer see the future they fight for. Nansart rules with order and equity. The citizens of the Empire will one day fall at his feet and thank the moons for his rule." At this, the man's eyes lit with lust.

Cradris broke from his trance to focus back on Zornan. "You should go free your wife. Gather what friends you can and extract her from them, then go hide somewhere in the north and watch the Empire burn. Once Nansart rules, you will again have a safe haven."

"Why the sudden change of heart? Why are you encouraging me to go find Calla, when moments ago, you were urging me to give it up? What purpose does it serve you?"

"Chaos." Cradris smiled. "We can use that chaos. With the Dundraz embedded at that level, our current plan will not work. But if you and some friends rip them apart . . ."

"You'd use us."

"Yes, you could phrase it that way. But unlike your friends, the Kuthraz, I will be honest about it. My friends and I want you to be happy. In fact, my counterpart, Trillia, is quite fond of your family. She would want what's best for Lady Calla."

Trillia was part of this somehow. High Counselor Lanthia was the leader of the Dundraz. Had his whole life not been caught is this chaotic whirlwind, he wouldn't have believed it.

"So what flight do you choose, Peak Crosser?"

"I'm going to the Kuthraz," Zornan replied, "to gather whoever will join me to fight through whatever that stick of a woman has put between me and my wife."

"Good," Cradris said. His satisfaction bothered Zornan, but he pushed it aside. "One word of caution." He looked back at Mairie. "Don't put all your trust in the Kuthraz. Laran Magistrate was correct. The Kuthraz may be less ruthless than the Dundraz, but that's like comparing a prairie cat to a shark; both will eat the skin off your bones if they can."

Zornan nodded, though he hadn't needed this strange man to tell him what he already knew. Now that Zornan's interests intersected with the Kuthraz, he could use them as they'd once used him.

"Sad parting, Zornan Peak Crosser. I hope when our paths cross again, a new era will have dawned on this moon-forsaken continent. I also hope we meet as friends. Understand, anything we do is for the best interest of those we serve: the people of this Empire."

Zornan sighed inwardly. He tired of these types. Loothdram, Cradris, Stethdel — men who thought they knew better than anyone else the flight of everyone else's lives.

"Mournful parting, Cradris." And he added nothing else, doubtful they'd ever be friends. Two meetings with the slippery man were more than enough.

13

A FLAILING INVESTIGATION

T he last time he'd been in Laran Magistrate's home, Crisdan had felt in control probing the feelings of the corrupt Kandrinali. He'd felt thrilled to uncover a possible Dundraz. Now, the home had the feel of a funeral, the end of Crisdan's effectiveness as an Investigator and servant of the Empire.

This feeling of futility reminded him of the investigation three years ago of Zornan Peak Crosser. Last time, it was a dead High Magistrate. This time, a missing one. In both cases, Crisdan's credibility and reputation had been questioned. The investigation into High Magistrate Stethdel's death had, of course, ended in Zornan's exoneration, which marked Crisdan's rapid ascension within his High Trade. He doubted this investigation would end so nicely.

"I still don't understand why you were questioning Laran in the first place." Sitting across from Crisdan, in the same opulent room where he'd questioned Laran, was High Investigator Mabbe. Though she was older than Crisdan by more than a decade, her face defied her age; she was strikingly beautiful — a trait she'd used expertly throughout her career, with high cheek bones, a perfectly symmetrical nose, and blonde hair mixed with gray that hung to her shoulders. And she wasn't just any High Investigator; she was the lead High Investigator, representing their High Trade on the Council of High Trades.

"I had a tip that he might be connected to the Dundraz," Crisdan answered for what felt like the one hundredth time.

"Yes, so you've said." Mabbe's blue eyes were always intense, always probing, and she personified what most outsiders thought of Investigators: judgmental, intimidating, lacking a sense of humor. Other Investigators did not intimidate Crisdan; his own abilities made him emotionally invisible to his fellow Investigators. Yet, even knowing that, Mabbe intimidated Crisdan. "But what source? What tip?"

"I told you. I'd cultivated sources as I searched for the rebels. I'd like to keep those private."

"When you were elevated to the High Investigators and given the charge to chase down the Kuthraz and the Dundraz, I wholly supported it." Mabbe brought her hands together in front of her face. "Hykvan had always spoken so highly of you, may the moons bless his soul."

Hykvan — Crisdan's mentor and greatest friend. He'd died of pneumonia less than a year before.

"He praised your integrity and your skills," she continued, "but after two years of constant investigation, all we have is a missing Magistrate who disappeared from beneath you during an investigation into his possible connection to the Dundraz."

Mabbe paused. Crisdan refused to take her bait, no matter how well she'd set it on the hook; he would not let her badgering force him into a misstep. She had to know he would resist her efforts, though he admired her persistence.

"I think it's time to consider changing your assignment," Mabbe said after a few moments.

"That would require a majority vote of the High Investigators." She knew that, but Crisdan said it anyway.

Another might have smiled at Crisdan's gamesmanship. Not Mabbe. Her eyes, her face, rarely showed any emotion, at least not in front of other Investigators. Rumor said the woman was not entirely human. Nonsense, of course. But in that moment, he understood the superstition.

"I believe I can get those votes," she said. "Listen Crisdan" — her voice softened, but not her eyes — "I want to find the Dundraz, but they seem very good at avoiding us. You are too close to this. You may need some separation, some new perspective."

"Meaning you're sending me back to Bristrinia until you figure out what to do with me." Crisdan held back the bubbling anger. "Meaning you think I've screwed up — that Laran's abduction is somehow my fault."

Mabbe's own face remained blank. "Meaning this all-consuming investigation of yours is possibly clouding your judgment. Investigations of this sort require many eyes and many hands, and I fear we gave you too much by making this assignment solely yours."

Crisdan knew she was right, which made it even worse. Had he been in her chair, he would have advised the same thing, but that didn't make it any easier to swallow. Trillia would not be happy if Crisdan was removed, and Mabbe would be even less happy if she knew of Crisdan's complicity in these events.

Crisdan stood. "Then I shall return to Bristrinia." He'd been resisting this, but it might be for the best.

"Sad parting, High Investigator Crisdan." Mabbe also rose. "Take some time off when you arrive. You've earned it." Though it wasn't a command, as they were nearly equals, the intent was clear: stay out of the way.

Crisdan turned to leave, feelings bouncing from relief, to annoyance, to anger.

"Crisdan." Mabbe's voice stopped him, and he turned to the other High Investigator. "Seek the Emperor's audience when you arrive — he should be updated on this." Another political set-up, of course, this time sending him in front of the Emperor to deliver bad news. Whatever previous support Mabbe might have felt when Crisdan was elevated to the High Investigators was now gone, evaporated like water on hot sand.

He could refuse the assignment; he was a High Investigator, same as she. Or he could send a messenger, a lower administrative Investigator, to deliver it for him, but Trillia would certainly take advantage of getting him in front of the Emperor. *By the moons,* he thought. *I've even started acting on her orders before I get them.*

"I will give Emperor Tothdarin and High Counselor Lanthia your regards," he replied with a slight bow of his head.

Crisdan walked quickly through the foyer and out into the street. He would gather his things from the inn, then catch a coach to the tunnel outside Kandrinal and secure a private ferry to the capital.

As he marched, he saw Stargarn keeping pace at his side.

"I wouldn't tie your raft to mine," Crisdan said. "It will be a good way to sink, my Enforcer friend."

"I do not give up on others as fast as some," was his reply.

They walked in silence, which Crisdan reveled in, until Trillia's thoughts interrupted his own.

We know who has Calla; we know who leads the Dundraz.

Deep inside, emotions stirred. Despite everything he worked under, he still wanted to bring down the Dundraz, even if Trillia and whomever she worked for might be worse. The thought of freeing Calla from her current terror tried to break through his frozen heart.

But his soul was slowly dying under Trillia's fierce hand. The passion he had known before for justice, his love for Calla — these motivations that had at one time stirred his soul like nothing else could, were now fading into an abandoned part of him. The prospect of solving those two puzzles should have filled him with determination, maybe even joy. Instead, they stirred him like a slight breeze might rustle a great tree.

I've been ordered back to Bristrinia, he replied to Trillia's mind.

Perfect. Calla and our treacherous Dundraz leader are in the capital.

May I ask who the leader of the Dundraz is?

Trillia's response crackled with glee. *None other than High Counselor Lanthia.*

Surprise bubbled up, quickly dissolving under scrutiny. Of course it would be someone who was well woven into the fabric of the Empire, which would explain the resources and the rebels' ability to stay one step ahead of his investigation. High Investigator Mabbe and Lanthia were rumored to be friends; his fellow High Investigator might be a Dundraz collaborator, or maybe just a source for the High Counselor. Either way, Lanthia knew nearly everything, and the Dundraz were even better positioned than Crisdan had feared.

Then it's convenient that I am supposed to brief the Emperor the moment I return to the capital.

Most convenient. We are close, my friend. Close to revealing these fools to the Empire, close to tearing them down. Trillia's mindspeak grew distant as she pulled away.

Crisdan stopped and faced Stargarn. "Do you trust me?"

Stargarn regarded him, ever-skeptical eyes hardening into something like respect. "I do, High Investigator Crisdan. I don't always understand what you're thinking, but you were right about Laran Magistrate being a part of this. So, yes. Yes, I trust you."

"Then I'm going to need your help in Bristrinia."

"Bristrinia?" The Enforcer's eyebrows scrunched together. "But the investigation here is ongoing."

"I'm not needed here," he said simply. He didn't need to tell the man he'd been dismissed. "The bigger reason is, I think we're close to unmasking the face of the Dundraz, and I need to be in the capital to do it."

Stargarn's eyes widened.

"I need you to have my back," Crisdan continued. "I need you to follow my orders without question, even if they make no sense. As soon as I'm able, I'll tell you everything. We're on the cusp of something important, Stargarn, something that will change the course of the Empire," he said, though he did not feel the revolutionary zeal he tried to impose on the Enforcer.

Stargarn seemed to lap it up. "I am your man, Crisdan."

"Good." Crisdan resumed his march toward the inn. "Let's go stir up the capital."

1 4

A WAY TO THE PEAKS

J ayzca spent the next four days walking between worlds with Mizcarnon, Chage, and Jo, with Mizcarnon spending most of the time commenting on how walking between worlds was amazing and effortless. The muted colors, the strange echoes — for the Peak Crosser, all of it was a wonder. Since Jayzca had lived with it most of her life, she'd forgotten how truly amazing it all was, if she'd ever even known that. But before this, Jayzca had been the only living person who could walk between worlds. Now, there were two of them, and it was comforting to have someone else to share this with her, especially now.

"If you like walking between worlds so much," she said to

Mizcarnon, "then we should travel all the way to your Empire like this."

"We cannot walk across an ocean," Jo warned. "Water and air flow between worlds. We would all drown, just as if we tried walking through the ocean in either world."

"Then how will we get across an ocean?" Chage asked.

"We'll steal transportation," Mizcarnon said, and he explained about giant flyers, lizard-like beasts, and how the Nansartans had created these, which could even carry two Hol'Feel'Koo across a great ocean.

"But that won't help us," Chage moaned. "You two could fly across, but how would we cross in our world?"

Mizcarnon paused, eyeing the two Hol'Feel'Koo. "Jayzca and I will take your forms in the human world. Then, we can fly on the miotop and get us all across."

His suggestion ignited a strong debate: Chage was still angry about being forced to destroy the Nansartan camp, while Jo was hesitant to let Mizcarnon take control. She'd agreed to travel with them, but the realities of their bond frightened her.

"I don't want to control you," Mizcarnon said. "I don't ever want to subvert the will of another. But I see no other way."

They discussed it for some time, and despite Chage's pouting, they all agreed Mizcarnon's suggestion was the only way. They walked south, headed for the former Croxshinese capital of Jigraile. No miotops had been in the camp outside of Kalsrah, but Mizcarnon was sure Jigraile would have some. If the Nansartans had conquered the capital city, they'd have a full complement there.

A day later, they passed by the White Mountain, the great peak that had for centuries been mined. Jayzca had been too small to remember being this far south, and twice her companions had to admonish her to keep moving even as the torn mountain kept pulling her eyes toward it.

"What do you know of those giant birds?" Mizcarnon asked, pointing to some dark shapes circling the mountain.

"Are they giant?" Jayzca squinted to try and bring the distant shapes into better focus. "Hard to tell from here, especially from between worlds."

"I sensed them when I was headed down the mountain to Kalsrah. They are like our giant birds, the mrakaro, but very different. Wild."

"Father says they helped the White God pull the mountains from the ground." At the memory of her father teaching her about their world's creation, a sudden sadness took her breath away. She inhaled deeply to regain her composure. "They have been here since the world began."

Mizcarnon's face furrowed in confusion, but he asked no more.

Nine days after leaving Ria'Fin, they arrived on a high ridge overlooking Jigraile, the former capital, which sat at the junction of three large rivers. The city extended across every shore. Jayzca's eyes widened at the sight of it. What many called River City was larger than she'd ever imagined a city could be; three or four times larger than Kalsrah. From this distance, rivers looked like snakes hoarding a shining jewel.

But as they got closer, Jayzca saw the heavy price paid at the hand of the Nansartans. Bile welled up at the back of her throat as she recognized scorch marks from the Sun Demon. Most of the skyline showed damage, like a giant had flicked away roofs or pieces of buildings, and the eastern shore was a enormous pile of rubble; whatever had been there was no more. It made the destruction of her city seem small in comparison. So much death. So much devastation.

West of the city, on the southern banks of the western river, sat a massive army camp, its outline three times the size of the one they'd encountered near Kalsrah. Even at this distance, Jayzca saw the miotops Mizcarnon had mentioned.

"There." Mizcarnon pointed out the hulking flyers.

They spent the rest of the day walking into the valley and crossing the western river by a bridge near the camp, and when they reached the edge of the camp, night had fallen. With all three moons bright in the sky, Mizcarnon led the way; even on a clear, three-moon night, Jayzca struggled to see, while Mizcarnon moved as fluidly as if it had been midday. They passed several patrols, but their presence between worlds went undetected.

As they reached the edge of the camp, Mizcarnon sighed. "The miotops are chained."

Jayzca squinted. She could not distinguish the chains from the giant lizards' dark shapes.

"The chains won't be a problem," Chage said. "Those will come apart as easily as you would break a piece of bread."

"I'll cross into the human world and try to speak with the miotop," Mizcarnon said. "I'm not sure how intelligent they are. If they are as aware as our mrakaros, this may not work. The moment I reveal myself, the thing could just alert its human master through mindspeak."

"You did not mention this risk when you shared the plan with us," Jo replied.

"We only had foolhardy options, Jo, and this seems the best perch of a bad lot."

Mizcarnon glided into the human world. Moments before, he had been clear. Now, he existed like a smeared painting, features blending into the dark.

The miotops were strange-looking creatures. Their heads were like a common lizard's, only a thousand times bigger, with a rounded snout and eyes on either side. Their legs and feet were thick like a lizard's, with massive talons on the toes of each of its six feet. Green scales covered them, forming a thick armor. As Jayzca's eyes adjusted to the darkness, she saw one of the miotops yawn. She gasped. Its mouth was like a small cave; she could have comfortably crawled inside and played on its tongue.

Mizcarnon, for his part, approached slowly, head rotating back and forth.

Standing next to the miotop, Mizcarnon scanned for guards, but saw nothing. Confident he'd invaded the miotop enclosure unseen, he opened his mind, trying to reach out to the sleeping creature. He could feel its mind; it was like a child's, simple and direct. He asked it to wake.

The miotop's eyelids flicked open, while the rest of its body remained still, save for its deep breathing. Yellow eyes glowed in the moonlight, its pupils focused on Mizcarnon.

We need to fly, Mizcarnon thought to the creature.

Its response did not come as words but more like desires he could feel — fatigue and thirst.

You can drink from the river, Mizcarnon told it, *but we must go now.*

The miotop slowly stood and stretched its massive wings, eyes fixed on Mizcarnon expectantly.

Just then, Chage appeared next to Mizcarnon, his massive form in Jayzca's control, and stepping back, the miotop let out a soft squeal like the surprised cry of a human child.

Easy now, Mizcarnon comforted. *You will be carrying two of these on our journey. You will not see me, but you will see them.*

At first, confusion leaked from the miotop's mind, but it soon calmed and did not squeal again. None of the other miotops stirred.

"You shouldn't have come without warning me," Mizcarnon scolded Jayzca with a whisper. "If it had woken its companions or alerted a guard, our plan would have been finished."

"It had to get used to these forms sooner or later." The deep voice was Chage's, but the tone and manner was Jayzca. "Bring Jo here while I take care of the chain."

Mizcarnon calmed his mind and began the process they'd practiced on their journey. It seemed strange, and his mind had rejected the thought. How could he become another thing? Could a human become a mrakaro? Could a horse become a man?

But then Jayzca had reminded him that his own blessings seemed miraculous to the Croxshinese. His ability to see, to fight, to heal — all enhanced beyond typical human limits. If the blessings of the Bendathdrans and the weapons of the Cazdanthians were real, then why not the magic of the Mazzdu?

Mizcarnon focused on Jo and, feeling her presence in his mind, he reached for her . . . and felt nothing but her distant presence, like he might feel a sunset hundreds of miles away. Then, slowly at first, and more rapidly as the moments passed, Jo seemed to rush toward him, as if about to lock him in an embrace.

Mizcarnon opened his eyes. The darkness seemed thicker than before. He blinked twice, but his sight would not adjust to the dark as it typically did. And his perspective was all wrong, he now looked down on the startled Miotop instead of looking up at it. He looked down at his hands and saw the thick hands of a Hol'Feel'Koo — Jo's hands. He stepped back, startled.

You and I are now one, Jo's voice echoed in his mind, not unlike mindspeak with a mrakaro or another member of the High Trades.

One? he thought back. *Not exactly. I control your body; we are not one.*

Cha'Farsa told me that as our bond matures, we will be as one when you bring me into the human world.

Cha'Farsa had not mentioned this, and Jayzca had made it seem like total control, like a Shindar with a Baldra with one creature's will completely subject to the other. Mizcarnon didn't know which was more terrifying: completely subjugating another's will or losing one's own to a combination of both.

He looked back at the miotop, crouching nearby, eyes wide. He couldn't see its skin's detail like he had before — couldn't see the ground moving as it nervously dug in its claws.

Of course. The physical gifts he'd had most of his life would not be in Jo's body. As Mizcarnon reached out to the miotop to mindspeak, he hoped his mental blessings weren't gone as well.

His momentary fear disappeared when he felt the confused, scared mind of the giant lizard. *It's me. Don't be frightened. I'm in another form.* The returning thoughts made it clear the massive flyer did not understand, but neither did it retreat or squeal.

"We must go," Jayzca said from Creature's mouth, setting the broken chain down onto the ground. "Someone will notice us soon."

Mizcarnon looked around. The other miotops still slept, but she was right. The longer they stayed, the greater the chance they'd be discovered.

Come, mighty flyer, we must go. We shall both get on your back. A cautious agreement echoed in return, plus an intense hunger. *We will find you something to eat once we've put enough space between us and this place.*

The miotop took a wary step toward Mizcarnon.

"Where's the saddle?" Jayzca asked.

"We won't need it," Mizcarnon replied. "And we're too big for a human saddle, anyway."

Mizcarnon, as Jo, stood by the miotop's side. Mounting the flyer wouldn't be much different than a human mounting a horse. Easier than getting on the back of a mrakaro. Still, he hesitated. How high could this body jump? He'd have to find out.

With a powerful leap, he bounded onto the front of the miotop's back, almost falling over before steadying himself on one of the flyer's ridges.

Be careful not to hurt my body, human. It's the only one I have, Jo chastised, though the thought was more mirth than rebuke.

If I get hurt as you, how does that effect you in your world?

Whatever wound you take follows me into my world. So, please be careful; I'm the only one who knows how to heal a Hol'Feel'Koo. Again, humor coated the thought, though Mizcarnon felt a pang of guilt for any harm he might bring Jo's body. The responsibility of her safety was a burden he didn't want to carry.

A sudden whine broke his thoughts, and Mizcarnon looked toward the sound. A nearby miotop bleated at them, its yellow eyes wide with alarm, and the remaining creatures awoke, joining the chorus.

To the air! Mizcarnon commanded their stolen flyer.

The miotop moved quickly, rumbling along, stretching its massive wings. Moments later, it jumped and the air caught beneath its wings, forcing them upward more smoothly than Mizcarnon would have imagined.

As they launched off, Mizcarnon scanned the camp, but saw nothing; Jo's eyes were not good enough in the dark to provide detail. He imagined the Nansartan soldiers trying to make sense of it all and hoped they hadn't gotten a good look at the thieves.

Behind him, Jayzca gripped tightly to a ridge on the miotop's back, legs locked fiercely against the flyer's side.

"You don't have to hold on so tightly," Mizcarnon shouted against the wind. "Chage's strength should keep you in place. And these things were blessed to carry many passengers, so it won't dump you."

Jayzca, however, continued with her fierce grip, and she held Chage's eyes shut as if opening them might make her fall. "Easy for you to say, Peak Crosser," she replied. "Some of us don't find flying so natural."

Mizcarnon laughed, though it came out differently from the sound that was in his head — a deep, guttural Hol'Feel'Koo laugh. He turned back to the front, orientating himself against the stars and the three bright moons. Circlarl, Dithdee, and the Fire Moon hovered in bright beauty; Circlarl was full, with blue Dithdee waning and the Fire Moon waxing. He'd obey the miotop's hunger, landing them in the northeastern Thick, where the animal could eat its fill, and then they could fly to the coast before flying to the Peaks.

The flight fueled Mizcarnon, despite his occupying another's body, and reconnected him with himself. He'd worried the Hol'Feel'Koo bodies might not take to flying, that he might feel sick, like many do on top of a giant flyer. But the Hol'Feel'Koo's world was harsh, so their bodies had been blessed by their gods to be strong and enduring.

Though his sight was not as good in the dark and his skin tempered the wind rushing across his face, being in the air again thrilled him. How long it would take for them to reach the Peaks, or how soon the Nansartans might import their terror to his homeland, he was unsure. But now he had hope. He had a chance to get home and warn the Emperor about the imminent threat. He had hope now that he could fulfill his duty.

FRIENDS AND PLANS

"There's no way she's coming with us to see the Kuthraz," Mairie said, eyes nearly as fiery as when she raged against attackers. "She's a criminal, Zornan, not a friend."

"She stayed, Mairie," Zornan replied, voice tired. When had he last had a full night's sleep?

"She just sees something in it for herself. She's selfish, Zornan, and your old friendship makes you blind." Standing with Zornan next to Moonie, Mairie shot a vicious glance toward Maeltha, who waited thirty feet away near the cliff overlooking the ocean.

"Maybe." Zornan couldn't believe he was arguing to take Maeltha with them. He didn't really trust her, of course, but they needed help.

Zornan had no idea if the Kuthraz would use the information about Lanthia for their own designs. If Loothdram again refused to give aid . . . "We need her, Mairie. Are you with me until the end on finding Calla?"

Mairie's eyes softened. "Of course. If we don't rescue Calla, then no one will. And she doesn't deserve to be in there, all because I exist . . ."

Zornan looked at his young friend, her eyes filling with tears, lips twitching with buried emotion. "Mairie, this is not your fault. The Dundraz did this. Maybe some blame lies on your father and Loothdram, but none on you."

"But my very existence threatens everyone around me . . ." She turned her head and closed her eyes against a rush of tears.

Zornan reached out and put his hands on her shoulders, turning her to face him. "We are both in that boat now, my friend. And we will make them pay. Anyone who stands between us and Calla will pay. They will see just what two Destroyers can do." Zornan had never thought of himself part of that ancient class of High Tradesmen who'd been wiped out for being too powerful to control. But the moniker had often been used to describe Mairie, and it described him now, too.

She took a deep breath. "Yes. They will pay — every bloody one of them."

Zornan stepped back. "But as strong as we are, we're going to need help. I don't trust Maeltha, and I don't think the Kuthraz will approve of us bringing her into their valley. But we need her; we need the help. Poor friends are better than none."

"We could just fly out over the ocean and dump her." Mairie's eyes sparkled, even under Zornan's disappointed glare. "Fine," she said, "we'll do it your way. But I am right sometimes, Zornan."

I agree with Mairie, Moonie mindspoke to Zornan. *Let's dump her into the ocean. She might be a wonderful swimmer.*

Not you, too, young friend.

Moonie giggled in Zornan's mind.

Zornan reached Maeltha at her spot near the cliff. "You're coming with us," he said.

"By the Destroyer's little glare, I'm taking it the decision wasn't unanimous," she replied.

"If it's any consolation," Zornan said, "I think Three Moons disagrees with me even more than Mairie does."

"Yes, Zor, very comforting."

She had used his nickname again. This time, though, he let it slide.

"We should at least blindfold her," Mairie said.

Zornan sighed. "Won't matter," he said, tired of arguing. Mostly, though, he was tired of the whole fiasco, which made their bickering even more unbearable. "Blindfolded or not, her Peak Crosser abilities will tell her exactly where in the Empire she is."

"The Kuthraz might not let her leave."

"Aren't you just a ray of moonbeams," Maeltha shot back to Mairie, who replied by sticking out her tongue.

"They will," Zornan said. "If a war is coming, they won't be there for long." And when the time came, he would like to see them stop him from taking her out.

* * *

Atop Moonie and Nightgrip, Zornan, Mairie, and Maeltha approached Fallen Mountain on their third day away from Kandrinal. They'd flown across much of the Infinite Mountains, inland, to avoid fierce ocean winds and spying eyes.

Lascrill, Zornan spoke to the Peak Crosser's mind.

Welcome greeting, Zornan. Have you found Calla?

Sort of. I need you to fly out here and meet us. I've brought a guest.

The older man's apprehension seeped through their mindspeak. *You'd better say it's Calla.*

No, not Calla. Come see for yourself.

A few minutes later, Lascrill's gray mrakaro broke through Fallen Mountain's cloud cover, and their old master immediately recognized his former student. *Maeltha is a traitor and a criminal. By the moons, Zornan, she left you and Mairie for dead on Doorie.*

Will you let her in?

I should kill her on the spot! She killed her own mrakaro, Zornan! She'd sell out her wing hand if it served her needs.

Then we will find help and safety elsewhere, Zornan replied.

Lascrill's anger burned. *She can come into our stronghold, but we're going to need a good explanation. If we're not satisfied, Josha might kill her.*

Fair enough, Zornan thought back. He could hardly fault the man; only a week ago, he'd nearly killed Maeltha himself.

They followed Ash and Lascrill through the clouds and down into the same clearing, where a dozen men and women waited, weapons drawn. Lascrill had been serious about not taking chances with Maeltha.

After they landed, Loothdram emerged from the crowd, his own hatrindi drawn. "You'd better have a good reason for bringing that demon spawn into our safe haven," he said.

"Welcome greeting to you, too, old friend." Zornan slipped down from Moonie's back, onto the dew-wet grass. He stretched his legs.

Mairie dismounted Nightgrip, but Maeltha remained in the saddle, her eyes, as usual, holding little of anything she felt inside. If Zornan hadn't known the situation, he'd have believed her expression was that of someone arriving in a new place as a welcomed guest.

Loothdram muttered, "Of all the stupid things to do—"

"Stop," Zornan said. "You don't get to question my intent."

"I do when it's about my people and my cause. You have endangered us—"

"You sent me, Ballin, and Mairie on our own across the Empire!" Zornan stepped up nose to nose with Loothdram, and Loothdram's hatrindi shot away from his hand, hitting the ground with a thud and pressing the grass like someone had stepped on it. "And now you question me? Maeltha may have betrayed us to the Dundraz on Doorie, but you sent us down that road, pointed straight at them!"

Loothdram stared at his hatrindi. "How did you do that?"

"Do what?"

"Pull my hatrindi from my hand?"

Zornan looked at Loothdram's fallen weapon, sensing the brastilia, feeling its edges and its weight; its power surged toward him like an insect pulled toward a candle's flame. Zornan relaxed, let it go, and the brastilia sword lifted ever so slightly, riding atop the thick grass.

"I'm sorry for being so sharp" — Loothdram met Zornan's eyes — "but we work hard to keep this place secret. You shouldn't have brought her here."

"And you shouldn't have sent me out without any help." Zornan edged back from his friend, forcing his throbbing, hot anger to lessen. "I think you'll want to hear what we have to say. We found a Dundraz agent in Kandrinal — a Magistrate called Laran."

Disbelief colored Loothdram's face. "That fat, old cow?"

"Yes," Zornan replied. "He'd been Maeltha's contact when she worked for them, and he told us who's behind the Dundraz, told us that High Counselor Lanthia is the group's leader, and that she likely has Calla. I need your help to find my wife."

Loothdram's face moved from disbelief, to surprise, to joy. "Lanthia! That witch leads the Dundraz?" He turned to Lascrill. "What do you think? Is it possible she's the leader?"

"That explains a lot," Lascrill replied. "The Dundraz seem to have incredible resources, and they are always one step ahead of us and the Empire. The High Counselor could do that."

"Come inside the cave." Loothdram turned to Mayfran, who stood at the head of the gathered guards. "Hold the traitor out here," he said. "Be nice, but not too nice." The former Enforcer nodded.

"I think I have plan," Loothdram said as Zornan followed him in, "one that will free Calla and bring down the Dundraz at the same time."

* * *

THE GROUP STOOD inside the Kuthraz's brightly lit planning room. Zornan hadn't seen Ballin yet; he certainly wasn't in this type of discussion. Instead, Zornan stood facing the three Kuthraz leaders: Loothdram, Lascrill, and Josha, a woman he knew little about except that she didn't trust Zornan.

"He brought a Dundraz agent into Fallen Mountain," Josha said to her fellow Kuthraz, eyes never leaving Zornan. "I recommend we execute Maeltha Peak Crosser and throw Zornan's stupid ass into a hole."

"You haven't even heard what he has to say," Lascrill responded.

"I don't need to," said the former Enforcer. Angry lines on her face matched her body's tension under her tight-fitting tunic. "Maeltha works for the moon-cursed Dundraz, and you two flitter brains are too close to Zornan and his family to see past his stupidity."

Zornan opened his mouth, then closed it. He couldn't let anger again get the best of his tongue.

"You're a thirsty deer with your eyes off the wolf," Loothdram said. "Lanthia is the leader of the Dundraz, Josha, and we have an opportunity to strike."

Her face softened, though only a gradation from one form of stone to another. "I recognize that, Dram. But he's not one of us. He has refused to join our cause. What happens if Zornan's agenda conflicts with ours? The moons align today, yes, but what about tomorrow?"

"Let's first figure out today," Loothdram replied, his usual mirthful countenance holding more weight than usual. "Today, Zornan's interests and ours are perfectly aligned."

Zornan furrowed his brow. "So, you'll help me free Calla?"

"Yes." Loothdram ignored a pointed glare from Josha. "But we'll need something in return."

"Only if it aids in freeing Calla," Zornan said back.

"See?" Josha faced her two fellow Kuthraz. "We shouldn't even involve him."

"We need him," Lascrill said, finally entering the conversation. "We need people like Zornan and Calla on our side — good folks."

"We don't need cowards who run from the fight," Josha said, returning her frosty glare to Zornan.

Her insult dipped the small room into an icy silence. Power surged inside Zornan, like it had outside with Crisdan, as her words drew forth his angst, and he could feel their brastilia weapons, sense the energy pulsing from the surrounding ore hidden deep within the surrounding rocks. When he closed his eyes, glowing green versions replaced them.

"I won't be called a coward," Zornan said, trying and failing to level his voice, "by a group that has stood in the shadows for decades, doing nothing to push its own cause."

"You sky-bound little—"

"Enough," Loothdram cut off Josha. "We already voted on this, and you lost, Josha. We bring Zornan in on this."

Josha looked as though she might unleash a profanity-laden tirade, but instead, she held her peace.

"The plan," Loothdram continued, "is to free Calla and three other political prisoners Lanthia is keeping in a basement prison below the palace."

"Calla's being kept in the palace?" A nervousness grew in Zornan's gut. The palace was the most heavily guarded place in the Empire.

"We believe so," Lascrill said. "Our inside source says Lanthia is keeping three men, all Kuthraz, outside official channels. About the same time Calla went missing, a woman was added, one who matches your wife's description."

The moon-graced palace of the emperor! They faced even fiercer headwinds than Zornan had ever considered taking on.

"And we have a plan to rescue them," Loothdram added. "Three of our people have been hired on as palace servants: your brother, Ballin; Bandrank; and Galla. You met the tailor and his wife in Grizthall." The couple had helped Zornan, Ballin, and Mairie escape Skathall Valley.

"You've entangled Ballin in this?" Zornan asked.

"He volunteered," Josha replied. "Showed great courage in doing so."

Zornan let the obvious insult slide.

Loothdram also ignored Josha's barb. "But our plan requires a distraction," he said. "We need to ensure Lanthia is not in the dungeon. Our source says either Enforcers, her own guards, or even sometimes Imperial guards escort her palace travels. We need her occupied and out of the secret dungeon."

"Not sure how I can help," Zornan said. "The High Counselor and I aren't exactly friends."

Loothdram's eyes were alight, like when, as children, he had an idea likely to get them into trouble. "Yes, but you have a standing invitation from the moon-blessed Emperor himself to visit his court. If you show up at the palace and request an audience, you will be granted one. Lanthia is required, by law, to join any official conference between Emperor Tothdarin and a subject. Once Lanthia and her band of evildoers are occupied with your visit, we will strike, freeing the three Kuthraz and Calla."

"How?" Zornan questioned.

"We don't have to tell him everything," Josha objected. "Circlarl, we don't have to tell him anything!"

"Bandrank and Galla were hired on as master gardeners, with Ballin as their assistant," Lascrill said over Josha's protest. "They will smuggle us in, in big wagons of fertilizer for the palace's central garden."

"You'll have all the force we can muster," Loothdram said. "Mayfran, Enforcers, myself, and a few others."

"And once you find them, how will we escape?" Zornan asked.

"That's where I come in," Lascrill said. "We extract everyone by giant flyer out through the central garden. I have ten Peak Crossers, including five from the military, all ready to keep the skies clear as we leave."

"Seems like a lot of risk to rescue four people," Zornan said. "Why expose yourself like this?"

"You don't get to question our tactics," Josha said.

"Theatrics," Loothdram replied. "Pulling four prisoners out of the palace will be a dramatic way to show what we, the Kuthraz, are capable of. And it will discredit Lanthia, maybe even destroy her. If she's hiding prisoners under the palace without the High Magistrates', High Investigators', and the Emperor's knowledge, she will at least receive uncomfortable questions, and maybe we can bring down the Dundraz's leadership structure along the way."

Yet even after Loothdram's impassioned explanation, Zornan could not see their goals. Would a group who'd waited decades for open involvement in Imperial politics really risk so much for four prisoners? Zornan did not pretend to understand politics and intrigue, but the action felt like they were flying blindly into a dark, raging storm because a favorite hat had been left behind.

But one of those prisoners was Calla, so did he really have a choice? Now that he knew she was in the palace, he could plan his own rescue, but how beneath the moons would he get Calla out of the palace dungeons? He and Mairie could fight through the guards, try it by force, but they would eventually be overwhelmed. And Zornan had no mind for intrigue. Even if he did, setting up an elaborate rescue would take months, maybe years, of planning, and depending on what the Dundraz truly wanted with Calla, that could be too late.

"I can be your distraction," Zornan said, not half as comfortable as the words had made him sound. "But I want Mairie to join the raiding party."

"Shocking," Josha shot at him. "He has a crazy demand. She's also not Kuthraz — not really. And she's a jagged edge, just as likely to cut us as she would a palace guard."

"Opinion noted," Loothdram replied. "I'm inclined to agree with our ever-frowning companion, here." Mirth had returned to the former Investigator's eyes as he poked at Josha. "What about you, old man?"

"I will disagree," said the old Peak Crosser, "both about being old and about your worry over Mairie. She will fight for Zornan and certainly for Ballin."

"But maybe not for us, although Ballin is as loyal as they come," Josha said, then she answered her own internal question. "All right, I agree to letting Mairie join the raiding party, assuming she wants to join us."

"Is your mrakaro up for the long journey to the capital?" Lascrill asked.

"Moonie is tired, but he'll be fine after a night's rest and some giant lizard eggs."

"Good." Loothdram laid his hand onto Zornan's shoulder. "Then we leave tomorrow morning for the capital."

16

THE HIGH COUNSELOR

Despite his ascension to High Investigator, Crisdan had never spoken to Emperor Tothdarin or to High Counselor Lanthia, though he'd heard plenty about both — the young, naive Emperor, and the scheming, petty High Counselor. Some of his colleagues had gone before the pair many times, which should not have been a big deal. Crisdan was one of the High Investigators, the ruling body of Investigators, and, in theory, he was one of the Empire's most powerful people. No, his authority did not match the Emperor's or the High Counselor's, but neither was he a commoner, nor a groveling merchant, and neither the Emperor nor the High Counselor could affect his status in any way. The law protected him from their wrath.

Yet, as he stood before the great brastilia doors separating him from the pair who ruled the Empire, he shook like an initiate on blessing day.

Was it the revelation that Lanthia controlled the Dundraz that made him nervous? Her group operated outside the law, outside of common decency; on Doorie, Crisdan had seen evidence of their depravity when they'd tortured High Magistrate Stethdel's daughter, and she hadn't been the only one tortured there in the time before the Empire's raid on the outpost. These rebels ignored the law, ignored morality. Even without Trillia's moon-blasted compulsion, Crisdan would hunt down the Dundraz to his dying breath. They were the sick herd animal that needed to be culled to ensure the survival of the whole. He faced down their leader, yes, though he could give no indication he knew that fact.

Worse, she was a Counselor. His blessing and training should protect him against her abilities, though it would require effort and care. The Counselors were High Trade cousins to Investigators; they, too, could read emotions, although usually not as well as an Investigator. They were more adept at manipulating emotions — if you felt fear, a Counselor could stoke that, make you manic. With sadness, a Counselor could drive you into a deep, unyielding depression. With anger, a Counselor could transform an irritating moment into a spring of fervent ire.

Crisdan's training and ability would protect him from Lanthia's inspection and deflect any manipulation of his emotions. Despite these mental assurances, the prospect of facing her formidable skills sent a chill through his body. Maybe he feared her discovering his compulsion; no one in his High Trade had yet discovered his altered state, but Crisdan truly feared someone would see it in him. This threat excited part of him; maybe this nightmare would come to an end. Maybe it would just start another.

An Imperial Guard pushed open the chamber doors, and Crisdan entered the throne room.

Reading about the throne room and hearing secondhand accounts did little to prepare him for its majesty. Massive columns held up a ceiling high enough that a large shipping boat could have been built inside the room's walls. The afternoon sun beamed through tall windows, casting the room in an eerie, celestial light, with deep shadows stretching from the pillars and raised throne. And on that throne sat Emperor Tothdarin.

"Greeting, High Investigator Crisdan." The Emperor's voice echoed through the chamber, deep tones giving it weight.

"Welcome greeting, Greatest Emperor of the Peaks, Tothdarin, son of Gathrizdel. It is my pleasure to serve you." Crisdan turned to his left where High Counselor Lanthia sat in a gold-inlaid brastilia chair, her formal posture giving strength to her thin frame. She wore a burgundy gown, form-fitting in the style she'd cultivated; the clothing hugged her body in a way Crisdan imagined was uncomfortable. The neckline plunged between her breasts, and he blushed thinking of Calla dressed in something that provocative.

"Greeting, High Counselor Lanthia," Crisdan said.

"Welcome greeting, High Investigator Crisdan," she replied, though her tone and eyes held no welcome.

"You come with a report on your investigation of the Dundraz rebel group," the Emperor said, focusing the conversation on the task at hand.

"Yes, Greatest Emperor. We've had some leads, though it has become complicated."

"Please elaborate."

Crisdan told them of Lady Calla's abduction, and how they believed it was a Dundraz retaliation for Zornan Peak Crosser's defiance three years before. He provided all details, including the young man's murder on Calla's back doorstep.

"What evidence connects it to the Dundraz?" Lanthia asked, her voice even.

"Just circumstantial evidence at the moment," he replied. Crisdan met her probing gaze, blocking her abilities. His nerves should have increased. Instead, his confidence returned. He would not be intimidated.

"And what of Laran Magistrate?" the Emperor asked.

"I had a tip he might be connected to the Dundraz. I met with him to question him, and his feelings betrayed him. I don't know how deep, but he was hiding a connection to the rebels." Crisdan didn't glance over at Lanthia to measure her reaction. Similar to his doing, she'd blocked her feelings from his senses. He couldn't read the Emperor, either; his throne protected him from any High Trade probing or influence.

"He disappeared hours after I spoke with him," Crisdan continued. "We believe he either fled, or was taken by the Dundraz or their rival, the Kuthraz. The abductors had worked with his manservant to perform the abduction."

"Do you have any evidence, besides your interrogation, that connects him to the Dundraz?" Lanthia questioned again.

"My interrogation would be enough to convict, High Counselor. Had we been able to question him again, a dozen other Investigators would have come to the same conclusion. We're combing the Magistrate's home for physical evidence of his involvement, similar to the evidence we found connecting Master Lascrill and High Magistrate Stethdel to the Kuthraz."

"But you never found any physical evidence of the Dundraz," Lanthia said.

"I would disagree." He turned to the High Counselor. "We found an entire military base. That's pretty substantial."

"And what of your source?" the Emperor asked. "Could they shed light on Laran Magistrate's disappearance?"

"They are dead," Crisdan lied. "I received word that my informant was murdered a day after I last spoke to the man."

The Emperor drew in a deep breath, then looked away, and Crisdan wished he could read the man's emotions. Was Tothdarin worried about the Dundraz and the threat they represented? If only he could accuse the High Counselor right then and there, exposing her to His Grace. But Trillia had commanded him not to, and her order trumped his instinct.

He didn't have to remain voiceless, though. He didn't have to be a coward.

"The Dundraz are the biggest threat facing the Empire," Crisdan declared. "They are vicious, devious, and single-minded. Like the Kuthraz with Lascrill and Stethdel, I believe the Dundraz have penetrated our councils. They stay ahead of my investigation due to their extensive resources and high-placed sources. They are always a step ahead, Greatest Emperor, and I fear they may have influence we can't fathom." Trillia's presence had crept into Crisdan's mind, though she did not object to his skirting close to revealing Lanthia.

"What do they want?" the Emperor asked.

"From what I've gathered," he said, "which is little due to their secretive nature, they want to replace you with a ruling council of High Tradesmen. They believe only the blessed are fit to rule."

Emperor Tothdarin flashed a weary half-smile. "Seems many of the Empire's citizens will not be content until I'm removed from this throne."

"Not a sentiment I share," Crisdan said, welling with former pride, though he had no idea what cause he actually served. He wished he served the Empire's cause, as he had before Trillia had trapped him.

The Emperor nodded at Crisdan's reassurance, eyes flashing with understanding and strength, his prior weariness having evaporated to reveal a deep resolve. Though Crisdan could not feel the Emperor like he felt most people, he didn't need his blessed Investigator abilities to recognize strength. He recalled Mizcarnon Peak Crosser's intense reverence for Emperor Tothdarin, a feeling Crisdan had once judged as naive and misplaced. Yet standing before Emperor Tothdarin, as Mizcarnon had done, filled Crisdan with a similar admiration.

The movement of the door behind Crisdan made all three of them turn, and in scampered a small, young woman dressed in servant clothing, head bowed and face red with embarrassment. She held a small piece of parchment.

"Beg my moon-blessed pardon," she said. "I carry an urgent message for the High Counselor."

An act. The young woman wasn't a servant, at least not in her portrayal. Crisdan felt her arrogance leaking through her performance. Her feelings burned with love and admiration for Lanthia, and he would have bet his father's last fish she was Dundraz.

High Counselor Lanthia took the parchment, read it, and for the briefest of moments, her own facade fell. Fear. But as quickly as it had come, the exposed feeling dropped back into the well where the woman hid her emotions.

Lanthia folded the paper, placed it into her lap, then dismissed the young servant with a wave. "Please go on, High Investigator Crisdan." Her smile didn't reach her eyes. In fact, it barely reached her cheeks.

"I have nothing left to report," Crisdan said. "I plan to remain in Bristrinia for the time being. As we have updates, I will return and report."

"Before you go," the Emperor said, "do you have any update on the whereabouts of Lady Calla? We met Zornan Peak Crosser three years ago after the Kuthraz upended his life and the Dundraz took him. I pray to the moons we might be able to find her and restore their family."

"I share your prayer," Crisdan replied. "Unfortunately, that trail has gone cold for the moment. A team of Investigators remains in Fallindra, however, to try to discover something that may lead us to Lady Calla."

"Thank you for your report," Emperor Tothdarin said with kinder eyes than Crisdan had imagined they would be. Was it as authentic as Mizcarnon had thought, or was it a cultivated attempt to inspire his subjects? "Sad parting," the Emperor continued. "May the moons bless your efforts in finding these rebels and freeing those whose lives they've ruined."

"Sad parting, Greatest Emperor of the Peaks, Tothdarin, son of Gathrizdel."

In the middle of Crisdan's bow, High Counselor Lanthia left the room almost in a run. Crisdan turned to follow.

What are you up to? he thought.

* * *

STARGARN, Crisdan mindspoke to the Enforcer as he walked quickly down the palace front steps. Ahead, Lanthia walked smoothly down a broad avenue, surrounded by a retinue of guards and Enforcers. Wherever that viper was going, she was going swiftly and in force.

What? came Stargarn's drunken reply.

Crisdan cursed under his breath. Of course, the one person he could count on in the whole moon-cursed capital was drunk, and likely in the arms of a woman. Blast him.

Where are you going? It was Trillia's voice.

I'm going to follow Lanthia.

And you don't think they'll notice a High Investigator following them? Had Crisdan not known better, he would have believed her thoughts had contained a little sarcasm.

Crisdan kept moving; she hadn't told him to stop. *That witch is up to something.*

Indeed. I have someone following her; you shouldn't risk exposing yourself.

Still, not an order. He kept moving.

Stop, Crisdan.

His legs froze, stopping abruptly enough that anyone observing him might have thought it strange. None of the pedestrians around him seem to take any notice, though. In fact, one man nodded respectfully as he passed.

Crisdan's bitterness blossomed. *Will you share with me what your spy sees?*

Stop sulking. His bitterness waned, but the part he kept separate, even from Trillia, screamed in rage. He couldn't even feel without her permission. *You can follow, but at a distance. Move toward the Cross District, but do so casually. A High Investigator should never be in a hurry.*

Crisdan obeyed, slowing his pace toward Bristrinia's most lavish residential area. He'd only been there once, to visit a wealthy merchant who had been a suspect in a murder case by the docks. The houses there defied sufficient description, especially for a fisherman's son who'd been raised in a wooden, one-room house, with the ocean out one window and the Jungle of Crazdar on the other.

Koofpash was a poor, provincial place, so opulence like that of Laran Magistrate made Crisdan uncomfortable. And Laran's house would have been, by far, the smallest in the Bristrinia's Cross District.

The residential streets of Cross were mostly bare; just a few servants moved about on errands. Overhead, the sun burned hot, and sweat coalesced under Crisdan's arms and along his back. Those rich enough to live there were either hiding inside or off at the coast at another lavish residence.

Turn left on the next street, Trillia commanded, and Crisdan obeyed. The next avenue was as nearly deserted as the last, with no sign of Lanthia or her guards.

A woman rounded the corner — the pretend servant who'd interrupted their meeting — and she stopped when she saw Crisdan, eyes widening with recognition before they lowered and she renewed her subservient act. Even at distance, he sensed her surprise and apprehension; he shouldn't have been here, and she knew it.

That servant recognized me, Crisdan thought to Trillia. *She works for Lanthia, Dundraz most likely.*

By the fourth moon, Trillia said, a curse Crisdan had never heard before. *Stop her. Engage her in conversation.*

"Excuse me, miss," Crisdan said as she passed, and the woman stopped, fear and curiosity burning in equal measure. "I'm looking for the home of Jugin Merchant. I was at his house once, but some years ago. You wouldn't happen to know where he lives, would you?"

Fear trumped her curiosity — muscles tensed; her heart beat faster. "No, my lord, no. I'm not from around here."

Crisdan let go of his easy tone. "Then what are you doing here?"

She stared, and he could feel the lie building in her mind. "My lady sent me on an errand." She turned to go.

Crisdan grabbed her arm, and she stopped. "I'm an Investigator, and you're not a servant, so let's stop playing games."

Before his next breath, the woman pulled her arm free and stabbed at him with a previously hidden knife. Crisdan moved to dodge, but too late, and she slashed him across the chest, cutting through his shirt and vest, slicing a line in his skin. He stumbled and fell to his back.

The woman turned and ran, and another servant across the street screamed, pointing at his fleeing attacker.

Crisdan sat up, watching her run. Though the wound stung, he was hardly bleeding; his clothing had absorbed most of the attack. She'd tell Lanthia where she'd seen Crisdan, and the High Counselor would realize Crisdan had been following.

His mind reached toward to the fleeing woman's and found only rudimentary defenses, not the strong will of a High Tradesman. No matter.

Crisdan unleashed his mind at her, and she stopped, dropped her knife, and fell to her knees. Then he pushed as hard as he could, and she screamed.

Crisdan rose and strode toward his attacker while the other servant glanced between them in disbelief, eyes wide. Others had gathered, shocked by a servant having attacked a High Tradesman in the light of day.

What they couldn't see was what Crisdan would do to the woman. He knew what had to be done, and it sickened him: either he should destroy her mind with the force of his own or use her weapon to end her life.

No. He was not a killer, not an executioner. And attacking another's mind was unpredictable and messy. There had to be another way.

Destroy her mind, Trillia commanded, echoing the argument raging in Crisdan's own.

And then what?

Walk away. My agent will clean it up. You need to be gone, and there can be no trace of you in that woman's mind.

Trillia's command had broken through his hesitancy, and Crisdan closed his eyes, unleashing his mind's full strength on the woman's. Slowly, her psyche fell under his will, like a sand sculpture beneath a wave, and as her terror rippled over him, he almost faltered under its torrent. But Trillia's command drove him beyond his own limits.

Crisdan gasped, and his eyes snapped open. Her mind was gone, leaving an emptiness more hollow than he'd find in a madman or invalid. She lay on the street, eyes open but vacant. Alive, but not alive.

Move away, Crisdan. Quickly. Trillia's strong command barely elicited a response from his weary mind, which felt his attacker, though only as echoes of memory within himself. As he moved, tears came unbidden. What had he become?

After a few steps, Crisdan fell to his knees, and he looked down at his wound, which shouldn't have been enough to drain him. No, it had been the mental exhaustion of attacking another's mind; it was rarely done, partially because the risk to the aggressor was nearly as great as to that of the victim.

Get up and move! Trillia shouted into his mind.

His muscles tried to obey, but a blackness came as he fell to the street. His last thought brought him joy: perhaps he'd be free today, slipping from Trillia's claws and into the peace of death.

17

UNEXPECTED HOPE

Nights filled with visions of Crisdan and Zornan were gone, replaced now by visions when she called them. Now that she knew about her abilities, that her visions were not just the nighttime effects of a worried mind, she could exert some control. Not complete control, but some. And her sleep had become blissfully free of jumping into the minds of her husband and the High Investigator.

The night before, however, she had dreamed, not a vision, but what she believed was a creation of her own imagination: she'd been trapped on a small ledge at the edge of a great cliff, a red-and-orange liquid fire burning beneath. Crisdan had rescued her, had crossed the fiery liquid without harming himself, though somehow her dream self knew she'd die if she stepped into it. Crisdan had glided across the roiling surface like he was walking across an empty field, and when he reached her, he carried her in his arms, her face tucked into his chest. Once they'd reached the other side, he'd kissed her, and unlike the one time in reality he'd tried kissing her, her dream self fell into the kiss.

Now, Calla blushed thinking of it. Somehow, her feelings toward Crisdan had blossomed again, with the knowledge that the man she'd begun falling for three years before had been transformed. That's why he'd been different; that's why he'd awkwardly tried to kiss her. The man she'd begun to love had not been fake. He'd been replaced.

Both her husband and Crisdan searched for her — she knew that now from her connection to them — and unless she was extremely tired, she could enter their minds at will. Well, not their minds, exactly. She never heard or shared their thoughts, and even though she'd tried thinking to them like mindspeak, neither man had ever responded. She could sense their active consciousness, but nothing else. If only she could find Windsa's mind so easily . . .

Did Crisdan still have feelings for her? It shouldn't matter if he did. But then why did her cheeks burn when she wondered about it?

Calla pushed Crisdan, both real and dream versions, from her thoughts while she sat at the same table she'd used for weeks now. The routine remained the same: three meals came and went each day, and the glow globes dimmed when it was time for sleep. Leanda came most days, their talk small and inconsequential, and Calla's angry outburst had not been mentioned again.

For the past several days, Calla had experimented with pushing her visions beyond Zornan, Windsa, and Crisdan; she'd tried connecting to her parents, to Trillia, to Zandia and, most of all, to little Caldry. Her heart ached to know more — to know what Trillia and that giant had done with them, to know they were well. But this desire did not fuel any additional visions.

Her latest attempt at focusing on the girls broke when the door creaked open.

"Good afternoon, Leanda." Calla looked up, but Leanda did not look like herself. She usually kept her hair in a tight bun; now, stray strands dangled like wisps from a ball of cotton.

Leanda did not close the door behind her as she usually did. "We need to go," she said.

"Go where?" Calla asked, not standing despite the woman's urgency.

"I need to get you out of here. We haven't much time."

Calla stood, though she didn't make for the door. "What are you talking about? What's going on?"

Leanda frantically glanced behind her, as if the stick-like woman who'd interrogated Calla might appear in the doorway. "Trust me, Lady Calla. Please, trust me."

Calla stood firm. "Why should I trust you? You're one of my captors, not a friend."

"I will answer any question you ask," the woman replied, "and I will answer honestly. No more lies, no more deception. But quickly."

"What is your name?"

The older woman smiled slightly, despite her frantic air. "Leanda Shindar. That was always true."

"All right, two more before I willingly go anywhere. Where is here? And who ordered this?"

"We are in Bristrinia," the Shindar said, "and High Counselor Lanthia ordered this, the same woman who interrogated you last week."

Lanthia, the Emperor's moon-blessed High Counselor! The woman had met the description Calla had heard of the woman: young, thin, and severe.

"But she did not do it under the orders of the Emperor," Leanda continued. "I believe she is Dundraz, or Kuthraz, or something entirely separate, but equally as dangerous. Come now, child. We need to get out of here."

The information was almost too much for Calla to process. Was Leanda telling the truth, and why would she help her escape? What would the High Counselor to the moon-blessed Emperor want with her?

Leanda reached out her hand. "Please, Lady Calla."

Calla took the older woman's hand, and Leanda pulled Calla out of her lavish prison.

Outside was a large sitting room, though not as lavishly decorated — the walls were stone, with plain chairs and a small table. Calla brought a hand to her mouth. In one of the chairs slumped a figure: a man in a soldier's uniform. Blood seeped from his neck, his head unnaturally tilted to the side.

"Come, Lady Calla."

Leanda pulled Calla through the sitting room and into a narrow, stone hallway where, at the end, they climbed some stairs. Covering her mouth, Calla tried to keep herself from retching as they stepped over two more guards lying in their own gore at the top of the stairs.

Before they reached the front door, Leanda stopped short, and with the shock of the dead soldiers waning slightly, Calla noticed her surroundings. The air was warmer; she'd been holed up in a basement. Now, they stood in a large kitchen, larger than any Calla had ever seen, where a huge brick oven dominated one side of the room, like in the back of the Water's Edge in Fallindra, except even larger. They stood next to a long, thin prep table. Though all the food had been put away and the dishes had been cleaned, Calla could smell the scents of her last meal still clinging to the air.

"Something's wrong," Leanda said, her voice just above a whisper. "I can't feel either of my Baldra."

Calla didn't dare look back at the corpses at the top of the stairs. "Your Baldra did this?" she asked.

"Killed the guards? Yes. But I can't feel her now." Leanda took in a deep breath through her nose. "Come. We must be gone now. We've been discovered."

They hurried through the kitchen and across a large dining room that could have fit Calla's entire Fallindra home. The next set of doors revealed a large room, and then another, until they finally reached the front entranceway.

This time, Calla could not control herself, and she lost her break-fast on the tile floor. Two more dead — one woman and one man, both dressed in the maroon of an Enforcer. Neither of their heads were attached to their bodies.

Leanda stopped, her expression worried but not angry. "I am sorry you had to see this, but we had no choice. Getting you out meant . . ." She looked back at the two bodies. "Come, Calla."

Calla closed her eyes as Leanda pulled her around the dead bodies. She could not banish the image of their headless forms, and she couldn't dispel the acrid taste in her mouth.

Leanda opened the front door, and they stepped out onto a stone stairway. Calla thought the sunlight would blind her, but it didn't. Instead, the sun's warm glow refreshed her after weeks in a basement. She looked around the long street filled with massive homes, each two or three stories high, dwarfing even the largest buildings in Fallindra. The wealth and scale was more than she could have imagined.

Leanda led her down the steps, and they walked down the street at an even pace. "Look like you belong," she said. "We must blend in now."

No one else walked the street, but Calla did as she was told, wearing one of the fine gowns Leanda had given her — a nicer dress than any she'd ever owned.

Leanda stopped again, holding Calla's arm. Up ahead, two men approached, both wearing the tell-tale Enforcer maroon. Calla glanced behind her, where four more men, similarly dressed, strode toward them. All wore the brastilia hatrindi at their hip. They were trapped.

Leanda's face fell into a resigned sadness. "I'm sorry, Lady Calla. I thought I'd played my part well enough to avoid suspicion."

The six Enforcers surrounded them, but stayed several feet away in a silence so complete, Calla could hear her own shallow breaths echoing like shouts in her ears.

A door shutting broke the silence, and a tall, thin man walked down the steps of one of the homes, dressed in a black-and-blue robe. He looked back at the group, then raised his eyebrows. He said nothing, just walked down the street, glancing back at them, both wanting and not wanting to see.

Calla was unsure how long they stood there before another group, a mixture of Enforcers and other armed men and women, led by High Counselor Lanthia, walked onto the long, broad avenue. The six Enforcers surrounding them parted for the tall, thin woman, and she stood inside their circle, facing Leanda and Calla.

"I'm disappointed in you, Leanda Shindar," Lanthia said. "I never pegged you for a Kuthraz sympathizer."

"You know I'm not that," Leanda shot back. "I've been loyally serving the Empire since before you were born."

"You will address me as High Counselor Lanthia or My Lady" — her expression had gone even colder — "and your prior loyalty does not absolve you from having Baldra kill guards and Enforcers to help a rebel fool's wife escape."

"Where are my Baldra?"

"Your Baldra?" Lanthia sneered. "The Baldra belong to the Empire, not to you. As do you. Now, let's step back inside and speak like civilized people." Lanthia motioned back toward the house they'd just escaped from, and Calla's heart sunk into despair, the hope from the last few minutes swept aside like fog before the sun.

As they walked back toward the house, another man walked onto the street, long, blond hair hanging to his shoulders and bright blue eyes visible, even from a distance. He wore servants' clothes, and he carried a small basket full of fruit. He saw Calla, frowned, then his eyes darted away and he hurried down the street with his head bowed.

They stood in the home's front foyer, with Lanthia flanked by a half-dozen Enforcers. Calla forced her gaze away from the corpses, though the stench of her own vomit forced another heave.

"What now, Lanthia?" Leanda had spoken the other woman's name with contempt. "Does the Emperor know of your treachery? Does he know of your little secret—"

An Enforcer thrust his hatrindi through the Shindar's stomach, and Leanda gasped her final breaths, stunned by the sudden violence. Calla screamed.

The world spun, and one of the Enforcers caught Calla, her own screams still echoing in her ears. Or was she still screaming? Calla hadn't noticed the movement, but within moments, the Enforcer had dumped her into her prison room, where she lay there and wept.

Crisdan woke to the glow of brastilia light, his body supported by softness. His eyes had adjusted to the light, and far in the distance arched a high ceiling above him. Peace and calm prevailed, though a vague thought tried to pull it apart.

The peace shattered as memories flooded in.

He'd fallen to the street after dismantling a woman's mind. He remembered feeling his cheek warm against the stones baked by the sun, with the mindless woman visible, her drool coalescing on the cobbles.

Crisdan closed his eyes, trying to wish himself dead.

"You're awake."

Crisdan opened his eyes. Stargarn sat beside him.

"Where am I?" Crisdan croaked.

"The palace hospital. The healers say you passed out from losing too much blood."

Crisdan felt the bandages across his bare chest. The wound stung beneath his touch.

"How long have I been asleep?" Crisdan asked.

"Just overnight," the Enforcer said. "They gave you something to help you rest and heal."

Crisdan peered around the cavernous room, where dozens of beds lined the space, each large and comfortable-looking. Only one other patient was with him, an older man who looked near the edge of death.

"They never found your attacker," Stargarn said to Crisdan's unasked question. "The woman who found you said another woman carried your attacker away."

Trillia, Crisdan thought. She had taken care of it. Despair crested again. What had he done?

"I spoke with High Investigator Dupon," Stargarn said. "They believe you are getting too close to unearthing the rebels, so one of the groups decided to have you killed."

A plausible hypothesis, based on who he was and what he was doing. Both the Dundraz and the Kuthraz certainly wanted him dead. Of course, it was wasn't entirely true.

"I've been assigned by the Council of Enforcers to be your personal guard," Stargarn continued, his stare serious. He looked to the floor. "I'm sorry I wasn't there to protect you." Then he looked into Crisdan's eyes. "I won't fail you again."

Crisdan took in a labored breath, the sting of his wound peaking with the effort. "You do not owe me an apology, Stargarn. I was foolish to leave the palace alone."

"What were you doing in the Cross District?" he asked.

Lies. Crisdan's life had become a series of lies, even to his friends, and Stargarn Enforcer might have been the only true friend he had left. "I needed some air and some time to think, after meeting with the Emperor and the High Counselor. I was wandering without a destination."

The Enforcer merely nodded, which made Crisdan feel even worse.

Stargarn forced a smile. "I'll let you get some rest," he said. "I or another Enforcer will be posted nearby at all times. And the Emperor has ordered you to have every convenience, so don't hesitate to ask for anything. I'll be just inside the door. We won't let you out of our sight again."

Crisdan sat in silence, staring at the ceiling, as the Enforcer walked away, boots echoing through the cavernous room. Even though he knew this wasn't his fault, Crisdan hated himself. All his hated actions were forced by a compulsion he could not ignore, but that knowledge, however, brought little consolation.

Good morning. Trillia's voice had broken into his mind like an unwelcome tide. *It is good to feel your mind awake.*

What happened to the woman who attacked me? he thought back, ignoring her platitude.

Don't worry about that, came her reply. *I would guess Lanthia and her people know what happened, but the mystery will keep them from action, at least in the short term. Our plans move unmolested.*

I'm glad my near-death didn't interrupt your plans.

Stop being so dramatic, Trillia thought. *You just passed out. You were in no real danger from the knife wound or from your mental exertion.*

Easy for her to say. She hadn't been part of either event.

You'll be happy to know we discovered what Lanthia had fled so quickly to do. Trillia's thoughts danced with glee. *She went to catch Lady Calla from escaping. We know where they are keeping the Peak Crosser's wife.*

A small ray of hope pierced into Crisdan's melancholy soul. He could free Calla from her nightmare.

He sat up, ignoring the chest pain and a sudden dizziness. *Then let's get going.*

Lie down, Crisdan. The force of her order pushed him back down onto his bed. *You're still recovering. The healers won't let you leave for a day or more. Do not fret, though; I have someone watching the house in the Cross District where Calla is being kept. When the moment is right, we will free her.*

Trillia's attention drifted away, and once again, Crisdan was thankfully left alone in his thoughts. Despair pulled at him, its anchor heavy and unrelenting, though he pushed against it with hope. At one time, he'd always acted according to what he felt was right, and he'd been proud of most of his decisions. Now, terrible decisions marred his existence, even if they weren't his, and his life had become a nightmare he couldn't wake up from. If only he could help Calla again, help her get back to her family, he could at least feel good about that. He dared not hope for her love or affection; he didn't deserve that. And she'd be better off if she kept those feelings buried beneath her contempt. No, this one good act would not absolve him of his atrocities, but it could make his life carry some meaning beyond Trillia's whims.

18

MIDWAY

The ocean stretched below them, reflecting the bright sun. The previous day had been cloudy, so Mizcarnon appreciated the warmth and the light. He missed his blessed eyesight, especially at night. Only two hours past sunrise and he felt fatigue, even through the incredible endurance of his Hol'Feel'Koo partner.

He looked behind him at Jayzca, appearing as Chage. Her eyelids hung heavy, sleep pulling at her. He nudged her awake, and she sat back, eyes wide.

"No sleeping," Mizcarnon said through the wind. "That's one of the most important rules of a Peak Crosser."

She rolled Chage's eyes. "Thank the White Goddess I'm not a Peak Crosser."

Mizcarnon returned his attention to their destination: a chain of three islands growing larger beneath them. He'd dubbed the largest Midway, though it was closer to the Peaks than to Croxshine, and it was the only place to stop and rest during the entire wind-blasted journey between the two lands.

During their flight toward the coast from the Nansartan camp outside Jigraile, Mizcarnon had detailed their route across the ocean, describing this one stopping place. The islands were rich in animal life; there would be plenty of food to fill the bellies of two Hol'Feel'Koo, two humans, and one giant miotop.

Less than an hour later, Mizcarnon guided the miotop to land on Midway's southern shore, and as soon as he dismounted, he reached out to Jo. *Does this island exist in your world?*

Yes, came Jo's response. *It's rocky and barren, but you can take your form if you need to.*

Mizcarnon returned to his own form, and hunger hit him like the beat of a mrakaro's wing. While humans resting between worlds needed not fear harm or fatigue, Jo had explained, they did keep growing hungry. And Mizcarnon felt the entirety of his three days of hunger.

Jayzca appeared next to him.

"I'll go hunting in a bit," Mizcarnon said, his own voice sounding strange to his ears. No, not just his voice — his own language. It felt strange to speak one he didn't really know.

Jayzca nodded absently, stretching her legs. She'd mentioned that staying too long in Hol'Feel'Koo form not only damaged the health of the human, but it could also damage the mind of the Hol'Feel'Koo. But Jo had not seemed worried, and Mizcarnon decided to trust the trained healer.

Mizcarnon worried about Jayzca, though. The curious, precocious girl he'd met weeks ago in Mazz was now gone, replaced by a sullen, depressed version. After he'd started a small fire, she stared into it, solid black eyes vacant, shoulders slumped, and mouth turned down in a seemingly permanent scowl.

"We should rest here this afternoon and night," Mizcarnon said. "We need food and sleep. We can start again in the morning."

"What will become of me when we reach your Empire?" Jayzca asked, her dark eyes not leaving the crackling flames. "You are a Peak Crosser and a servant of your Empire. How will I ever fit into that life?"

Mizcarnon had spent much of their journey considering this. With his Empire facing an inevitable clash with Nansart, he would be called to duty. Indeed, where would a young girl fit into that life? Maybe even more worrisome than her place, though, was his own. How would his own people feel about his now-black eyes and a bond with what many would consider a supernatural monster? And he brought with him a girl with the same black eyes, unheard-of golden skin, and her own supernatural beast? The Emperor was open-minded, but Mizcarnon could only imagine the scorn High Counselor Lanthia and others of her ilk would heap upon him and Jayzca.

Despite all that, he could not abandon Jayzca. As of now, Mizcarnon, Chage, and Jo were the only family she had, but Mizcarnon was ill-suited to play the role of father. He was the oldest of six siblings, having been sold into the High Trades at the age of twelve to ensure his family's future. He'd visited often with his brother Cal, and his wife and their children, who were all so loud, so full of energy and movement. Others found Mizcarnon stoic, maybe even boring, and when the chaos of children surrounded him, he felt overwhelmed, yearning for the quiet mind of a mrakaro or for his own solitude.

But Jayzca was not like his nieces and nephews; she was filled with passion and feeling, yes, but she did not squeal and play like other children he'd been around.

"I don't know, exactly," Mizcarnon said, speaking the truth. "I'm not even sure what my life will be like when I reach home, but as my father always says: 'Let's save tomorrow's worry for tomorrow.'"

"Do you see your family often?" A thick longing coated her question.

"I don't see them as often as I'd like."

"And no children of your own?" She finally looked up into his face.

"No. Peak Crossers are allowed to find a spouse and have children, but not Peak Crossers with my specific calling. We are wedded to our work, wedded to the needs of the Empire of the Peaks."

Jayzca looked back at the fire, her questions revealing how little they truly knew about each other.

Tears brimmed in her eyes again, and shaking slightly, she tucked her knees to her chest. "Did I make a mistake?" she asked.

"What does your heart tell you?" A frustrating question to a question, the kind Mizcarnon had despised when he was younger, even though it felt like the adult thing to say.

"I feel different depending on the moment." She closed her eyes against her tears for a few silent moments, then added, "How can saving a man's life be wrong? Father speaks of sacrifice, but what right did I have to not help you when I knew I could?"

Mizcarnon let the silence linger, unsure whether her questions were rhetorical. He certainly had no answer that would likely satisfy. "What do you want?" he asked. "What will make you happy?"

Her eyes opened, then narrowed, intent on the dancing flames. "The death of the Nansartan emperor and the end of his conquering."

Mizcarnon examined her hard, determined face. No, he was not dealing with one of his nieces or nephews who carried the troubles of youth on his or her back. Jayzca carried the troubles of her people, of an entire conquered continent, as if the future depended almost solely upon her.

Part of him urged himself to rebuke her, to convince her that she need not shoulder the world's problems. But wasn't he driven by similar feelings? Didn't he carry the burden of his own people as they rode this miotop across an unfathomable sea? Though she was small and young, didn't she have the same right to yearn for her people's safety and prosperity?

So Mizcarnon didn't put salve on that wound, wouldn't try to get her to ignore the desires of her heart.

Instead, he replied, "Then we are united in what we want. And I can assure you that, once we reach my land, I will do everything I can to ensure your sacrifice was not made in vain."

She looked up and managed a weak smile before staring back into the dancing flames, and Mizcarnon went to find food.

In Jayzca's view, a mountain danced, alight with earth fire. Everything else around the oozing lava was blackness, as if the surrounding space held back the light. She edged forward down a small path lined on both sides by the burning, liquid earth. Though she should have felt hot air churning with the lava's heat, a chill had wrapped around her, and she tightened her arms against herself.

Instinctively, she reached out for Chage through her mind, but no connection came. Was he still asleep? Where had she been before this? Her last memory was one of eating a meal with Mizcarnon on an island in the middle of an endless ocean, but as she tried to recall what they'd eaten, the memory slipped from her grasp like a mountain fish in a stream.

She was driven onward by some growing desire she couldn't quite identify, and she didn't even look back to see how far she'd come. Moving forward was the only way to satiate this inner desire.

At the foot of the mountain, Jayzca came to a small switchback path, and despite tired legs and doubt hanging in the back of her mind, she pressed on, up the burning mountain.

Some indeterminable time later, Jayzca stood on a ridge, finally looking back across her path. The sight snatched away her breath, and she pressed back against the mountainside. She was thousands of feet above the valley floor with its rivers of winding lava. How had she climbed so high so quickly?

Despite her growing doubt and fear, she pressed on again.

Soon, she reached a flat ridge, though she did not look over the path's edge again. Instead, her gaze met a giant man standing on the other side of the platform. He glowed like the earth fire, yet was surrounded by an impenetrable darkness, and his skin was as gray as stone, completely exposed but for a garment about his loins. Jayzca did not know who he was, but she hated him; a part of her demanded she rush across to claw his eyes from his head. But she simply stopped walking and just stared at him. He stared back.

"You think you can destroy me, little girl?" The stranger spoke in Mizcarnon's language.

"Who are you?"

He merely laughed, and Jayzca's growing terror urged her to run back the way she'd come, yet she remained, as though the liquid fire had hardened about her feet.

"Who are you?" she repeated.

He answered again in laughter, and the chill in the air grew colder.

A moment later, her father stood next to the man, his face adorned with his usual expression of piety. He looked at Jayzca, not with the angry stare she'd seen before her exile, but with the kind gaze her memories told her had been common in the years before the Nansartans, before Mother and Juso had been killed.

The giant gray man grabbed Father's throat and lifted him into the air; Father's feet swung wildly.

"You think you can stop us?" the giant man bellowed. "Nothing will stop us. Nothing will stop the death that comes."

Jayzca ran forward, but each step took tremendous effort, and as she struggled to get closer, the giant man flung Father over the edge of the cliff. Jayzca screamed while Father's body plummeted to the valley floor, disappearing in a puff of smoke as it disintegrated against a fiery river.

Jayzca turned to the man and screamed again, though not in her voice but in the roar of Chage's powerful howl. The giant, gray man only laughed.

Jayzca's eyes snapped open. She sat up. Darkness still prevailed, but not the unnatural darkness she'd just seen. The outlines of the trees stood against the White Goddess' light, and a soft rumbling, the gentle snore of the miotop, drifted nearby. She wanted to jump to her feet, to charge at the gray giant, but instead, she sat tensed on the soft ground, unsure of what she'd seen or even of what she saw now.

"Are you all right?"

At first, she didn't recognize the form's outline, but the voice brought his identity: Mizcarnon. Yes, she was on the island, sleeping, or had been. Her father's death, the laughing giant — it had all been a dream.

"I had a dream," she muttered, holding back tears. Why should she cry? Surely, her father was alive, hidden deep in the mountains.

But the intense feelings lingered, even in the light of reason, and Jayzca began to sob, fearing her father had met an end similar to the one in the dream, or that he soon would. Despite her best efforts and intentions, her father's death seemed inevitable — all her family, dead at the hands of those monsters.

Strong arms wrapped around her, and she buried her head against Mizcarnon's chest, her body pulsing with each sob. She wanted to tell him about the dream, about the dread it left in her heart, but she couldn't find the words. So, she continued to cry, and Mizcarnon continued to hold her, until she fell back into a dreamless sleep.

19

TWO BALDRA

Zandia drifted on a tunnel sled, flying through the empty passageway. She was close to Nabfryn now. Soon, she'd be reunited with Nin'Kindo — no, she would think of him as Dirik, his given name, not his Baldra name. She was Zandia, and he was Dirik.

Though she tried to hush her growing excitement, it felt good to feel hope and maybe even a hint of something else she didn't want to name, as her feelings for Dirik were complicated.

Yet there were a thousand reasons to be cautious and not let these emotions cloud her. Dirik was still Baldra, slave to some unknown master. As she glided through the tunnels, she reexamined their mindspeak conversation. Dirik never mentioned his new masters, never mentioned how he'd found her. And finding her father would be the most convenient to ensnare her.

Part of her wanted to seek out Mayfran's advice, but the bitterness of his recent compulsion lingered. She knew what he would say anyway: steer clear of her fellow Baldra. His mind seemed heavily occupied anyway by something else, and Zandia was content to leave him alone.

She refocused her thoughts on Dirik. Could the sincerity she'd felt through her bond with Dirik . . . could that be faked? Baldra were not accomplished deceivers but blunt weapons, so she chose to believe Dirik's intentions were pure, even if Mayfran's pretend voice screamed for her caution.

She turned her attention back to guiding the tunnel sled — a small speck floating through the dimly lit passageways. These tunnels had been cut with two large tunnel ferries able to pass by, one opposite the other, with no risk of collision. A one-person sled was much smaller, and Zandia kept it low in case she encountered a ferry.

Until she'd been bound to Mayfran, she'd never wondered about the power that allowed her to fly through the tunnels, believing only Baldra and Ferry Guides could keep the brastilia ferries and sleds floating through the brastilia-lined tunnels. But the spell Mairie's mother had cast that had connected Zandia to Mayfran had opened more than just freedom; it had returned Zandia's childlike curiosity. How could she keep this sled flying through the tunnel? It was an ability she'd had for fifteen years, yet she'd never considered the how and why behind her blessings . . . until recently.

As best as she could figure, she used the sled's brastilia to push against the tunnel walls' brastilia, and like the magnetic metals she'd seen sold in Dasnath, the refined ore reacted against each other.

Zandia slowed until the sled landed softly on the tunnel floor. Was there something special about the brastilia in the walls or in the sled that made this possible, or would it work with any form of the ore? Could she use her hatnuthri like that?

Zandia pulled out the hatari she'd taken from Zornan's home and placed it onto the brastilia-lined tunnel floor. She thought about the empty space between the hatari and the floor, just like between the sled and the tunnel, trying to create a cushion. At first, nothing happened. But after less than a minute of concentration, the shortened brastilia staff drifted up into the air to float at her waist.

She plucked up her weapon and smiled. So, there was nothing special about the sled. What about the walls? She tried the same exercise between the sled and the hatari, and nothing happened. So yes, the tunnel lining was special, but not the sleds.

Zandia extended the hatari into a full-length staff, then returned it back to its shorter form. Zornan had once told her he'd seen a man form a fisherman's hook on the end of a hatari. How malleable was this ore? She focused, and as the staff extended into a thin scythe, she smiled again. Zornan's experience on Doorie had cast doubt on all the limits of High Trade abilities Zandia had been taught. Using this knowledge, Zornan had become nearly as lethal as a Baldra, so what could Zandia become?

She shrunk the scythe into a short staff, tucked it behind her back and, with a self-satisfied thought, made her sled rise back into the air as she continued toward Nabfryn.

Nabfryn was the largest underground city in the Empire, several times larger than the Bowels. Though few people actually lived there year round, it was the tunnels' largest connection point, with seven separate tunnels stretching out to the rest of the Empire. If Bristrinia was the Empire's mind, then Nabfryn was its heart. From there, one could reach Skathall, the distant plains of Fandrill, Rinderel, the southern coasts, Kandrinal, the capital — all from one of the underground city's tunnels — and its central location made it a hub of trade and culture. Each culture across the Empire mixed here, more so than in the large cities and trade centers, and all kinds walked its streets: mustachioed men from Kandrinal, dark-skinned people from the Ice Mountains or Crazdar, folks wearing strange fashions from Shisnath or Nadria. Food from across the Empire filled the air with their exotic scents: berry tarts from Corbay, meat pies from the nomads of the Bauzyj Desert, fresh salmon from Koofpash.

Zandia would enjoy none of it.

Even in Nabfryn's diversity, she was an outsider. In fact, Baldra were not openly welcome anywhere in the Empire, merely tolerated in the lawless cities. She'd traveled once to the Ice Mountains, and the dark-skinned natives there had treated her like a curiosity. Monsters roamed those mountains, and a Baldra seemed tame in comparison to the nightmares those people encountered.

As such, Zandia skirted about in the darkness in the far reaches of the massive cave that held Nabfryn and waited for a pair of ferries to enter and exit, then slipped into the cave carrying her sled.

Exotic smells tempted Zandia, but she ignored them. Even though she adored the Bauzyj meat pies, sneaking into the city with her hood pulled over her head might bring the guards' or Enforcers' attention, and she didn't need that trouble today. She wanted to see Dirik, despite her growing fear this might all be a trap.

For several minutes, she waited outside the Rinderel tunnel as three ferries came in and out. Once the three ferries had passed, Zandia slipped into the tunnel, sled under her left arm, her borrowed hatari ready in her right hand.

"Zandia," hissed a voice from the darkness between the tunnel's first two glow globes. "I am here." Dirik's voice. Zandia resisted the urge to drop everything and run to him.

As her eyes adjusted to the darkness, she saw his face — pale and unnaturally white, like hers. Zandia's eyes were the blue she'd had since she was a child, but the Bendathdran who'd blessed Dirik had been more inventive: his eyes glowed yellow when placed in the light, like a jungle cat's. He smiled as she approached, razor white teeth visible in the dim light. The combined effect made him one of the scariest-looking creatures in the Empire. He was beautiful.

But she had to be careful, had to be sure. Zandia closed her eyes, opened herself up to the second sight and saw his familiar orange glow. No green on his person. She also saw the blocky forms of his hatnuthri lying behind him on the cave floor, too far away for him to retrieve them quickly. No other orange glows sat in the darkness; they were alone.

Unable to hold back her enthusiasm, she dropped the sled,

sheathed her weapon, and ran the last few feet between them, falling into his arms. He embraced her, lifting her smaller frame up into the air.

"I can't tell you how I've missed you," Dirik said, his whisper like a shout with his lips so close to her ear. "When Talalah died, I thought I'd never see you again."

Zandia pulled back to look into his yellow eyes. What did she see? Happiness, yes, but was there regret? Maybe sadness? Before she could examine more, he kissed her.

When they'd been Tha'Strukra and Nin'Kindo, they'd never been romantic, just two Baldra who shared the same Shindar who'd become best friends. Lust was not unknown to Baldra, but their blessings reduced their natural urges that could become a distraction.

But, since they'd first been connected, Zandia had harbored romantic feelings for Nin'Kindo, for Dirik. Most of the time she'd dismissed those fantasies as girlish nonsense, unfit for a Baldra. Now, she gave in to the kiss. She'd never kissed anyone before, had never felt the warmth of another's lips on hers, and it was a thousand times better than she'd imagined.

After an indeterminable moment, Dirik pulled away slightly to lean his forehead against hers. Zandia kept her eyes closed, enjoying the touch of his skin, of his body against her own.

"I love you," she said before she could check the words. She didn't regret speaking the truth.

"I love you, too," he replied. Then Zandia felt something new on his skin: tears.

She started to pull away, but he clutched her in his strong arms, and she felt a prick against her skin, the puncture of something sharp. Zandia brought her head back and slammed her forehead against his chin at the same time stomping on the inside of his foot with hers.

He made no sound, but jerked away, and she spun out of his arms' reach, pulled out her hatari and extended it to full form.

But he just stood there, more tears falling. "I'm so sorry, Zandia. I didn't want to do this." He looked into the sky. "Shut up!" he cried between clenched teeth. "I will say what I will!"

He was trying to defy his new Shindar, whomever it was.

"Fight it," Zandia whispered, hardly daring to hope he could. "Don't do this."

He looked back at her, his yellow eyes steeped in sadness. Another Baldra, Dres'Dargpa, had once told her the only way to see the truth in a Baldra was through its eyes. "I'm not strong enough," he sobbed. "I'm sorry, Zandia. I'm not strong enough."

Zandia felt something stir inside her, a dreadful feeling she recognized — the same feeling from moments after she'd been drugged by Trillia and her giant, a dampening of her abilities and strength. Her muscles slowed, and an intense grogginess pulled at her. She stabbed at Nin'Kindo, but the movement was sluggish and he dodged easily. She slashed again, though even slower. He stepped out of the way.

"I am sorry, Zandia," he said again. His lip bled from where her forehead had struck his chin. He still looked beautiful.

"I know," she slurred. She'd trusted Trillia, trusted Nin'Kindo. Trust was for fools, and she had proven herself as foolish as could be.

She tried to reach out to Mayfran to let him know she was again in trouble, but the drugs Nin'Kindo had used were fast, and she could not even feel Mayfran's mind in the distance.

The last thought she had before darkness engulfed her was of Mayfran, hoping he might come to find her.

20

DESPAIR AND HOPE

Zornan sat in his room at the Peak Crosser keep in Bristrinia, where he'd been for three days, waiting to meet with Loothdram and his men to discuss their moon-cursed plan to storm the palace. Just thinking about it made his stomach flip and his hands fidget.

To pass the time, he'd been playing with the disks the Cazdanthian High Priest had given him. Three floated in the air, orbiting each other in a pattern. For three days, he'd been manipulating them. On the first day, he'd been able to do little and it had exhausted him. On the third day, however, he could move the brastilia in the air and manipulate its shape.

Zornan's argument with Loothdram at Fallen Mountain had convinced Zornan he could do what the High Priest could. Zornan had pulled Loothdram's hatrindi from his old friend's grasp and had anchored it to the ground, all without consciously trying. Anger seemed to bring Zornan additional magical strength, but he needed to be able to call on these new abilities at will, not just in times of crisis. So, he practiced.

The three disks floated to his hand. He placed two back into his pack, held onto one and, with a concentrated thought, transformed it into a small knife. With another thought: a hammer. Once transformed, it would hold its shape until he changed it again. Each time, the disk wanted to return to its original shape and would, unless Zornan pushed it in a different direction.

Zornan stowed the third disk into his bag, then checked the position of the sun. Time to go meet Loothdram and his band of rebel fools, a band Zornan had apparently joined.

Zornan took the disks and left his room, headed for the yard, where Moonie walked, squawking at another mrakaro, a larger female with white wings and light brown feathers covering almost everything else. Moonie looked up at Zornan, then hopped over to him.

Please tell me we get to leave, Moonie said expectantly.

Zornan smiled. *Not yet, friend. But I need you to watch something for me.*

Moonie followed Zornan to where the mrakaro's large saddle hung on a peg, and Zornan stuffed the sack of brastilia disks into a saddle bag.

These disks are very valuable, Zornan thought to his companion. *I can't walk around Bristrinia with them, because if I'm stopped, they will raise suspicion. I need you to guard them.*

I will guard them with my life.

I know you will.

Where are you off to now? Moonie asked.

To meet with Loothdram and finalize our plans.

I don't like this plan. You're walking into a prairie cat's den with a stick and a hope. During the entire flight from Fallen Mountain to

141

Bristrinia, Moonie had lectured Zornan about how much he disagreed with Zornan aligning himself with the Kuthraz.

Zornan patted Moonie's neck. *I know. But it's the only route I can see to get Calla back. And I know when it's time to escape the palace, you'll be there. The morning I go to the palace, I will saddle you and send you into the air. With you coming to carry us out, I know we'll make it out safely.*

At the praise, Moonie stood a little taller and squawked. *I will be there. The three moons could not stop me.* The young mrakaro's confidence pulsed through their bond.

Zornan nodded at his mrakaro, then left the yard toward the docks.

Zornan wished he had the confidence Moonie had shown; though he hoped to see Calla soon, his dread grew with each moment he drew closer to the rescue attempt.

His path toward the docks took him through a lavish residential district, then onto a busier street filled with vendors and merchants. As he neared the tidal zone, the air turned salty and he could hear the roar of the ocean, though he could not yet see it.

Turning down a familiar street, he came upon the docks with dozens of small fishing vessels. Larger merchant ships floated farther out in the bay, their sails tied against massive masts. They braved the tides and the storms to bring goods from Kandrinal around Ninsath and to the capital then back again. Tunnel travel was safer, but broad sailing ships could carry more cargo, so risk-tolerant merchants accepted the dangers, tempted by the promise of large financial returns. By tunnel, the journey took less two weeks; by ship, a month, depending on the wind and the sea. Most sailors probably thought riding on the back of a giant flyer thousands of feet above ground to be insane; Zornan thought it insane to trust one's fate to a fickle ocean.

He stood on a dock, looking out upon the ocean. Not that long ago, he'd been in Kandrinal, another seaside city bordering the constantly shifting ocean and filled with hundreds of thousands of people. They hadn't spent much time by Kandrinal's shores, but

Bristrinia's dock area wasn't much different. The wooden dock stood dozens of feet in the air, with the ocean hanging in the distance. The entire district was built on raised platforms. The three moons had pushed the tide away, and the ships floated in the distance. Great ocean storms often destroyed buildings and platforms here, so the place had a newly built feel, smelling of both salt and fresh lumber. As a Peak Crosser, Zornan avoided storms like the ones that hammered seaside cities, but the seaside residents had no such luxury. Bristrinia and Kandrinal took a beating, then awoke to the sun and fixed the damage.

Zornan felt like they had flown into a great storm, and a large portion of himself wanted to find shelter, to get out of its tumultuous winds and stay away from its deadly force, exactly what a smart Peak Crosser should do. The tempest of the Empire's political fate swirled around him with forces he didn't understand and couldn't control, threatening to dash the lives of his family against unforgiving rocks. Now, looking out at the unfathomable ocean, standing on the edge of a city of more than a million people, Zornan felt suddenly small. No, he wasn't a Peak Crosser on a mrakaro, navigating a great storm; he was an ant riding a sparrow.

"I was raised here on the docks," came a voice that startled Zornan, and he peered over to see Bandrank, the man who'd helped Zornan and Mairie escape Skathall three years prior. He looked much the same: wrinkled and old, a bold tuft of white hair moving in the ocean breeze. "I used to come here when I was lonely to watch the tides."

"Welcome greeting," Zornan said, leaving out the older man's name.

The older man simply nodded, eyes still on the ocean. With a heavy sigh, he said, "Follow me." He turned to walk down the boardwalk. Zornan followed.

Several blocks away, they entered an empty warehouse that had seen better days. Broken outer boards had been patched with lesser ones, and the place smelled of moldy wood and rotting fish. Inside, the stench only increased, and without Zornan's blessed sight, he would have been blind. Filtered light from the late afternoon sun provided only dim illumination as Zornan, stepping carefully, followed Bandrank deeper into the building. They reached a small room in the center and stepped inside.

Since Leanda had been murdered in front of her, all of Calla's pretended civility had disappeared. Later that day, men had come and taken the bed, table, chair and books, leaving nothing but a thin, feather mattress and a worn blanket. They'd also taken the clothes that Leanda had provided. Meals were served twice daily, and though the food was still edible, it was not the extravagant fare she'd been treated to for the first few weeks. The water closet, cleaned three times a day before, was cleaned only once now.

That first night had been cold on the basement floor, and Calla had shivered constantly, sleeping in small increments, fairly certain she could hear mice squeaking in the room. Unlike before, when she'd had the faint light of a glow globe, her nights were now spent in complete darkness.

No one interacted with her. The small woman who brought her meals and cleaned the water closet kept her gaze on the floor and moved with high efficiency, and an Enforcer guarded her door at all times, not the unblessed guards she'd had before.

When she did sleep, her nights were haunted by the hatrindi blade piercing Leanda's torso. She'd never seen such violence, and she couldn't rid her dreams of the Shindar's blank, stunned expression, or of the cold look in the Enforcer's eyes. She hadn't looked at High

Counselor Lanthia, but in her dreams, the foul woman cackled as Leanda fell dead to the ground and an Enforcer carried Calla away like a child's doll.

On the eighth morning, she sat in the light of an oil lamp, finishing her first meal. When she finished, she set the meal aside and closed her eyes, fighting back tears of despair. Leanda's attempt to free her might have been her best chance at escape. Zornan was an incredible man, and now a fierce one, but he was just one person. Lanthia commanded Enforcers, Baldra, Shindar, and soldiers. What could Zornan do against that? Could Crisdan, with his connection to whatever Trillia was, best the High Counselor and maybe even the Emperor? And would they even want to? Crisdan would want to free her, yes, but his will was not his own.

She kept her eyes closed. Over the last few days, she'd been hesitant to reach out. She'd seen through Zornan's gaze as he flew across the Infinite Mountains on Moonie's back, but she hadn't been able to discern his destination. Was he coming to Bristrinia? Had he discovered where she was?

Her mind suddenly filled with his sight. He was walking in a city, which looked a lot like Bristrinia, and in an instant, she knew it was. Zornan was here.

He strolled through a lavish district. Was it the same neighborhood in which she was kept? She couldn't tell. She'd only been outside for a few moments and had been so frightened, she hadn't noticed many details. The homes had been huge and the street wide, but every street he walked down fit that description.

He left that area to walk through streets filled with shops and merchants until he finally neared the ocean, descending a steep street to an area filled with warehouses, docks, and giant ships. Calla gasped. She'd never seen the ocean with her own eyes, though she'd now seen it twice in Zornan's sight. The mountain range in the Empire was called Infinite; the same word could have been used for the ocean, as its blue-green stretched forever past the horizon. The wooden ships were tall, masts towering over almost any building in Fallindra.

Zornan waited at the dock for some time before a voice startled him and, in turn, Calla. "I was raised here on the docks," the voice said, and Zornan turned to an older man with an ocean-wind weathered face. "I used to come here when I was lonely and watch the tides."

Zornan followed this man back into the maze of warehouses, and they entered one that looked abandoned. Soon, they reached a room inside it, and Calla's hopes lifted when she saw the residents.

Calla had never met Mairie or Ballin, but she knew them instantly from her previous dalliances in Zornan's mind. Loothdram, the mischievous blond friend of Zornan's youth, was there, as well. Before long, another man joined the group—a large man, older than Zornan by maybe a decade, muscles tight on his face and his exposed forearms.

Zornan embraced and greeted his brother, and Calla's closed eyes filled with tears at the reunion.

"Where are the others?" Zornan asked as he stepped away.

"Josha and Lascrill are in Corbay," Loothdram said. "They wait there with the giant flyers for our escape."

"Oh, look," Zornan said to his brother, "Loothdram shares a detail of the plan. I didn't think we'd get any of those." After a moment, her husband asked, "How are you getting everyone besides Bandrank and Ballin into the palace?"

"Inside manure," Loothdram replied with a boyish smirk. "The morning after next, when you request an audience with the Emperor, Bandrank and Ballin will bring me, Mayfran, Mairie, and a few others into the palace in wheelbarrows full of manure."

"Easy for you to say," Mairie said. "You don't have blessed smelling."

"You can always back out," Loothdram replied.

The young woman stared at Zornan's childhood friend, eyes smoldering. Was Loothdram foolish enough to antagonize a woman like Mairie?

"I'm still nervous about escaping through the gardens," Zornan said. "Won't the Imperial Guards just stop us? Feels like there's a hundred different ways this could end poorly, and maybe only one or two ways it doesn't."

Loothdram grinned. "We have a second distraction planned. I promise, we'll all fly out. It won't be without danger, but for once, we are one step ahead, and we have the Fire Moon's luck on our side."

"Let me guess," Zornan said, "the distraction is a surprise."

"Something like that," Loothdram said. "The details are in place. You'll just have to trust us."

"Fine," Zornan said, though Calla knew through his tone that he wasn't fine at all. "I will be at the palace the day after tomorrow at dawn. Be ready to get Calla and get her out of the palace. I'll join you in the garden, but make sure Calla is safe. Get Calla out of the palace. Don't worry about me."

Calla couldn't hold the image any longer as a sick realization slammed against her mind: They were coming to rescue her, but they would be in the wrong place; Zornan had secured the Kuthraz's help to extract her, but it wouldn't work.

Please, Zornan! she pleaded, trying to push her thoughts to him. *I'm not in the palace! Please find me!* But only dark silence answered her.

After several moments of crying into her lumpy mattress, Calla sat back up. Was she destined to live out her days as their prisoner? Would they kill her, like they'd killed Leanda, if they thought she was of no use? No doubt they would; a monster like Lanthia didn't leave scraps of her depravity.

Was there any hope? Zornan and his friends would storm the palace, only to find her not there. What would Zornan do then? Die, trying to search the palace? Kill mercilessly, as he'd done in that tavern? Why did they think she was in the palace? She wanted to scream, wanted Zornan to hear her. He was in Bristrinia — so close, though he might as well have been on the other side of the Ice Mountains.

This time, she closed her eyes and reached out for Crisdan, hoping for some comfort. Where was he? She had resisted reaching out to him, fearing her own fickle feelings, especially in her current state. She'd been emotionally weakened by her imprisonment, by Leanda's death, by all of this, but she had to try to find some hope.

Crisdan was in a small room, with light streaming in through a small window. He sat in a chair facing a large, maroon-clad Enforcer whom Calla recognized: Stargarn, one of the Enforcers who had assisted Crisdan all those years ago and now called Fallindra his home.

"It seems like an impossible plan," Mayfran said. "Why not approach the Emperor? Or the Imperial Guard?"

"Lanthia is the traitor," Crisdan pleaded, voice sounding tired. "Who knows who else we can trust? For all I know, the Emperor is involved."

The Enforcer furrowed his brow. "Come now, Crisdan, that doesn't make any sense. Why would the Emperor have a rebellion against himself?"

Crisdan laughed, though short and forced. "You're right there. But the larger point still stands: We can't trust anyone other than ourselves."

"How many guard Lady Calla?"

At the sound of her name, her eyes opened with surprise. She closed them again.

". . . though I'm not sure the entire number," Crisdan finished, the first part lost to her surprise. "We can handle it."

"I appreciate your confidence in my abilities, but even I can't best that many men." Though the Enforcer's expression said he thought he might be able to do just that.

"We'll bluff our way in," Crisdan said. "And if that doesn't work, I'll attack their minds and you can take care of their bodies."

Stargarn shuddered. "Attack their minds? You can actually do that?"

Crisdan looked at his feet, answering without meeting the Enforcer's eyes. "I can, if I must." He looked up at the large man. "We have to rescue Lady Calla."

Stargarn leaned back and sighed. "This wouldn't have anything to do with personal feelings you might have for the woman, would it?"

"Stargarn, please, it's not—"

"I know you think I'm an idiot much of the time," the Enforcer interrupted, "but it was clear back in Fallindra three years ago, and I can see that fire in your eyes now. As unlikely as it might seem, I've loved myself. I know how that can motivate a man."

"She's a married woman." Crisdan's words sounded like a caretaker's final prayer over the dead.

"But you're going to rescue her," said the other man. "And if everything you say is true, she can't go back to Fallindra. You'll have to protect her. You know better than I how ruthless both of these rebel groups are. You can protect her, offer her refuge." The Enforcer smiled.

"She won't choose me," Crisdan said. "She chose Zornan three years ago. Nothing has changed."

"Perhaps." Stargarn peered out the window, his gaze searching for a love he might have lost. "Regardless, the next time Lanthia is called to the throne room, we move. I'll stay in the Cross District and watch the house. We'll be ready."

Crisdan stood, placing a hand on the Enforcer's shoulder, which, even with the man seated, nearly reached Crisdan's chest. "Indeed, my friend. And I don't use that term lightly. You might be the only person I can trust in this entire Empire."

"Besides your lady friend," the Enforcer replied.

"Don't call her that. She's—"

Stargarn raised his hands. "Banter between friends. You are a righteous man, High Investigator Crisdan. I don't always understand you, but I always admire you."

Calla opened her eyes, and the scene dissolved. Joining minds often wearied her and she couldn't hold it any longer. She hadn't realized she'd been crying, her cheeks stained with tears.

Crisdan was coming. She had no idea if he could actually free her, but she hoped he would. And what would she do when he arrived? The part of her she'd rather bury deep yearned for his embrace, his strong arms around her, his face close to hers.

She wiped away her tears. When the time came, she would figure that out. Freedom might be at her door, and she wouldn't ruin this return of hope by wallowing in guilt for something she hadn't yet done.

She lay back down on the flimsy mattress, the cold seeping through it and into her, and fell into a thankfully dreamless sleep.

21

CHAINS

Before she could see anything, Zandia could smell and feel. Wherever she was smelled of mold and rot — someplace old. The dirt beneath her face, its earthy smell, mixed with something ancient and something dead, and the air was colder than the last time she'd been above the surface. Probably north somewhere; possibly very north.

For some indeterminable time — maybe minutes, maybe hours — she could only smell and feel; trying to open her eyelids did nothing. After that time, however, her eyelids finally responded despite the paralysis of her other muscles. Prostrate on the damp earth, she couldn't see much; light filtered in through a window. She could see only dirt, wood and light.

Sensation in her torso and her arms came next, muscles tight and in pain. But she was Baldra so it would not bother her. She realized her arms were pinned back behind her. She'd never worn Baldra cuffs, though she recognized the sensation; brastilia binders bound to her forearms kept arms tightly behind her. Even when her arm muscles returned to her command, she wouldn't even be able to squirm.

Neck muscles came next, and Zandia turned her head to get a better look at her surroundings. She lay in a small, one-room building with a dirt floor, the rest of it coarse wood. The structure was old, though it was hard to determine how old until she discovered the climate and how that might age things. She focused on these analytical details so her mind wouldn't get mired in the reality of her capture.

When feeling came back to her legs, she sensed two more Baldra cuffs: one set around her thighs, the other around her ankles. Her captors were taking no chances with her. Zandia growled. If she ever escaped, she'd gut each of them in turn.

Would she, though? Her memory was hazy . . . but Nin'Kindo had captured her. Could she kill one of her only friends? A man whom she loved but was under compulsion to harm her? Part of her said yes she could, without hesitation. But she wasn't sure that part of her ruled as much as it once had.

Zandia turned onto her back, which only made it more uncomfortable with the cuffs behind her, so she rolled onto her side instead, and in her drugged state, even that small motion took considerable effort.

Meeting with Nin'Kindo had been the stupidest act of her life. Of course this had been a trap. Part of her pleaded for internal mercy, saying she hadn't been trained to think but to follow orders; her life under the compulsive heel of another's will had left her unprepared to face these decisions. She should have consulted Mayfran. If she had, she knew she wouldn't be here.

Most of her knew this wasn't true, though; she had considered what Mayfran would have likely said and dismissed it. Speaking with him might have changed her mind, but she'd refused to reach out to him — a conscious, emotional choice to follow this unwise path. She was to blame — not her former Shindar, not the Empire nor the Dundraz. Zandia had made a poor decision, and she would have to live with the consequences.

"You're awake."

The voice startled her, as her senses hadn't all broken through the drug-induced haze. She turned her head, her mind suddenly alight with fear, anger, and hate. Zandia knew that voice, though she hadn't heard its sickening tone in many years, and she shifted in its direction, recognizing the man behind it: her father, Zortranc.

"Surprised to see me?" Zortranc smiled. He'd always enjoyed the discomfort of others, especially those closest. "You've been hunting me for so long, it must be gratifying to finally reach me. I imagine, though, dear little Zandia, that you thought this would be a little different. I'm sure your stupid little mind fantasized about removing my head or some such nonsense. No, you're the same cowed bitch you've been since you were born. The Priestesses might have given you Baldra abilities, but they can't change your soul."

Zandia growled. She thought she could speak, the feeling having returned to her tongue, but she chose not to, not willing to play his sick games.

"The Dundraz have been great employers," he continued with an overly satisfied grin. "They came to me to get insight into Zornan. They thought that, perhaps, as his father, I might understand him better than they did." He smiled the smile that had chilled Zandia's heart as a child. "I helped them plan his demise, which is underway as we speak. And then I learned of you, my stupid little girl, all grown up into a monster."

"You're the monster," Zandia said before she could keep the words from her lips.

Zortranc laughed that familiar, terrible laugh, as when one of his kids or their mother had questioned him. The kind of laugh that said pain and anguish would come soon at his hand.

"That would make it easier for you if I was, wouldn't it? And how can a stupid little girl who's been transformed into that" — he motioned at her — "call anyone else a monster?

"But," he continued, "you're not really a monster, even if you are the subject of nightmares. No, you're more like a knife. The real monster is the Shindar, the genius behind you. So, perhaps you are a monster in a way, yes, but not a good one." His smile widened, like he'd made an extremely funny joke, and Zandia wished she could cut the smile off his face with a hatnuthri.

"I'll leave you alone," he said after several moments of silence. "I'm sure seeing me has given you a lot to think about." He smiled once more before walking out a door and closing it behind him.

Zandia growled again. She wanted to scream. Again, she tested her cuffs, but they gave her no room to maneuver. She could roll over a few times, maybe, but for what purpose? She was trapped in Circlarl-knew-where, bound like a feral cat. No escaping from this. If Zortranc was being honest, and if the Dundraz were behind this, they would not leave any openings for her to exploit.

So Zandia lay there, visualizing all of the painful ways she could kill her father, though the imaginings did little to calm her soul.

If only she could reach Mayfran, reach out for help, and tell him where she was so the Kuthraz could find her. Baldra were solitary creatures, and in her partial freedom, she'd embraced that isolation too much. She could have been with the Kuthraz, or with Zornan, searching for Calla. She didn't have to be Baldra anymore; she didn't have to be alone. Yet, here she lay on the moon-cursed floor of a small shack, as alone as she'd ever been.

She reached out anyway, guessing the Dundraz would keep her drugged or maybe use one of those brastilia spikes Trillia had used to dampen her abilities and cut her off from Mayfran. To her astonishment, she could sense herself on the map inside her mind. The shack sat several miles from the city of Dasnath, facing the Plains of Fandrill, which explained the colder, damper air. And if she could feel her location, she could probably . . .

Mayfran! her mind shot out into the space between them. *Mayfran!*

Can you hear me? she called, hoping to capitalize on their mistake of letting her mind fully wake.

His response came a moment later. *Zandia! Where have you been? I could barely feel you, nothing more than a flicker. I couldn't even tell where you were.*

Dasnath. A village outside of Dasnath.

I can sense you now. What is wrong?

I've been captured, she responded. *I was an idiot. Nin'Kindo, the other Baldra who'd been attached to my former Shindar, he reached out to me and I met with him. But he's been rebound by the Dundraz. I'm such a fool.*

Zandia worried he might confirm her stupidity, but he only said, *I'm sorry, Zandia. I'm sorry I wasn't there with you.* Intense regret drifted in along their bond.

I'm a stubborn beast, she explained. *I should have listened to your warnings. And there's more. My father is here. He's part of the Dundraz.*

What? How can that be? Why would the Dundraz employ someone like him?

He was hired to provide insight into Zornan, she replied. *But now he has me.* Just thinking the words filled her with a dread so heavy, she could hardly breathe through it.

I am coming your direction. I'll leave this moment.

Excitement over Mayfran's potential rescue blossomed within her, wiped out by a sudden thought: the Dundraz would not make a sloppy mistake like this; they would not allow her to reach out to Mayfran and let her awaken unless they wanted it so. And if the Dundraz were letting her do this, then. . .

You must not come, she said.

His irritation peaked. *Why beneath the light of the moons not?*

It's a trap. They would never have let me wake fully unless they'd planned on drawing you and more Kuthraz here.

Of course it's a trap, he said, *but we'll figure out a way. There are some Kuthraz in Junnindra. I will meet them there and come to you.*

Zandia opened her mind to Mayfran's location: Bristrinia. Even by giant flyer, he was more than a week's travel from Dasnath. He'd first meet his friends in Junnindra, then come here, which might take weeks before they reached her. And the Dundraz would see them coming. Zandia herself could resist any torture they saw fit to inflict upon her, but if they captured Mayfran or any others, the Dundraz would break them like they had Mairie on Doorie.

No, Zandia commanded, knowing she had no ability to do so. *Stay where you are. Stay safe.*

I'm Kuthraz on the eve of a war, Mayfran replied. *There is no safety for me.*

You're doing something important in Bristrinia.

It doesn't matter, he said. *Loothdram can do without me. You cannot.*

You're helping Zornan, she guessed, and felt his confirmation though he didn't speak it. *Stay and help Zornan. Stay and help your friends.*

Nonsense, Zandia. Others can take my place here. I'm coming for you, trap or not. The Dundraz won't know what hit them.

As he broke their connection, Zandia burned with equal parts frustration and admiration. The idiot Enforcer would walk into a trap set by devious Dundraz who had at least one unbound Baldra at their disposal. But no one had ever sacrificed themselves for her like Mayfran was doing. No one had ever tried to save her. Neither her brothers nor her mother had rescued her from Zortranc's persistent wrath. Ever since she'd become Baldra, no one had ever needed to save her. Part of her was annoyed she needed saving, needed the help of a man. But the warmth of his affection quickly drowned that out.

Some time later, the door opened again, and she looked to see who might prod her now.

Nin'Kindo walked in first, though it took a moment for Zandia to identify the second face — a familiar older woman, but her identity did not fit with the Dundraz. After several moments, Zandia recognized her: Priestess Kisthana of the Bendathdrans, lover of Stethdel and mother of Mairie.

For a brief moment, hope flooded Zandia. Kisthana was aligned, if loosely, with the Kuthraz. She'd saved Zandia from unspeakable pain after Talalah Shindar had died and their connection had been severed. Kisthana had been the one to unite Zandia with Mayfran and free her from the depravity of the Dundraz.

But it quickly dissolved into confusion. The Priestess should not have been there, not among the Dundraz, not escorted by Nin'Kindo. Zandia hadn't seen the Priestess among the Kuthraz in the past three years, though, and Mayfran had said Kisthana did not care for Loothdram or the principles behind the rebellion.

The Priestess looked much like Zandia had remembered: dressed in plain gray clothes, the generic colors of High Trade initiates, and she carried her habindhi, the brastilia staff used by the priestesses to bless and curse. Her long, dark hair was pulled back and hanging near her waist.

"Leave us," Kisthana said.

"My orders are to—"

"I don't care about your orders, Baldra," the woman spat back. "If you don't leave now, I'll sever your connection to your Shindar with a wave of my habindhi. Remember what that felt like, you little vermin?"

People did not insult and poke at Baldra. But, then again, Kisthana was not most people. Nin'Kindo's face paled with the memory of the last time he'd been severed from his Shindar, and, as he nodded, withdrew.

"I am sorry, Zandia." The Priestess's face, which had been as immutable as the peaks, softened.

"Sorry for what?" Zandia asked.

"What they are asking me to do."

"Why are you helping them?"

Kisthana knelt next to Zandia. "The Kuthraz are fools, Tha'Strukra."

"Zandia," she corrected.

"Yes. Zandia." Kisthana tried to smile, but it collapsed before she could form it. "The Kuthraz continue to involve my daughter in their peak-foolish schemes. She's been with them since Doorie, caught in their schemes and falling for another idiot idealist, just like her mother.

"The Dundraz," she continued, "have promised me that when this war comes and they move to rule the Empire, Mairie will be safe."

"War? What war?"

"It's coming, Zandia. The Empire, the Kuthraz, the Dundraz. It's bubbled up, and it will fall out and over."

"What makes you so sure the Dundraz will win?" Zandia asked.

Kisthana laughed. "Please, Zandia. You know their strength better than I. They have more people, more power, more resources. The Kuthraz are a bunch of fervent fools playing at rebellion. The Dundraz are a movement, a militarized organization ready to step in and lead the Empire, and replace Tothdarin with a stronger leader. I think their reasoning is flawed, and the moons know they will be just as corrupt and inefficient as the current Imperial government. But they will win."

Though Zandia wanted to argue, she knew it was true. Compared to the Dundraz's strength, the Kuthraz were small. And the Dundraz were just as dedicated to their own cause, believing that righteousness fell on their side of the philosophic line.

"You apologized before," Zandia said. "What are you sorry for?"

Kisthana stood back up to look out a window. "For what I've been asked to do."

"You're going to sever me from Mayfran."

The Priestess nodded. "Yes. But that's hardly the worst part."

"I'll be bonded to a new Shindar." Zandia's gut knotted with dread.

"Not the worst part." Kisthana turned her head slightly, like she might look at Zandia, but looked back out the window instead. "They've asked me to bind you to your father."

The knot in Zandia's stomach exploded through her body. She'd been under that man's rule before; for thirteen years, his despotic cruelty had governed her life, but during that time, she'd had her mind as a refuge, a place where his cruel hand could not touch. Once bound, she would fulfill his sick will, act as his mighty hand. And she'd have no refuge, even in her mind. This thought made her so ill, she thought she might vomit.

"I'm sorry," Kisthana repeated. "Zortranc is a sick man, a despicable man. But your fate was sealed when they called you to be Baldra."

"You can't do this." Zandia's own voice sounded foreign — not the strong hiss of a Baldra, but the weak squeak of a cowed little girl. No, it wasn't foreign. She just hadn't used that voice in more than fifteen years.

"I'm sorry," the Priestess said for the third time.

Silence reigned as the revelation that Zortranc would soon become her master crashed against Zandia's mind, threatening to break her sanity. She struggled against the Baldra cuffs, but an extended effort resulted in little more than a wiggle. As Kisthana said, Zandia's fate had been sealed; her future and her will would never be her own. She'd become frustrated with Mayfran, but the thin tethers to the Kuthraz would be infinitely preferable to the chains that would tie her to her father.

"They won't give you Mairie," Zandia said, breaking the silence. "I know these people. They do not extend courtesy; they do not make deals. They impose their will. Mairie is a threat, a power they can't control. They tried to break her on Doorie and couldn't; they'll want her dead."

Kisthana turned, looking down at Zandia with eyes that held a deep sadness that seemed to mirror Zandia's own soul. "Mairie is all I have left in this world, all I have that matters. I don't care about politics; I don't care about their silly games. I just want my daughter to be free of them."

"Her fate was sealed when you blessed her as a child," Zandia said, a cruel but true retort. The comment only served to intensify the Priestess's sadness.

"I'm sorry, Zandia," Kisthana said for the last time, leaving the small room, steps leaden with remorse.

As soon as the door closed, Zandia screamed.

22

PLANS IN PLACE

C risdan waited in his sitting room, in the quarters the Emperor had given him following his attack and recovery. There, he resisted the urge to reach out to Stargarn for a report on the goings-on at the house where they kept Calla. Stargarn didn't need the distraction of an impatient Investigator. Thinking back to his prior conversation, he didn't feel nearly as comfortable as he'd acted with his Enforcer friend about his plan to rescue Calla. It had multiple problems Stargarn hadn't even asked about.

First: Crisdan's constant escort. Ever since the Emperor's healers had released him, an Imperial Guard had accompanied Crisdan on his two trips beyond the palace. Apparently, the Emperor feared for Crisdan's safety, that his role of uncovering the rebels had exposed him to danger. Doubtless, true. But he didn't need a guard to watch him; he needed all eyes off what he planned to do.

Second: Crisdan didn't know if he could again physically attack minds and disable people. Even under compulsion, attacking that woman's mind had rendered him unconscious. Plus, his first victim hadn't had the mental shields given to all High Tradesmen. The Enforcers watching Calla would have those blessings. If his bluff or Stargarn's abilities were not enough, would they be arrested? He'd witnessed the heavy hand of the Dundraz, so there would be no clemency. If Stargarn and Crisdan were discovered, they would be killed.

But he was a High Investigator; the bluff would work. Lanthia, in order to preserve secrecy, must have been keeping details from most of her minions. He needed surprise, not force.

Although, extra force wouldn't be a terrible alternative.

Trillia, he spoke to his master's mind.

Yes, Crisdan?

Is your helper still around? The woman who moved my attacker's body?

Yes, she is in Bristrinia still. Why?

Crisdan hesitated. Trillia had already approved his mission to free Calla, and she'd left the details up to him. Involving Trillia more deeply tainted the act. But that was foolishness. Freeing Calla was more important than his pride. Trillia could help assure his success.

I think I need some help, Crisdan continued. *I'm bringing Stargarn, and I think I can bluff my way through this. It may end in a fight, though, and Stargarn won't be enough.*

My helper is extremely capable, came Trillia's reply. *Her abilities exceed that of an Enforcer's. What help could she provide?*

Crisdan revealed his entire plan to Trillia. She may have known already, with her window into his mind, but he told her anyway. *Can your helper watch the house and come in if we need help?*

After a few moments, Crisdan felt a tickle in the back of his mind

— the familiar sensation of another High Tradesman trying to connect through mindspeak. Despite his natural tendency to block it, he let down his guard and let in the new mind.

Hello, Crisdan, fellow servant of Nansart. The woman's voice was rich like chocolate, steeped in a unique accent, even through mindspeak. Like himself, she wasn't a native speaker of the Empire's tongue. Judging by the extent of her accent, though, she probably had learned it as an adult.

Servant of Nansart. Crisdan didn't know what that meant. He'd never heard the name of that person, place, or organization, and he wanted to ask the woman, probe to see who they worked for and why they did what they did. But the task at hand was more important.

Welcome greeting, he replied.

How can I help you? Trillia says you have a mission for me.

Crisdan again explained the plan, adding in her part. *I want you to meet us and watch the house. We may call you inside to help if we can't get past the guards.*

Spilling more infidel blood will please me, if it comes to that. Her reply was almost gleeful.

What do I call you? he asked.

My name translates to Dagger in your language.

Crisdan shook his head. *Okay, Dagger* — he could hardly think the word without lacing it with sarcasm — *I will reach out when we need you.*

Until then.

Again, Crisdan shook his head. Unbelievable. His allies were a psychotic foreigner and an Enforcer too obtuse to realize how much trouble they were plunging into. What could possibly go wrong?

He considered Stargarn. Crisdan had thrown this net into the sea, with Stargarn on the other end. With so much duplicity everywhere, though, how could Crisdan be sure the Enforcer wasn't a rebel? No. He had to trust someone, and when Crisdan probed Stargarn's feelings, they were transparent, easily readable. Most High Tradesmen tried to hide their feelings from Investigators, with mixed success. Enforcers were not blessed with extreme mental protections. In fact, most seemed to make those useless through emotional bravado, as if daring the Investigators to probe them to find nothing but thoughts of killing soft, fuzzy things and violently defending the Empire.

So, he would place all his trust in Stargarn. He had little choice; his list of friends was short.

Is your plan in place? came Trillia's voice to his mind.

Yes, Dagger knows the plan. Where is she from?

She was born in Boothdrinka.

Crisdan had, of course, heard of the far-off kingdom across the sea, though he'd never met anyone from there. Visitors from Booth-drinka were extremely rare. Traveling the vast ocean was dangerous, and only Peak Crosser scouts and risk-taking sailors ever traveled between the three continents. He thought of asking Trillia about Nansart, but decided against it. He could push her to reveal more after Calla was safe.

The plan is ready, he thought to her.

Very good. Trillia's mind drifted away from his.

Crisdan stood. He shouldn't bother Stargarn, but his anxiety could not be contained, so he decided to take a walk, maybe get some fresh air in the palace courtyard. Sitting alone in his lavish room was making him claustrophobic.

An Imperial Guard greeted him outside his door and followed Crisdan as he walked toward the palace entrance. For the first few days, it had been difficult to find his way around the labyrinthine building; he still didn't know all its hallways, but he'd memorized paths to the front door and to the common dining area.

As they approached the palace's front door, he noticed it stood slightly ajar with voices filtering through.

"I am demanding an audience with the Greatest Emperor of the Peaks, Tothdarin, son of Gathrizdel," came a familiar voice.

"Demand is a strong word." The second voice was muffled — an Imperial Guard. "No one demands to see the Greatest Emperor."

Crisdan stopped short and did not enter the conversation but stood close enough to the door to hear it. And as sure as he was that the early-morning sun had lit the sky, he knew the one demanding an audience was Zornan Peak Crosser.

"Demand might be the wrong word," Zornan replied. "When I last visited the Greatest Emperor, he said his court was always open to me. I am here with urgent business, so now I claim that privilege he gave me."

"We'll need to confirm your identity before you enter the palace," said a different Imperial Guard, with a voice full of authority.

Crisdan slipped through the small opening in the door and out onto the front steps. Below, six Imperial Guards surrounded the Peak Crosser who, even though he'd come to address the Greatest Emperor of the Peaks, wore nothing more than his Peak Crosser uniform. Crisdan repressed a smile at the man's complete lack of pretense; Zornan was the same whether he came to address the Emperor or was headed to a tavern.

"I can verify the man's identity," Crisdan said.

One guard stepped forward, bowing his head slightly. "High Investigator Crisdan. You know this man?"

"Yes." Crisdan looked at Zornan. "This is Zornan Peak Crosser, and I believe you'll find he does have an open invitation from Emperor Tothdarin to visit."

The authoritative guard looked at another fellow guard, but said nothing. Mindspeak. The lead guard turned to Zornan. "Follow me, Zornan Peak Crosser. I will escort you to a waiting chamber while we alert the Emperor of your presence."

Zornan turned to Crisdan. "Thank you." Nervousness wafted off the Peak Crosser. Nervousness, yes, but more than that: fear. Something he hoped Crisdan would not suspect. Zornan fidgeted, like a boy with a plan to do something his parents would not approve of. And despite knowing Crisdan's efforts to free Calla, the Peak Crosser didn't even ask for an update.

"The least I can do," Crisdan replied, his mind burning with questions, though he held on to them. Zornan was in a hurry, but so was Crisdan, and whatever scheme Zornan made to hatch would only benefit Crisdan. If all eyes were on Zornan, that meant fewer eyes watching Crisdan and Stargarn.

The lead guard returned, and four others followed him and Zornan into the palace.

Dagger, he called out to the woman with his mind.

Yes, fellow servant? He hated that she called him that.

The plan has been accelerated. Go to the house and tell me when you have eyes on it.

As you command.

Next, he reached out to the Peak Crosser's mind. *Zornan, it's Crisdan.*

High Investigator? came Zornan's cautious reply.

Yes. I need to ask you a favor.

Zornan felt annoyed by the intrusion, but replied, *What can I do for you?*

Just let me know when you've entered the throne room.

Why? Zornan's mind burned with wary curiosity.

I have audience with him later today, Crisdan lied, *and I was hoping to visit him soon. As soon as you start your audience, I will proceed to the waiting area.*

As you wish, High Investigator. Clearly, Zornan didn't fully trust Crisdan's explanation, but that was fine; Crisdan didn't need his trust, just his information.

Crisdan walked back into the palace to change into his High Investigator clothing. If his bullying of the guards and Enforcers was going to work, he'd need to look like a High Investigator.

"You don't need to watch me so closely," Crisdan said to his Imperial Guard escort.

"Emperor's orders."

"And what if an Enforcer friend of mine escorted me from the palace? Would that satisfy the Greatest Emperor's command?"

The man considered this. "Yes," he said, "as long as he promises he won't leave your side."

Crisdan smiled. After Dagger reached the house, he'd have Stargarn come to the palace, and together they would await Zornan's word that he was about to stand in front of the Emperor. High Counselor Lanthia would then be occupied, and Crisdan would go to free Calla. He tried not to think of holding her in that moment, of kissing her softly on the cheek, but he couldn't contain his feelings, and after a moment's hesitation, he let the thoughts build without resistance.

23

FINDING HUMANITY

They came for Zandia after two days of almost complete isolation, and in that time, she'd only seen Nin'Kindo when he'd come once a day to spoon-feed her some soup. They'd not spoken. When they'd finally come for her, she didn't resist; the Baldra cuffs made that impossible.

For the first time since she'd awoken, they took her outside. Had it not been for the impending terror, the fresh, cool air might have felt nice against her skin, and escaping the stench of confinement might have been a relief. But there was none. With the future she faced, even the sweet tasted bitter.

The view stretched from the foothills of the Infinite Mountains, across the snow-covered plains of Fandrill, to the looming Ice Mountains beyond. When she'd been here before, Zandia had loved this view; she'd traveled across those desolate plains to the dark-skinned natives of the snow-capped mountains. They'd been the only people she'd met who didn't view her with disgust. Instead, Baldra were treated as guests; foreigners, for sure, but not monsters. Ever since she'd been bound to Mayfran, she'd often thought of one day living amongst those hard, humble people. She'd become used to considering the future. Now, she didn't have one.

With that thought, Zandia screamed, her shrill voice echoing across the foothills. Nin'Kindo did not look at her, but Kisthana and Zortranc did. While the Priestess regarded her with sad eyes, as if marching to Zandia's funeral, her father's lip curved up into a smile on one side. How she wanted to cut that from his face!

Mayfran! she called out with her mind. *Mayfran, please help me!*

We're coming, came his worried reply, *but we're days away. Can you stay safe?*

She hadn't wanted to worry him since he could do nothing, and he'd feel the severed bond as soon as it happened. A severed bond was maddening to a Baldra. How would it affect a Shindar? Would it break Mayfran like she'd been broken after Talalah died? Or would she simply fade from his mind?

Mayfran deserved to know what was coming. *Kisthana is here. She is going to transfer my bond from you to Zortranc.*

Mayfran's disbelief and rage floated to her. *Impossible. She can't — she wouldn't!*

They've guaranteed her that Mairie will be spared from the current conflict.

Tell her that won't happen! Mayfran yelled through the bond. *The Dundraz will not spare Mairie! They don't show mercy.*

I tried to explain that to her. Even the small bit of mindspeak heightened the fatigue in Zandia's mind. She'd barely eaten in days, had barely slept; she had almost nothing left inside, nothing left to resist what she faced.

We're coming. A phrase likely meant more to comfort, though it lacked any hope. Mayfran knew he couldn't be there in time.

I'm sorry, Mayfran. Zandia fought back tears. She would not let Zortranc see her cry. *I should have listened to you. You were right. This path of revenge has ruined me. It might ruin you and my new friends. Once I'm bound to Zortranc, I will reveal everything, I'll—*

Stop. Mayfran's voice halted her agonized rambling. *You need not apologize to anyone, Zandia. I failed you. The Kuthraz failed you. The Empire failed you. You are innocent, a victim of the evil inside our hearts. I will free you, Zandia. I will spend every breath freeing you. I will.*

With this, Zandia could no longer hold back her emotions and she cried, her sobs kept in check by her strong binds. She didn't bother to open her eyes to see if anyone watched; she couldn't endure another satisfied grin from her father or more sympathy and pain from Kisthana.

She pulled her mind away from Mayfran, unable to bear his presence any longer. His own mind resisted at first, and she worried he would compel her to remain in contact. But the resistance faded and their connection became a distant hum in the back of her mind.

When Zandia finally opened her eyes, the small procession crested a hill to face the mouth of a small cave, where wisps of snow dotted its edges and shade protected it from the sun. As they entered the cave, near-complete darkness gave way to the flickering light of several glow globes. The cave looked natural but for the two brastilia tables in the middle. It was a Bendathdran blessing chamber, hidden away on the edge of the Plains of Fandrill and controlled by the Dundraz, hundreds of miles from any Imperial force of strength — yet another sign of the Dundraz's superiority over both the Empire and the Kuthraz. Kisthana had been right, a fact Zandia had tried to ignore since joining the Kuthraz: the Dundraz would win, not just today, but forever. And nothing could stop them.

Nin'Kindo gently laid Zandia down onto one of the altars and stroked her bald head. Although the gesture might have been kind, Zandia could only feel its cruelty. Unfair to Nin'Kindo, yes. He'd been acting under compulsion, just as she had once done. Indeed, how many terrible things had she done under compulsion's cruel hand? Yet she couldn't even forgive her best friend for something he would have never done under his own will; her despair was too thick to let forgiveness through.

"So, how will this all work?" Zortranc asked, lying down on the altar opposite Zandia.

"I will utter the blessing and transfer the bond." Kisthana's voice hovered just above a reluctant whisper. "The transfer will take some time. I've never done this; it hasn't been tried in centuries. It might work, but as I told your masters, it might kill you both or just one of you. Transferring a severed bond is hard enough, but transferring a living bond . . ." Her voice faded off.

"I'm a gambling man," Zortranc said, bravado punctuating each word. "If there's even a chance at controlling a Baldra, well . . . that's worth the risk.

"Zandia," he continued, "did you know our family is special? The Priestess here says me, you, Zornan, maybe Hisvan or Ballin, all have something inside of us, a special proclivity toward magic. That's why this could work. Usually, a man my age would be unable to be blessed. But we're special, Zandia. Different. Isn't that wonderful?"

Zandia refused to reply.

"As I've warned before," Kisthana said, "this could be very painful for you both." Her voice was soft, like a healer's, not cold like when she'd bonded Zandia to Mayfran on Doorie. "The other possibilities include damage to your minds, which I cannot repair," she added. "Or it just might not work." Had Zandia heard hope in that last phrase?

"Get on with it, witch," Zortranc said. "I know the risk. And Zandia is in no position to object."

Zandia looked over at Nin'Kindo, who wouldn't meet her eyes. Tears stained his cheeks, and despite her prior anger, she knew how much this would pain him, how much this would scar him. Baldra carried so many unseen scars. She would bare the greater scar, of course, though she allowed herself a moment of grief for the scar Nin'Kindo, Dirik, would carry for the remainder of his days.

Kisthana began the ceremony, chanting in ancient Bendathdran, swinging her habindhi staff over her head in an elliptical motion. Last time, Zandia's mind had drifted toward madness, unable to focus on the words or feel their rhythm. This time, although grief drowned out the words, the rhythm of the ancient chant soothed her, and for the first time in days, she felt something akin to peace. Maybe it was a resolve to reality, or maybe it was acceptance. Either way, she drank it in. Her soul yearned for peace, yearned for anything but the turmoil she'd wrestled with for days.

In this clarity, however, she realized she felt nothing of the blessing. She should have felt something — a distant pull at her mind. Yet nothing came. Zandia felt Mayfran nestled in a corner of her mind, his haste echoing through their tepid bond. She could sense the world around her, the chant of the Priestess, the labored breathing of Zortranc, the soft weeping of Dirik . . . but the blessing did not intrude. It was not working.

Zandia opened her eyes just as Zortranc stood from his altar, one hand on his head. He shoved Kisthana, and with a sick crack, she struck Zandia's altar, then fell to the ground out of sight. Zortranc picked up her discarded habindhi.

Zortranc uttered a string of nasty curses and his meaty hands clutched the magical staff like a club. "The Dundraz warned me you might try something, that you might not be strong enough to do this. So I'd memorized the Bendathdran prayer you were supposed to use; otherwise, it would have just been gibberish. What were you doing to me, huh? Shredding my mind? Killing me?"

Zortranc swung the habindhi down in a vicious blow. Zandia heard another crack of bone and Kisthana's muted yelp. Then Zortranc kicked her, followed by a pained grunt from the Priestess.

"Did you think I wouldn't know?" Zortranc bellowed, his voice transforming into the rage speech Zandia had come to know all too well as a girl, and his eyes sparked with a familiar violence. She had only seen him this enraged once, at least sober, the time Zandia thought he'd kill Mother. Hisvan had stopped him, after Zortranc broke his oldest son's nose. The next morning, Hisvan had left the house and had never returned. Weeks later, Zandia had been sold into the High Trades.

Zortranc carried that same rage now as he kicked Kisthana again. He was going to kill her! Zandia looked over at Nin'Kindo, but he only watched, held back by his compulsion. His muscles had tensed, yet the other Baldra did not move to stop her enraged father.

Zandia struggled in vain with her cuffs. Kisthana had risked her life to maintain Zandia's freedom, so Zandia could not let him kill her just because Kisthana had gotten in the way of what he wanted. But the Baldra cuffs were unbreakable, and she was too weak to even try.

She drew in a deep breath, seized the hope she'd had before, and stopped struggling. Brute force could not free her. But something else might. She'd done it with the hatari, and she'd used a sled to float through the tunnels. Brastilia was hers to command. Maybe she and Zornan were indeed special, different, more in tune with the magic coursing through their veins, more in tune with the world and its power.

She focused on the cuff binding her arms behind her back — a large piece of brastilia, which had a lock with a unique key. She didn't need a key, though; she could re-form the brastilia to her will, just like the Priests of Cazdanth had done when they'd forged it. Brastilia wasn't shaped like steel through fervent heat; rather, it molded to the will of the Priest. She would be its master now. She would shape it.

Her concentration broke as the cuff expanded and slipped from her arms, and just as her father raised the habindhi in what might have been a killing blow, Zandia swung the large cuff at her father's chest.

A hatnuthri blocked it, and Zortranc looked over at her, eyes wide with surprise and fear. Nin'Kindo held his short sword in two hands, fending off the large cuff.

With another simple thought, Zandia reshaped the leg cuffs, and they sloughed off her legs. Then, keeping Nin'Kindo at bay with the arm cuff, she swung her legs around and kicked her father in his fat belly. Air rushed from his lungs, and he stumbled back against the other altar, hitting his hip and spinning face-first onto the cave floor.

The Priestess's staff flew in a different direction, and Zortranc landed with his legs in the globes' light, his torso disappearing into the darkness beyond.

Zandia rose from the altar and re-formed the brastilia cuff into a long broadsword. Nin'Kindo was taller by more than half a foot, but her long weapon would negate some of that advantage. As she stood, Zandia felt her knees threaten to buckle. She couldn't beat Nin'Kindo in this state, having had no food or sleep for days.

Yet Zornan had almost defeated the Baldra Dres'Darpa on Doorie in a similar state; he'd pulled strength from the brastilia around him. And so would Zandia. She felt the brastilia altars burning, their green glow in the second sight now visible with her eyes. The energy swirled around her and then rushed into her muscles, renewing them as if she'd eaten solid meals and slept for days. She was a fierce Baldra once more.

She looked on Nin'Kindo as tears ran down his face again. "I am resisting my Shindar," he said through gritted teeth and quivering lips, "but I can feel her avalanche approaching. It won't last long."

"You can fight it," Zandia said. "We can fight it."

"No." He shook his head. "There's only resisting; I will lose. But know that Dirik loves you, even if Nin'Kindo must kill you." His voice broke on the last word.

"You won't kill me," she said, feeling the power fill her like the sun filling a valley on a bright morning.

"Then you must kill me," he said. "Free me from this. Please, Zandia, don't let me live like this."

He struck with sudden ferocity, his Shindar's will finally eclipsing his own, and Zandia blocked with ease, using her long sword to keep his twin hatnuthri at bay. Despite his protestations that his Shindar's will would prevail, Nin'Kindo's movements were slow and predictable; Dirik resisted the commands, even as Nin'Kindo tried to obey.

Zandia spun and swung the sword in a powerful arc, which Nin'Kindo parried. But the blow was too strong and it knocked both weapons from his hands. Before he could reach for them, she kicked his knee, and it bent unnaturally, bringing him down to his other knee. He looked up at her, eyes pleading for his own death. She brought the brastilia sword to his throat, and he didn't move. He wanted to die — needed to die. Killing him would be a mercy, would free him from his prison. She should kill him. It would be the most noble kill she'd ever known.

Instead, Zandia slammed the hilt of her formed sword into his temple, and he crumpled to the floor. She listened to his heart and breath to confirm his unconsciousness.

She sighed, holding back a sob. She couldn't kill Dirik. He was still in there, resisting his Shindar like she'd never seen a Baldra do. There was hope to free him. Maybe she and Zornan could figure it out. Maybe, Kisthana, if she survived, could do it.

With that thought, she turned to Kisthana, who was a lump on the floor, breathing heavily, eyes open and distant.

Zandia turned back to Nin'Kindo, re-forming the sword into the cuff that had held her, this time, though, without the keyhole. She locked it in place to hold the Baldra's arms. She then did the same with the leg cuffs. He was incapacitated now, but he was Baldra; that might not last long. She picked up his discarded hatnuthri and holstered them in her sleeves.

Zandia turned back to Kisthana. Her long, dark hair covered much of her face, except for her bewildered eyes as her body lay unnaturally, twisted into a painful reminder of Zortranc's assault. Zandia pushed her hair aside. The Priestess's breaths came unevenly, each bringing a flinch of pain.

"Can you hear me?" Zandia said.

Kisthana's mouth moved like she might speak, but she nodded slowly instead.

"We need to get out of here. Others will come. Nin'Kindo probably communicated with his Shindar before I knocked him out. We need to find someplace . . ."

The other woman's gaze shifted to behind Zandia, widening with surprise, and Zandia felt a blunt smash against the back of her head.

She slumped down on top of Kisthana, the Priestess grunting with the impact.

Zandia could feel the significant wound to her skull — probably a fracture. Blood seeped from it and rolled down her neck and onto her back. Her vision blurred.

But she was Baldra. The sensation of her wound was not pain, just her body telling her what was happening. She'd fought with broken bones and significant internal injuries, so a fractured skull would not slow her down.

Zandia extracted one of Dirik's hatnuthri and extended it, looking back in time to see Zortranc raising the habindhi for another strike. Despite the momentum and ferocity of the blow, Zandia brought up the short sword and blocked his, cold, the strike of brastilia striking brastilia echoing through the cave. Surprise and terror replaced Zortranc's self-satisfied anger.

Zandia pushed the habindhi aside and came to her feet, wobbling a little. She steadied herself, pulled strength from the brastilia of the altars, from the raw ore buried deep inside the mountain, and with that strength, her legs steadied and her head stopped feeling like a confused lump.

Zortranc's shock wore off, and he took another swing. Zandia countered, striking the oncoming staff with both of her weapons, knocking it from his grasp. At almost the same moment, she kicked his stomach, forcing the air from his lungs again and pushing him against the cave wall. He pulled himself upright, as if he might scale the wall and escape his Baldra daughter. But there would be no escape and no mercy. Not this time.

She brought the twin weapons up, crossed them in front of his throat, and his eyes widened even further. A sudden smell of urine joined the other damp scents in the cave. His fear thrilled her.

She was about to take his head off, when Mayfran's voice came into her mind. Not his actual voice — she could feel him distantly in her mind, and she kept his presence at bay. No, his words were from her: morality spoken in his voice.

You don't have to be a killer, it said. *You are free to choose now. You don't have to keep walking their dark path. You can make your own way.*

Zandia kept the hatnuthri still. She was Baldra, and Zortranc was no match for her. He'd once been a strong man, but his vices had eroded this strength. His stomach hung over his belt, and his face was rounder and more wrinkled than it had been when Zandia was a child. She was a Baldra, and Baldra killed. Zortranc deserved to taste her blade more than any kill she'd ever made.

But Mayfran's words were right. She didn't have to be a Baldra anymore; she could choose to be something different, choose to be human. Even though she'd rarely made the choice to kill, each one had broken off a piece of her moon-cursed soul. She'd been kind once, witty and fun. Despite the terror that had often existed in her home, she'd been happy for much of her young life. Darkness existed in her, as it probably did in everyone, but she didn't have to give in to it. She could bind Zortranc or cripple him and leave him to the mercy of the Dundraz. Now, with his own piss soiling his pants and his fear as palpable as any emotion Zandia had ever sensed, he seemed pathetic. He was not the unstoppable monster of her youth but a shell of the man he'd been — an overgrown bully. She certainly did not pity him, but he seemed so non-threatening in this state, so helpless, she wasn't sure she could kill another unarmed human being.

Until he spoke.

"Zandia," he pleaded, voice raspy and frantic, "please don't kill me. This plan was theirs, not mine." Deflecting blame, as always. "And I know so much about their organization. I know the location of their hideouts, and I know the names of so many of their leaders. Please, don't kill me. I will serve whomever you'd like me to serve. I have no loyalty to the Dundraz; they were a means to an end. Please, Zandia, please . . ."

And before his slime-coated words could change her mind, she brought the hatnuthri together and cut off his head.

Zandia turned, hoping she'd feel something human. Was she regretful? No. Zortranc had terrorized enough people; he deserved his death. Did she feel satisfied? Part of her, yes, since that vile man would never hurt another living soul. He would meet Circlarl on the edge of the heavens and receive his eternal home among the flames of the Fire Moon.

But she couldn't find the joy in it she'd imagined she'd feel. Killing him did not erase the trauma of her youth, did not restore her family, but maybe . . . the world was now a little bit safer, a little bit brighter, even if she was a shade darker.

Zandia knelt back down next to Kisthana.

"That man deserved to die," the Priestess said, flinching as she spoke. "I would have loved to have done that myself."

"Next time, I'll let you kill the maniac attacking us," Zandia replied.

Kisthana laughed a small, short laugh, cut short by pain.

"We need to get out of here," Zandia repeated from before her fight with Zortranc. "How many others are there?"

"Three Enforcers staying in town," the Priestess said through gritted teeth. "They probably have more in Dasnath."

Zandia nodded. Even in her wounded, weakened state, she could handle three Enforcers. "We need to move you," Zandia said, "but it will hurt a lot."

"Leave me," Kisthana said. "I won't survive what he did to me."

"I'm not leaving you," Zandia insisted. "I'll carry you to safety if I must."

Kisthana croaked out another laugh. "You're such a fool. If I'd had half your courage, I wouldn't be in this mess and neither would you."

"I got captured through my own stupidity," Zandia replied, "and if not for you, the Dundraz would have found another Bendathdran to do their bidding. You saved me from a fate a thousand times worse than death. For that, I will always be in your debt."

Kisthana looked over at Nin'Kindo, then back at Zandia. "You are a good person, Zandia."

"I thought I was an inhuman monster," Zandia said, a brief smile lighting her face.

"My definition of humanity has expanded in the last little while," the Priestess remarked.

THE THRONE ROOM

One of the Imperial Guards nodded and guided Zornan past Crisdan and into the palace. The sight of the man who'd exonerated him made Zornan strangely tense. What was High Investigator Crisdan doing at the palace at the same moment Zornan was aiding the Kuthraz? The Koofpashi man had been tasked with rooting out and dismantling the rebels. Could his appearance be a sign the Empire knew something of this rescue attempt?

Zornan pushed aside his paranoia. Crisdan was a moon-blessed High Investigator. There were hundreds of plausible reasons why the man could have been in Bristrinia and visiting with the Emperor or with one of his staff. Crisdan's reasons for being in the palace likely had nothing to do with Zornan being there. Yet despite reason trying to stretch out and comfort Zornan's mind, fear and doubt kept hold.

The Imperial Guard walked Zornan into a small room not that much bigger than a closet though comfortably furnished with a richly decorated chair, a small table, and a glow globe. The room had no windows or other doors.

"Please, sit here," the guard said, his voice remarkably clear through his brastilia helmet. "We will convey your request to the Greatest Emperor."

Zornan sat and tried to calm his fraying nerves. Crisdan's appearance had been unsettling, even if it was unrelated to his plans with the Kuthraz. What was Zornan doing climbing into the teeth of the prairie cat? Even with Zornan's newfound abilities, the Emperor and his guard could crush him. And he'd also be facing High Counselor Lanthia who, if Laran Magistrate was to be believed, was the navigator of all Zornan's pain.

Zornan worried he might have given himself away with Crisdan. He'd been so nervous already, and a hundred times more nervous as the High Investigator looked on the Peak Crosser with his all-knowing eyes. What had Crisdan sensed? Enough to alert the Imperial Guard of a potential threat? How much of one's intentions could an Investigator divine?

Time marched slowly as he waited. Zornan stood to pace, but soon sat back down, stilling his hands in his lap. He closed his eyes and tried to dip into a meditative state, but peace was as slippery as a rain-soaked mrakaro, so he tapped his foot and tried not to think about facing Emperor Tothdarin and High Counselor Lanthia, which, of course, only made him think about it more.

After two hours of waiting, the door opened and three guards stood there, two holding large, ceremonial hatari almost twice as tall as they were. All three had hatrindi tied at their hips.

"Come with us, please," the one without a staff said. His voice had sounded like the one who'd escorted Zornan to the waiting space, but the Peak Crosser couldn't be sure. "The Greatest Emperor and his wisest High Counselor were not planning on holding court today. You should be honored they acquiesced to your request."

Zornan started to walk, but the guard held up a hand. "Please, leave your hatari here. We will also need to search you for weapons."

When Zornan had been here before, he'd had no weapon and he hadn't been searched. Their cautiousness seemed prudent and probably wasn't out of the ordinary, though it increased his nervousness all the same.

He withdrew his hatari, setting it on the small sitting table. Then the guard patted Zornan down from his shoulders to his boots. He finally stood, eyes unreadable behind his mask. "Follow us."

They followed the columned hallway, the ceremonial hatari snapping a rhythm against the marbled floor. They stopped at the nearly two-story brastilia doors leading into the throne room, where two more guards stood to the side, both with the massive hatari. They pulled the door open.

Crisdan. Zornan reached out his mind to the High Investigator.

Yes, Zornan Peak Crosser?

I am about to enter the throne room.

May your audience bring you what you desire.

Zornan hoped it would as he stepped inside.

Despite his relative familiarity with it, awe nearly took his breath away upon seeing the throne room. Most of Fallindra would have fit into this space, and the columns were wider around than the ancient trees of the Ice Mountains. Even though his awe mirrored his previous visit, procedure did not. Last time, no guards had accompanied him during his audience. This time, three did, including the one without the ceremonial staff.

Emperor Tothdarin sat on his throne, dressed in black and gold. His suit was form-fitting, not the flowing tunic he'd worn three years before, and the golden crown sat on his dark, curly hair, a matching gold chain holding a pendant dangling in the center of the Emperor's chest: his family's seal of two mrakaros flying past three moons.

"Greeting, Greatest Emperor of the Peaks, Tothdarin, son of Gathrizdel," Zornan spoke reverently, bowing his head. Voices seemed to get amplified in this hall, so he kept his tone low.

"Welcome greeting, Zornan Peak Crosser," the Emperor replied. "Your visit is unexpected, but not completely surprising."

"I apologize for my boldness in seeking your audience, Greatest Emperor." Zornan lowered his head yet kept his eyes on the younger man's face.

"I gave you an open invitation, Peak Crosser." His tone held kindness, not the frustration Zornan feared he might hear. "And you have earned a right to speak." The Emperor looked to his right.

Zornan turned to his left, where High Counselor Lanthia sat in her high-backed chair. She wore a burgundy dress, high-necked with a frilly collar of black lace. Her dark hair was pulled back into a large bun on the back of her head, making her seem even more severe, if that was at all possible. Her face appeared calm enough, yet Zornan thought he saw muscles tensing, a volcano of emotion hiding beneath the beautiful surface. The Peak Crosser hoped that was his nervous imagination.

"Greeting, High Counselor Lanthia," Zornan said, bowing slightly. She responded with an even slighter nod.

"I imagine I know why you're here," the Emperor said. "But I'd like to hear it from you."

"I come hoping to find help," Zornan said, face flushing. He'd asked the Emperor of the Peaks to help him, like a commoner might implore a Magistrate. But this was no Magistrate. "My wife Calla has been kidnapped by the Dundraz and I want to—"

"The Dundraz have been destroyed," Lanthia cut him off. "They died on Doorie when the Peak Crosser scout and his men stormed the ancient fortress."

"What my High Counselor is trying to say," the Emperor added, "is that we haven't had any evidence of them since that raid. How can you be sure it's them and not another group?"

This question caught Zornan in mid-flight. How had he known? He just had, and he'd stormed across the Empire under that assumption. In the end, he'd been correct, but he'd never even considered another possibility until the Emperor had now posited it. And he couldn't reveal what he'd learned from Laran; he needed to remain calm and say the words Loothdram and he had rehearsed.

"I can't know for sure," he said, "but I can think of no other enemies. They hate me, and I can't imagine they all died that day. I think the organization lives and breathes, and I need help to find them. I need help to bring my Calla home."

"I, too, believe they exist," the Emperor shared, ignoring a pointed glance from Lanthia. "Crippled on Doorie? Most certainly. Destroyed? Not likely."

"Then you can help me." As soon as Zornan had said it, he felt a hot anger burn inside him. The Emperor could not help him, would not help him. Calla had been under the Emperor's moon-forgotten feet for more than a month, and the fool hadn't even noticed.

"We are trying to help," the Emperor said, mournful, though his voice rang melodramatic in Zornan's ears. "We dispatched High Counselor Crisdan, and we still have an investigative team working on—"

"It's not enough!" Zornan's sudden outburst surprised himself, and the shock on the Emperor's face made it clear he'd gone too far.

Zornan tried to calm himself. But how could he remain calm? This idiot had allowed the Dundraz and Kuthraz to operate within his realm! He might not have been complicit in Calla's kidnapping, but he'd been derelict in his duties as a caretaker and as an emperor. He was a foolish boy, playing emperor in a game he could never truly master . . .

Zornan turned his head to Lanthia, where a grin crept onto the edges of her face. The hot anger boiled up in him, the rage of weeks pent up; he should have been able to control it. Would he ruin this chance to free Calla so he could chastise the moon-blessed Emperor? Why couldn't he control himself?

As if his mind suddenly awakened from a nightmare, Zornan pulled strength from the brastilia items around the room: Lanthia's chair, murals on the floor, even the throne itself. Filled with its intoxicating energy, his anger faded into the background, dormant. He looked back at Lanthia and held back a smile.

Zornan bowed deeply, his hair nearly touching the floor. "I beg your pardon, Emperor Tothdarin, brightest moon of your father's sky. The loss of my wife has driven me to bursts of anger. Your moon-blessed grace did not deserve my tirade." He stood erect. "I will face whatever punishment is deemed fit for my outburst."

Emperor Tothdarin sighed heavily with a grief Zornan could not understand. "You are forgiven. I have never loved like you, never had family like you. I can't imagine what you're going through. But we are doing what we can. The Empire is vast, and hunting down a single person is like finding a mrakaro feather fallen in a forest. Without understanding more of the Dundraz, I can't say with confidence what we can do to rescue your wife."

"Why don't you call on your Kuthraz friends?" Lanthia said, her voice colder than a windstream. "Loothdram, your childhood friend; or Lascrill, your former mentor. I'm sure they'd be willing to help you."

Zornan looked at her, and he felt something akin to a rope trying to wrap itself around his mind. Then Loothdram's warning hit, coming back to his memory. His friend had reminded him that a Counselor could push and stoke emotions. So he hadn't had that outburst on his own; it had been stoked by her power. Zornan pulled more energy from the surrounding brastilia, pushing her emotional attack aside.

"I did," he said, knowing the truth might be damaging, though revealed soon enough. Now that he was in the throne room, Loothdram's men might have been already storming the secret palace prison.

"You admit to an association with the rebels?" Lanthia replied, eyebrows raised in mock surprise.

"No, not an association," Zornan said. "But I was able to make contact, and I asked them for help."

"You would betray your Empire?" Lanthia spat. "You would stand here and admit to cavorting with those who'd wish the moon-blessed Emperor dead on his throne?"

"I would do what I must to find my wife." Anger stoked those words, unforged by the High Counselor; those words had been all Zornan's own. "But they refused to help me." The truth was close enough. "I then searched for other answers and found little."

The Emperor regarded him, an eyebrow raised. "But you discovered something, and you've come here because you know something about the Dundraz."

Zornan was now off his script, off the simple words Loothdram had told him to say. He was just to plead for help, cry, beg, and the more pathetic, the better, Loothdram had said, to make dismissing him uncomfortable. But Zornan would not follow Loothdram's script. In that moment, looking at the Emperor's kind eyes, Zornan decided to change tactics.

Mizcarnon Peak Crosser had loved the Emperor, adored the Emperor, and Mizcarnon was a man like Zornan, a man of principle. Mizcarnon thought the Emperor worthy of his throne, so Zornan would hold to that assumption.

"I captured a Dundraz traitor in Kandrinal," Zornan said. "He told me the identity of the leader of the Dundraz." He wanted to look over at Lanthia, to see her face pale or harden, but he kept his eyes locked with Emperor Tothdarin.

"What traitor?" the Emperor asked.

"Laran Magistrate."

Zornan could not help himself, now stealing a glance at Lanthia. Her face held nothing, though; it seemed even calmer than before. In light of this, for the first time since he'd learned the news, he doubted it. What if Laran had lied? Yes, Cradris had seemed certain Laran had spoken the truth. But what if Cradris had been manipulated, or what if the Crazdarian had manipulated Zornan?

"You kidnapped a Magistrate?" The Emperor's words hung, strong and accusing, and in that moment, Zornan felt an intense need to hide, to escape the room and Tothdarin's accusing glare.

"Yes." The words crawled out weakly, almost as a croak.

"That is a serious crime," the Emperor continued, "and one which, even in the pursuit of your wife, is inexcusable. You are not an Investigator of the High Trades. You have no right to employ vigilante justice like this."

"Well, we've heard of him killing the gang in Manmandoo," Lanthia added. "He's become unhinged with grief."

Zornan's stomach tightened into a massive knot. What had he just admitted to, in front of the High Counselor and the Emperor? A capital crime, probably. Even if the Kuthraz freed Calla, Zornan would not leave here.

Unless he could fly at the problem from another direction.

At that point, he had nothing to lose.

"Do with me what you will," Zornan said with a resignation he didn't quite feel, his own words forcing him away from Calla and the girls, "but know that the leader of the Dundraz sits in your highest councils, helps shape the Empire they strive to destroy."

"Do you have a name?" Lanthia asked. "Or just a general thought?"

"He named you, High Counselor Lanthia, as the leader of the Dundraz."

Zornan's words hung in the air for a moment, shock painted on both the leaders' faces. Then Lanthia laughed. Not a bitter, nervous laugh, but one you might hear from a patronizing parent.

"I think grief has clouded you beyond reason," Lanthia said, her laugh still echoing through the vast space.

"That is the most serious of accusations," the Emperor said. The kindness in his eyes had been replaced by something else. Anger? Disappointment? Zornan did not know the man well enough to know.

"I realize that." Zornan's voice tightened, threatening to not come out, and he pulled more strength from the room. "But think about it, Greatest Emperor. Who else could have hid a small army at Doorie? Who else could evade every attempt at discovery? Who else could avoid the greatest Empire on the face of this world? The Kuthraz had a High Magistrate, and look how much power that gave them. How much more could the High Counselor give?"

The Emperor looked down, forehead creasing in thought, as if he might be considering the possibility. Or maybe seeing something he hadn't wish to see.

"I will not sit here and take these ridiculous accusations," Lanthia spat, voice shrill. "Guards, take this man to the dungeon."

Zornan heard footsteps behind him, but he refused to look back.

"Stop." The footsteps died with the Emperor's loudly echoed word. Tothdarin leaned forward and rubbed his face with his hands, then sat up straight. "Do you have any evidence of this accusation besides the testimony of an abducted Magistrate?"

Under the Emperor's intense glare, with Lanthia's angry visage burning him like the hot sun, and Imperial Guards behind him ready to arrest him, Zornan's confidence shattered into a quivering fear. The accusation, which had seemed so absolute, now seemed weak under the unrelenting light of the Emperor's judgment. Zornan had nothing. Laran was not here, and Zornan had no other evidence. He hadn't just walked into a prairie cat's den with a stick; he'd worn a belt of meat around his waist.

"He's just a Peak Crosser," Lanthia said, breaking Zornan's uncomfortable silence. "He thought himself an Investigator, a Magistrate, and an Enforcer. But he should have remained on his giant flyer and stayed out of this windstream."

Most of the strength drained from Zornan's limbs. Loothdram had used him again. There would have been no way out. Eventually the commotion of the rescue would reverberate through the palace, and even without his accusation of the High Counselor, they would have never let Zornan leave. He'd been naive and stupid — again. They already knew about his assault in Manmandoo, and now he'd admitted to kidnapping a Magistrate. He might have had the strength of a Baldra now, but his mind had not kept pace.

"I just want my wife back." Zornan spoke just above a whisper, though it carried in the silence.

"You'll never see your wife again," Lanthia barked. "I'll see you thrown into a pit to never leave again. I'll see you publicly tried, your family humiliated and left destitute on the streets. I'll make sure—"

"Enough." Once again, the Emperor's word silenced the room. Lanthia fumed, though she said nothing. She'd won; she needn't say any more.

"Under my watch," the Emperor continued, "I've let the Empire decay almost to the point of collapse. The rebels control too much, and they destroy the lives of men like Zornan Peak Crosser without consideration. They take an innocent woman and use her as a piece in some sick game. They commit travesty after travesty, hoping the light of the moons never reveals their deeds."

He stood and faced Lanthia. "At one time, you were my greatest friend, my closest confidante. I even loved you. But I, too, was a piece in your game, nothing more. Weeks ago, I would have had Zornan imprisoned for his accusation, probably executed. But not today."

Lanthia's face curled with more rage. "What! He has no evidence of his claims. Just wild accusations with little—"

"I have witnesses," Tothdarin cut her off, "confirming that you are holding the Lady Calla. They watched you thwart an attempted escape. I should have acted then, but I didn't want to believe in your betrayal. Zornan's accusation, while flimsy on its own, pushes me from my disbelief."

Lanthia's face drained and her eyes widened. "Let me explain. We were trying to draw out the Kuthraz, and we thought, well, we knew Zornan would go to them, and we'd—"

"No more lies, Lanthia. No more deception." The Emperor's eyes now held a deep and weary sadness. "How could you betray the Empire? How could you betray me?"

Lanthia's expression softened, anger lines around her eyes smoothing out. But before she could answer, one of the two-story high windows behind the Emperor shattered, glass tinkling and skidding across the floor behind the throne. The Emperor ducked at the sound, crouching next to his throne as the Kuthraz stormed the throne room.

25

NO MORE PEACE

A small group entered through the broken window, led by a bow-wielding Mairie. Loothdram and Ballin entered next, followed by a dozen men and women, all armed with swords or hatrindi. The three Imperial Guards moved toward them but stopped when Mairie trained her arrow on the crouching Emperor.

"Stay where you are, guardsmen," Loothdram said, "or the Destroyer will kill your Emperor before you can raise a brastilia-armored pinky."

"What are you doing here?" Zornan spat. "You're supposed to be rescuing Calla!"

"No," Loothdram said without a hint of guilt. "This was always the plan. We needed an audience with the boy Emperor."

One of the guards stepped forward. "You will address the Greatest Emperor with respect or—"

"Or what?" Loothdram interrupted. "I know dozens of your kind swarm here, brought by your mindspeak pleas. But if they enter, we will kill him, and we're all prepared to die. Are you prepared to lose your Emperor? Are you prepared to see him assassinated while under your protection?"

"This is madness," Zornan said. "I had him. He knows Lanthia is Dundraz. He's on our side."

"On our side?" Loothdram laughed. "I didn't think you had a side, old friend." Then he turned to address the Emperor. "Have you finally found the snake sleeping in your bed, you moon-lighted fool?"

Emperor Tothdarin stood, the power and assurance having returned to his frame; he cowered neither under Loothdram's tone nor Mairie's arrow. "Loothdram Investigator, you have come into my throne room under the curtain of violence. But now that you're here, let's hear your grievances. What evil has the Empire done that the Kuthraz want redeemed?"

Loothdram smiled, though it barely reached his cheeks let alone his eyes. "We want freedom, Emperor. The ability to live our lives as High Trade without servitude to the Empire. And we want a voice in the government, representation."

"Those are interesting reforms," the Emperor said. "I have considered both in the past."

"But you dismissed them, Your Benevolence."

"No, I delayed them. I knew I didn't have the alignment of my council, that there were many of the High Trade leadership who wanted to maintain the current system. But my plan has always been to abolish compulsory service and the selling of the children by desperate parents. The system is flawed and cruel, and it needs reform."

The Emperor sat, his judgment looming large with his words and presence. "Representation is also under consideration," he added. "A new council would come into play, with elected representation from each of the many cities and valleys in the Empire."

Loothdram looked unsure, like he'd reached out in the darkness for a wall but found nothing. "You're just saying what I want to hear."

"No, I am not." The Emperor turned to Lanthia. "When did I make these proposals, High Counselor Lanthia?"

Zornan had almost forgotten about the traitorous woman, who also looked confused, the Emperor's accusation seemingly forgotten in the simple question. "Weeks ago, Greatest Emperor."

"Could be another lie," Loothdram shot back. "How can I know for sure? How can I know you won't bury us in the dungeon if we put down our weapons?"

"I never said you'd be set free," the Emperor replied. "Your group has stormed the palace and threatened my life. Your group has killed in the name of your cause, manipulated and destroyed. You will answer according to the law. My point wasn't to exonerate or placate you; it was to show you the futility of your cause. Had you sought audience at my hand, you would have found we agree on far more than we disagree."

Loothdram's and his men's postures slumped, their confident bravado washed away by a douse of doubt.

Except for Mairie. Her body remained tense, a coil ready to release, her arrow still aimed for the Emperor. And her expression. What was that on her face? Anger? Yes, with an intensity Zornan had seen before her murderous rampages.

"Mairie," Zornan said. "Lower your arrow."

The blonde woman glanced at him, arrow still trained on Tothdarin. "He's lying to us. Fooling us. His negligence created all this, and it killed my father, forced me to live in exile." Her voice cracked with rage, and her face twitched with it.

"Lower the arrow," Loothdram said. "We should hear what the Greatest Emperor has to say."

But Mairie did not relax at all. "I will finish what we came here to do."

"We came here to address the Emperor," Loothdram said. "Put the arrow down."

Zornan scrutinized Mairie. What had gotten into her? Yes, she could become angry and emotional, but he'd never seen her this unreasonable. Of course she liked to be right, liked to see things in her way. But her arrow should have been pointed at Lanthia, who'd killed High Magistrate Stethdel, her father. And the laws that made her a bastard were centuries old, not written by the Emperor who'd spent just a decade on the throne. Mairie knew all this.

Then the answer came to him like the light of dawn across the Infinite Mountains, and he looked at Lanthia whose smugness had returned, her eyes unwaveringly locked on Mairie.

Zornan looked back at his friend, her blonde, curly hair flowing behind her head. Was she under compulsion? Had they altered her mind while on Doorie? Even with his eyes open, Zornan's second sight overtook him. Mairie glowed a pattern of orange, yellow, and red, except for the green glow of her brastilia bow and arrows, and a shape of green in her head. It looked like . . . tendrils growing up from the base of her skull and moving their way across her brain. They had done something to her on Doorie, something Lanthia used now.

"Don't give in," Zornan said, infusing his voice with as much urgency as he could. "Mairie." She spared him a sidelong glance, arrow still trained on the Emperor. "Step onto the floor around the throne." She was only one step away from the brastilia that might block whatever the High Counselor was doing. "Lanthia is doing something—"

"All these machinations," Mairie said through clenched teeth, "Stethdel's death, Liven's almost death, your family. This man could have prevented it all. Instead, he sits there on a gilded throne. We need something better, something greater." Tears rolled down her cheeks, and she pulled back even farther on the bow. "We need a revolution."

Before Zornan could speak or move, Mairie's arrow flew, a blur he couldn't follow, and his eyes found the Emperor slumped against the arm of his throne, the fletching of Mairie's arrow protruding from the intersection of his neck and jaw. Zornan looked away when he spied the arrow's tip coming out from Tothdarin's scalp.

Mairie slumped to her hands and knees, sobbing, the bow discarded. "What have I done?" she muttered.

The lead guard raised his sword to cut her down, while Zornan still stood in shock, too far away to help. Ballin had moved toward Mairie, raising his sword in an attempt to block. But it had been timed poorly, and the guard's blow struck clean through Ballin's wrist.

Ballin screamed. Pulling his maimed limb into his chest, he fell to his knees as blood saturated his clothing.

Sounds and motion broke through Zornan's daze. The door opened, and dozens of Imperial Guard streamed in, weapons at the ready. They would all be dead in moments, traitors and assassins.

Zornan's daze melted. He had no weapon, and they were outnumbered and outclassed, but he would not watch his brother and his friends die as he stood there doing nothing.

He scanned the throne room and found one of the ceremonial hatari, twenty feet away. Too far. But maybe it wasn't. For days, he'd been practicing with the brastilia, moving it to his will. He could do so again. He could fight.

Zornan reached out, feeling the brastilia weapon's energy. It flew through the air, and he caught it, surprised by his own success.

"Zornan!"

Loothdram's shout broke Zornan's surprise in time for him to see a guard's hatrindi coming for his head. He moved the new weapon, easily blocking the blow. The guard paused; he hadn't expected a flying weapon, nor such an easy block. Zornan stepped back, shrinking the elongated weapon down to a more manageable size. It was thicker and heavier than he was used to, but it would do.

Three Imperial Guards came at him in a coordinated attack, but Zornan was faster than they'd expected. He spun in a fury, pushing the attackers back with his twirl. He ran between them, positioning himself between the guards and his fallen brother. Ballin clutched his wounded arm to his chest, his forehead covered in sweat.

More guards streamed into the room. Zornan fought off the three attacking him, and Loothdram and his six Kuthraz made for the new guards. They wouldn't last. These men wore brastilia, moved nearly as fast as Baldras. Some of Loothdram's men were Enforcers, but they could not stand against Imperial Guard.

"Lanthia's escaping!" one of Loothdram's men shouted right before a guard's hatrindi pierced through his side.

Zornan elongated his weapon back to its ceremonial length and swung it in a swift arc, knocking two of the guards off their feet, with the third one backing up before the arc reached him. Zornan turned to see Lanthia surrounded by six men in thick, dark clothes: soldiers of the Imperial army. Where had they come from? As if to answer his question, they backed her down stairs, a part of the floor having been pushed away. Before he could get there, they were through the hatch, the block slammed shut. Lanthia was gone, and his chance to find Calla had likely fled with her.

With Zornan's attention diverted, the third guard rushed him, and Zornan reacted too late. He dodged, but not soon enough and the guard's hatrindi sliced through his shoulder, cutting into his Peak Crosser uniform and gashing his skin. Zornan snarled and, bringing the hatari back into a smaller form, attacked the man with a fury. But even though he struck, it did little to the guard; his armor was too thick for Zornan's blows to do much more than bruise.

But brastilia obeyed his command. He had to end this, had to get to Calla, had to save his brother and Mairie. Zornan slowed his attacks, matching the guard's speed. After three strikes and blocks, he thrust the pointed end of his staff at the man's leg, and as he did so, he imagined the armor having a hole — then it did, pushing aside like clay! The hatari tip dug into the man's thigh, and the guard grunted, falling to one knee. Zornan brought the hatari to his chest, extended his arms, and slammed the weapon into the guard's helmet. The face-plate shattered, and the man fell to his back.

The others had not fared as well. The guards had Loothdram and two of his men on their knees in surrender. Four of the Kuthraz lay dead or dying. Only four guards lay on the ground. More would come.

No. No more would come. Zornan pushed on the large doors with his mind and, after some exertion, they closed. The Imperial Guards turned to look, then turned to him, rushing him with a collective shout and hatrindi raised.

Zornan dropped his hatari and closed his eyes. The second sight came. He could see their green energy, their armor and weapons gleaming with it. This was his domain to control, and so he did. He lifted each up into the air, then slammed them to the ground, pinning them down. It took will and force, but he could hold all of them. His muscles tensed, but he held strong.

Zornan opened his eyes. Loothdram and his men stood staring at Zornan like he was a moon that had fallen from the sky.

"Take their weapons," he commanded, and the two remaining Kuthraz moved to obey.

"By the Emperor's bloody bones," Loothdram muttered.

"Poor choice of words today, Dram," Zornan said.

Loothdram ignored Zornan's retort. "What are you? What can you do?"

"I'm a Peak Crosser. I'm a husband. I'm a father." He did not care to be more than that, even if he was.

"You could bring down the Empire, you could—"

"Look around you, Loothdram!" Zornan cried out, struggling to speak while he held the guards down and the door shut. He couldn't do this forever. "You've already brought down the Empire."

"No," said the Investigator, eyes wild, face twitching in anger. "This is just the beginning. Lanthia is still alive, Lanthia—"

"Is gone," he said, "and so is my Calla. You lied to me, Loothdram. You used me to get your audience with the Emperor. Do you have any idea where Calla even is?"

"This is bigger than Calla, Zornan. Bigger than us all. This is about freedom and justice. We can't be distracted by individual considerations. Come, Zornan, Lascrill is bringing the mrakaros to the courtyard. Come help us. We need you. The Empire needs you."

"I will stay and find my wife," Zornan said.

"Friend, we don't have time—"

"I am not your friend." Each word came with a biting sincerity. "I wanted none of this. The Emperor was a good man, and he could have been your ally. But instead, you—"

"Me!" Loothdram screamed, stepping closer to Zornan. "Mairie did it! She killed him! I didn't order that."

Zornan looked over at Mairie, who huddled together with Ballin on the floor near the throne. Zornan could see the green tendrils wrapped around her mind. "No," Zornan said. "Lanthia did something to her on Doorie, made her susceptible to the witch's influence."

The screech of mrakaros broke their argument.

Are you all right, little one? Moonie spoke into Zornan's mind.

I am not well, Zornan replied. *Calla is nowhere to be found.* Moonie screeched in reply, a plaintive call.

"It's time to go, Zornan," Loothdram urged in a kinder tone.

"Go, then. I'm not leaving without Calla."

"You don't have to," came a voice from the guard whose faceplate Zornan had shattered.

Zornan stepped up to the man, whose face had been bloodied, his nose likely broken. Locks of bloodied, blond hair hung over his exposed forehead. He looked young, ten years younger than Zornan.

"What do you mean?" Zornan asked.

"The treachery the Emperor spoke of?" the guard replied. "I was the one who witnessed it. The Greatest Emperor"—his voice choked on the phrase—"he had me follow her. I saw your wife. Open your mind. I can show you where."

Zornan did as he was told and saw a house in the residential district he'd walked through to meet with Loothdram. He knew where it was.

"You're sure she's there?" Zornan asked.

"She was there just a few days ago. We've had a man watching it and no one has come or gone. It's well guarded, but"—his eyes scanned the room—"I don't think that will be a problem for you."

"Thank you."

"You didn't kill us," the Imperial Guard said, then coughed. "You could have slaughtered us, crushed us."

"You don't deserve death for protecting or avenging your Emperor."

The man coughed again. "Mizcarnon was right about you. Sad parting, Zornan Peak Crosser. May the moons grant you light and wisdom, and may fortune bring you and your wife back together."

"Sad parting, Imperial Guard. May the moons grant you peace." Zornan looked around the throne room. Blood had pooled, and the smell of it almost overwhelmed him. None were likely to find peace any time soon.

Zornan turned to find Ballin standing, pleading with Mairie. "We have to go, Mairie. We have to go."

"No," she sobbed. "Oh, moons above, I killed him. I didn't want to. What's wrong with me? I killed him!"

Zornan picked up the ceremonial hatari and holstered it, glancing back at the fallen Imperial Guard. "Order your men to stay on the ground and I will release them. If they flinch, I will not show as much mercy as I have."

"Stay still men!" the guard shouted. "Stay still until I order you to move."

"Can't bloody move anyway," came a reply.

Zornan let go of them, but kept his mind on the door. None of the guards moved.

He walked over to Mairie and, grabbing her shoulders, lifted her to her feet. "You didn't kill the Emperor, Mairie, Lanthia—"

"I loosed the arrow! I am the dagger that starts a civil war, all of the blood—"

"Will be on Lanthia's hands," Zornan interjected. "They did something to you on Doorie, warped your mind. I'm sorry I didn't see if before. I didn't know I could."

"Take it out," she begged. "I can't live with them inside me. I'd rather die. Please, take it out."

Zornan closed his eyes, seeing clearly the green tendrils dancing around her brain, glowing, pulsing. "I don't know if I can."

"Please, Zor, please. I need to be free."

Zornan took a deep breath and focused on the green energy.

Would it be like parting the armor or calling the hatari? He hadn't time. He would want it gone, too, want whatever power they held in her mind to be gone. So he wished it gone.

The green glow dissolved into a mist only visible in Zornan's second sight. Mairie gasped and arched her back. Zornan had to hold her up to keep her from falling. He opened his eyes. Mairie's face was pale like she might be sick, but her eyes were alert. She steadied herself.

"Are you well?" Zornan asked.

She nodded.

"Good. We need to move." He closed his eyes one more time, and she glowed only orange, no green. Somehow, he'd done it, and he wasn't even sure what he'd done.

The three of them followed Loothdram and his men out through the broken window and into the courtyard.

26

FINDING CALLA

Crisdan and Stargarn had waited on the palace steps for some time before moving to the streets outside. Zornan was being made to wait, which would not be uncustomary for unannounced guests, though it frustrated Crisdan to no end. Calla could be free soon. They needed Lanthia occupied, distracted by whatever request Zornan had brought before the Emperor.

When Zornan's confirmation came, the sun hung high, the heat of the day nearly there. Sweat beaded on Crisdan's forehead, though he couldn't be sure how much of that was from the heat and how much was his nerves.

Let's move, he mindspoke to Stargarn, and they moved purposefully down the street toward the Cross District.

They did not want to seem to be in too much of a hurry — a High Investigator and an Enforcer sprinting through the capital would have brought unneeded attention — so their journey took longer than Crisdan would have liked. He wanted to run, to crash with abandon into Calla's prison house. But he would let wisdom trump enthusiasm.

When they reached the street and could see the lavish house, Dagger's voice entered Crisdan's mind: *Nothing has changed, fellow friend. Our prey is still inside.*

Calla is not prey, Crisdan replied. *She is a friend.*

I was speaking of the foolish men guarding the woman. We will spill their blood like cravsda draining its prey.

What beneath the moons was cravsda? Who was this woman?

Only if we need to, he soothed.

As you say.

As they approached, one black-clad guard and a maroon-clad Enforcer came out, closing the door behind them to stand at the top of the stairs.

"Where are you two going?" the Enforcer said.

"Watch your tone," Stargarn replied, voice hard. "This is High Investigator Crisdan."

The Enforcer and the guard both bowed slightly, faces draining ashen at Crisdan's name and title. "My apologies, High Investigator," the Enforcer mumbled. "We weren't told you were coming. I don't—"

"High Counselor Lanthia asked me to come question the prisoner," Crisdan interrupted. "Is that going to happen on the porch?"

The Enforcer glanced at the guard, then looked back at Crisdan. "Of course not, High Investigator, it's just that our orders—"

"Your orders, young man, are to let me in right now," Crisdan said. "There is an imminent Kuthraz threat, and the High Counselor needs intelligence to counteract it. If you'd rather explain that to High Counselor Lanthia herself—"

"Of course, Your Grace." The Enforcer opened the door. "Please enter."

Crisdan stepped through, but the guards blocked Stargarn.

"He cannot enter," the guard said. "By the orders of—"

"Fine." Crisdan acted as irritated as he could manage and tried not to seem too eager. "Stargarn Enforcer can stay here."

Watch yourself, Crisdan added to Stargarn. *They will mindspeak with the palace soon enough, and then things will get interesting.*

I like interesting.

The smaller guard led Crisdan down a broad hallway to a staircase leading to a basement.

"Speak with Bussa Enforcer when you reach the bottom," the guard said. "He will show you to the prisoner."

Crisdan took the stairs. The walls were lined with portraits of a family Crisdan did not recognize. Whoever had lived here was allied with the Dundraz cause, either be choice or perhaps by force.

At the bottom of the stairs, an Enforcer and two unblessed more guards stood forming a line between Crisdan and a wooden door at the far wall. Their rigid posture seemed to form a physical barrier.

"Greeting, Bussa Enforcer," Crisdan said, pausing on the last stair step. "I am here to question—"

"You're here to do nothing," Bussa said. "I checked with the palace. They did not send you."

"I am a High Investigator," he replied. "I do not need to be sent. Our council does not take orders from Enforcers."

"My orders come from above your ranks," the Enforcer said, eyes narrowing.

"Who stands above the High Investigators, save the Emperor himself?"

The Enforcer's eyes darted as if to find a suitable answer painted on the wall. "Well, the orders come from—"

"As a High Investigator, I command you to step aside, Bussa Enforcer."

His expression showed doubt, though his words did not. "I have been commanded by the Emperor's own council to refuse entry."

"So, High Investigator Mabbe has been informed? How lovely. I will reach out to her and see if she can set this straight. I'm investigating rebel groups, and I have a bit of autonomy."

"Not the Emperor's Council exactly," Bussa said, his confusion nearly as thick as his neck. "Just one member—"

"High Counselor Lanthia." Crisdan let his revelation sink in, and the three guards' eyes widened. "I don't answer to her, either. So unless you have a confirmed order from the Greatest Emperor, or one from the Council of the High Trades, you will move aside."

Before the man could answer, Crisdan turned to the sound of a sudden fight upstairs, the familiar singing of brastilia weapons striking each other.

"Go help him," the Enforcer said to the three others.

"Stay put." Crisdan's command stopped them just as they flinched to move. "By order of the High Investigators, stand down."

Bussa pulled out his hatrindi, and the two guards unsheathed their swords. "High Investigator Crisdan, by order of the Greatest Emperor of the Peaks, son of Gathrizdel, I arrest you for conspiracy to overthrow the throne."

Now, Crisdan narrowed his eyes. "I would reconsider your undying loyalty, Bussa Enforcer. Lanthia is not here to protect you."

The Enforcer's lip curved into an arrogant smile on one side. "I think we can handle a little Investigator, even a High Investigator."

Crisdan closed his eyes and pushed on the minds of all four.

At first, nothing happened but a vague awareness of their thoughts. Then, each face curled in confusion at the intrusion. Crisdan let his full power flow through his mind into theirs, and the two fell to their knees, grunting in pain. The Enforcer gripped his head, the hatrindi's pommel against his ear.

"You're . . . attacking . . . us," was all Bussa could say.

Crisdan did not reply. What could one say to someone whose mind might never recover?

Crisdan clenched his hands as he pushed forth a furious attack. All three collapsed fully to the ground, one screaming like a child and curling into a ball. The two unblessed quickly lost consciousness.

The Enforcer stubbornly held on, readying his sword. With two minds down, Crisdan refocused all of his efforts on the large man. Bussa screamed, pulled his sword back, preparing a strike to take Crisdan's head. But before he could swing, his face trembled and his eyes lit up with fear. He gasped as if he might pull strength straight from the air. A moment later, he gasped again, then collapsed.

Crisdan reached out to pick up the man's hatrindi, but his head spun, and he almost fell to the stone ground. He closed his eyes to steady himself, feeling tired with the kind of exhaustion his father used to aspire to each day out on the boat, searching for the fruit of the ocean. But Crisdan had not performed a good day's work; rather, he'd disconnected the minds of three others. He could feel their empty, simple minds, wiped clean to an almost infant-like awareness. When they woke, they would not be the men they had been.

Before Crisdan could collect himself to move toward the door, Stargarn rushed down the stairs, his breaths heavy. He pulled up just before slamming into Crisdan, and his eyes widened at the three fallen men.

"How . . . ?" Stargarn couldn't even finish his question.

"How is it upstairs?" Crisdan asked, brushing past giving an explanation.

"Some woman came to help. Strange accent, fights like a moon-blasted Baldra." Stargarn's admiration for Dagger's skills pulsed through their bond. "I could have handled it myself, but she's quite capable. She said she knew you, that she was here by your request."

Before Crisdan could respond, again the crash of brastilia weapons echoed above them.

"Go help her!" Crisdan ordered. "I'll get Lady Calla."

Stargarn nodded in agreement, then sprung back up the stairs, three steps at a time.

Crisdan stepped over the fallen guards toward the closed door, which had a lock. He jiggled it. It held firm. His mental attack would not work on the heavy, mindless object. He stepped back to Bussa and, taking a key from his belt, Crisdan stuck it in, turned it, and pushed the door open.

Against the opposite wall, Calla stood on a dirty mattress. She wore a tattered dress that had been, at some point, fine and beautiful. Her features were gaunt from too few meals to keep her usual, rounder figure. The room smelled of terrible food and of her own unwashed stench.

And she looked absolutely beautiful.

"Crisdan." Her expression held no confusion at his arrival, no shock, and her feelings poked at him: relief, admiration, and . . . affection. He hoped his own feelings weren't clouding hers. He wanted her feelings to be real. He needed something to be real.

"Calla. We must go."

Crisdan stood there, as she knew he would. She'd been in his mind all morning, hoping he would find her. So yes, while Zornan spoke with the Emperor, Crisdan had found her, and she could feel freedom calling to her.

"Crisdan," was the only word she could manage before falling into his embrace.

His arms wrapped tightly around her, and his heart pounded so fast that she could feel it in their touch. Calla began to pull away, but his arms held firm.

"Come," she said. Pushing against his chest, she grabbed his hand. Crisdan nodded, and she led him from the room.

Calla stopped short. Three men lay on the floor. At first, she thought they were dead, yet there was no blood and two still had weapons at their hips. One man's eyes were open, vacant, and his chest moved in shallow breaths. Drool pooled from his open mouth dripping onto the cold, stone floor.

"You did this?" Calla asked, looking up at Crisdan.

The man's face looked tired, sad, older than she remembered. In her visions, she saw through his eyes, so she rarely saw his face.

"I did what was necessary," he whispered, an attempt at convincing himself more than her.

She looked away from the bodies and pulled on him again. He came forward, but as they reached the prostrate men, Crisdan stumbled. Calla looked back. His eyes had started to roll back in his head, and she caught him in her arms, barely keeping her feet under his weight.

"Thank you," he muttered into his shoulder.

As he drew back, their faces were so close, she could feel his breath on her cheek. He stopped pulling away and kissed her, placing his hands on her hips. Calla kissed him back.

RESCUE AND BETRAYAL

Zornan sprinted into the courtyard through the broken window, where a flock of giant flyers descended into the massive open space — more cosows and mrakaros in one place than he'd ever seen since the Academy. Many of the flyers continued circling above, while six already-saddled mrakaros landed, including Moonie.

We need to move, Moonie spoke to Zornan's mind. *There are soldiers marching on the palace, a hundred archers or more.*

In one, smooth leap, Zornan mounted the multicolored mrakaro, and as he strapped in his legs, he looked over at the Kuthraz and his friends. Mairie helped Ballin onto one mrakaro, then she mounted another. Both birds spread their wings and, taking a few steps, jumped into the sky. Moonie soon followed.

Had they not been fleeing for their lives, Zornan would have loved the sight of a half-dozen mrakaros circling the courtyard, gaining altitude. Instead, he kept his gaze below, scanning for those who would try to kill them.

The green glow of the archers' bows became apparent before the archers had gotten into position on the palace's roof, and the giant flyers weren't high enough yet to be out of range. Lascrill and his mrakaro, Ash, circled above with another group of giant flyers, riders all armed with bows, as well. As they spotted the Imperial archers, Lascrill's group began firing to provide cover. But it wouldn't be enough. Too many archers stood on the roof, and some of their dozens of arrows would no doubt hit their marks, which could include his brother and Mairie.

The first volley shot forward, and Zornan reached out with his mind, controlling their energy like he'd done with the brastilia armor of the Imperial Guardsmen in the throne room. The arrows slowed, stopped, and then fell harmlessly back onto the roof or into the courtyard.

Despite the inexplicable, the archers nocked again and sent a second volley into the air. Again, Zornan reached out and the arrows fell harmlessly downward.

Now, the group of giant flyers was high enough to be out of range, and Lascrill's archers continued firing toward the soldiers below, gravity as their ally.

Get next to Ash, Zornan spoke to Moonie. The mrakaro flapped his wings, pulling in next to Lascrill's gray-feathered giant flyer.

I'm glad you are well, Lascrill mindspoke as Zornan met his eyes.

I'm not interested in pleasantries, Zornan shot back. *You all used me. I ask that you care for Mairie and Ballin until I come for them.*

We'll be at the old aviary near Corbay, Lascrill replied. *I am sorry, Zornan.*

Save your apologies, Zornan said. *I need to find my wife. I'll settle my score with you and Dram after she's safe.*

Do you need help? the old Peak Crosser asked.

Not your kind of help.

Zornan urged Moonie away from the group, guiding him toward the residential district the Imperial Guard had shared with his mind.

Moonie flew lower with no archers nearby, settling in just ten feet above the highest rooftops and weaving amidst the plumes of smoke streaming from chimneys, the smell of midday meals drifting from opulent kitchens. Moonie banked left, and Zornan soon saw the house the Imperial Guard had shown him. Its chimney had no smoke pouring from it. He closed his eyes and, finding the second sight, saw several orange glows, though they seemed to all run together; he could not tell how many people were there. He'd need to have Zandia teach him how to better understand what he saw.

Moonie landed in the middle of the street, head pivoting, scanning for danger. Several residents came out and stared at the mrakaro, eyes wide and mouths agape.

You'd think they'd never seen a mrakaro, Moonie said. *It's not like I'm going to claw their faces off.*

Back into the air, Zornan spoke as he slipped off Moonie's back. *Keep watch. Let me know if anyone comes for us.*

The giant bird nodded and launched into the air.

Zornan pulled his new, thicker hatari from his holster and grew it to the standard length. The door of the house stood open, and a dead, bleeding Enforcer lay just inside. Zornan took each step up the stairs with care. Another dead body lay next to the Enforcer inside, a man dressed in black. Panic gripped him. Was Calla dead? Who had killed these men? Had the Imperial Guardsman led him astray?

Before Zornan could conceive any answers, a staff came flying toward his head, and he blocked it just in time. A woman faced him, and she struck again. Zornan dodged her second strike, turning around and backing away into the foyer.

The woman was tall, with bright blonde hair cut chaotically in a short, spiked style, and her eyes were blue, the bright color of a deep lake. She swung again, Baldra fast. Zornan blocked, trying to gain footing, but losing ground. She was fast, strong, and aggressive.

"Stop!" a voice called from behind him. "That's Zornan, the prisoner's husband."

The woman stepped back and lowered her weapon. "My apologies, flyer," the woman said in a heavy accent Zornan could not place. "Infidels look like infidels, you know?"

Zornan did not know. Instead, he turned to see the man behind the voice — a thick Enforcer, a hatrindi in his hand.

"I'm with High Investigator Crisdan," the Enforcer said. "He's downstairs rescuing the Lady Calla."

Zornan looked back at the fierce woman adorned in green clothes, which he thought might have been a dress but was really a long shirt, with pants underneath. The style was strange, foreign, and her staff was even more strange. It looked like brastilia, a matte finish reflecting a little sunlight, but the color was all wrong, a sandy brown instead of the swirling browns of brastilia.

The woman turned her head away, then looked back at the Enforcer. "My master calls, infidel. The city descends into the abyss. I go to help." Her eyes danced with glee and, in one fluid leap, she sprung out the door.

Zornan turned to Crisdan's ally. "Where is Crisdan? Where is my wife?"

"Below," the Enforcer said, pointing to a open doorway with his hatrindi. "We must hurry. Lanthia's people will come for us."

Lanthia's people. So Crisdan knew Lanthia's identity as well? Zornan pushed aside the question; he'd find answers once Calla was safe.

Zornan led the way down the stairs, Crisdan's Enforcer friend close behind, and as he turned the corner, he saw three more men heaped on the ground. His heart danced when he saw Calla's feet, and he took the last four steps in one bound.

When he landed, he stopped short. Crisdan had indeed rescued Calla . . . and they were locked in an embrace and a kiss.

Motion caught Calla's eye, and she pulled away. At the bottom of the stairs stood Zornan, Stargarn Enforcer hovering behind. At first, her heart leapt to see him, but as Crisdan dropped his embrace, Calla watched confused hurt cross Zornan's face. Not anger, just a deep hurt.

"Zornan," she said, voice weak. She wanted to run to him, but the fallen guards and her moment of indiscretion lay between them.

"Calla." The word lacked its usual tenderness. "You are safe." He did not move toward her.

Calla stepped around the fallen guards and pressed against Zornan's chest. At first he did not embrace her, posture stiffer than she'd ever felt. Several heartbeats later, Zornan wrapped one arm around her, but the gesture, too, lacked its usual tenderness.

"You are safe," he repeated as she cried into his chest.

"The girls," was all Calla could say in reply.

"The girls are safe," he said, arms pulling her even closer.

"No," she sobbed. "No, Trillia has them. She took them."

Zornan pulled back. "What? No, Zandia is watching them—"

"She's right," Crisdan said. "I'll explain later. We need to move now."

Crisdan watched the Peak Crosser carefully, not wanting to move toward him. Zornan's eyes burned with anger, the hand not holding Calla gripped his hatari fiercly.

Crisdan did not know why Trillia had allowed him to confirm Calla's words, and he had no idea how Calla even knew that. Had the Dundraz or the Empire told her? Had Trillia somehow informed Calla during her captivity?

"Did you have something to do with this?" Zornan barked.

Stargarn, sensing the rising tension, stepped closer.

"No," Crisdan replied, grateful he was able to answer honestly. "But we need to go. Lanthia will be here soon, and she will kill us all."

"She will try." Intense anger drifted from the Peak Crosser, its power almost enough to overwhelm Crisdan's abilities.

Crisdan wanted to look on Calla, but he did not trust himself to do so. He could feel intense guilt and grief coming from her. Any affection she'd been feeling for him had been dashed beneath the stronger emotions brought on by the sight of her husband.

What had he become? Did he have to destroy everything he touched? Was that his moon-cursed destiny? All this sorrow, all this terribleness — he'd been a part of it, even if not by choice. And he would be forever. At least as long as the moons let him live beneath their damned light.

Grief and hopelessness slammed into him, their force enough to take away his breath. He'd held Calla, ever so briefly. But he would never hold her again. Could never hold her again.

"He's right." Stargarn glanced up the stairs. "Lanthia will send more Enforcers, guards, who knows what else. And that strange woman isn't here to help us anymore."

"The palace is a little distracted at the moment," Zornan said as Calla pulled away. Their complicated, mixed feelings swirled; a distance grew between them.

"What did you do?" Calla asked.

"I . . ." Zornan paused, eyes heavy, feelings thick with regret. He didn't finish his thought.

"Come on," Stargarn urged.

Zornan nodded, then led the way, with Calla behind him. Stargarn followed, Crisdan last.

As they reached the top of the stairs, Crisdan pulled in his Investigator senses. Calla and Zornan deserved privacy; he might have smashed their trust, but they deserved to piece it back together without his probing. When he pulled back, he caught a sense of Stargarn. In place of his usual bravado or casual indifference, Crisdan sensed rage. Hate. His Enforcer friend felt like murder.

"Stargarn, no!" Crisdan yelled just as the Enforcer drew back his hatrindi, aiming for Zornan's back. Crisdan slammed into the man, knocking the Enforcer against the wall. With his offhand, Stargarn punched Crisdan in the face, then stuck the brastilia sword into Crisdan's shoulder. It came out the other side, and the Investigator screamed as pain wiped away all other feeling.

Zornan pivoted at Crisdan's warning. As the High Investigator struggled with the Enforcer, Zornan pulled Calla behind him, and before he could react, Stargarn stuck his hatrindi through Crisdan's shoulder. The High Investigator's scream mixed with Calla's own.

The Enforcer yanked the sword out and looked like he might strike again. With a thought, Zornan wrenched the hatrindi from the Enforcers grasp. The weapon flew across the atrium to slam against a far wall. The Enforcer looked down at his empty hand in surprise, but recovered quickly and charged at Zornan.

Zornan waited until the man was nearly on top of him, then twirled his hatari in a wide arc, taking the Enforcer down at the knees. The large man's head hit the stone floor with a loud crack. Holding the back of his head, the Enforcer tried to sit up, but Zornan kicked him in the face, the man's cheekbone shattering under the impact. The traitor fell onto his side, limp. Zornan raised his hatari, arms arched above his head, and prepared to thrust the point into the man's chest.

"Don't kill him!" Calla pleaded.

Zornan turned. Calla looked as though she was going to reach out to him, but fear sat in her eyes. He lowered his weapon, draining off some of his anger. He had been ready to kill the Enforcer, and would have, had she not stopped him. Zornan looked down at his attacker. That kick to his face might have killed him anyway.

"You're not a killer," Calla said, as if she feared he was exactly that.

Zornan lowered his gaze, guilt replacing rage. He had almost killed a defenseless man, something that would have seemed impossible just weeks ago.

"I'm not a killer," Zornan repeated, hoping Calla's words were true.

Zornan followed Calla to assist the fallen High Investigator. Crisdan held his shoulder, hands covered in his own blood.

"We need to get him out of here," Calla said. Her concern for Crisdan stoked a dark jealousy.

"You have to leave me," Crisdan said. "I am not on your side."

Zornan considered saying something about Crisdan trying to steal his wife, but held his tongue instead.

"I know," Calla said. "I know Trillia has you."

Crisdan looked at her, eyes sad, face furrowed. "How? I—"

"What are you talking about?" Zornan demanded. "Trillia has him, how?"

"Compulsion," Calla replied, eyes still on the High Investigator. "Trillia controls him like a Shindar does a Baldra."

Zornan shook his head. Had her captivity driven her mad? The Magistrate of Fallindra controlling a High Investigator? And Trillia had taken the girls? Zornan's mind struggled to put it all together, but all this, and Calla's betrayal, made reason more slippery than a rain-soaked cliff.

"Ridiculous," Crisdan said, echoing Zornan's thoughts. "That's ridiculous."

But Zornan could know. Calla was superstitious, though not prone to lying. Zornan could find out.

He opened his second sight, like he had done with Mairie, and like in her mind, Zornan could see green swirling within the High Investigator's head. Yet it was different. The green force around Mairie's mind had been tendrils, like wisps of smoke off a candle. The green magic that wrapped around Crisdan's brain moved in a complex, braided pattern, like an intricately woven basket.

Hot anger boiled again. Trillia. Zornan had trusted her, but he could trust no one who'd subject another person's will to their own.

"Tell your master that I know," Zornan spat. "I can see it in your mind, her green magic."

Crisdan's eyes widened. "She's impressed," he said, voice hollow and unimpressed. "You've become more than she'd imagined."

More than she'd imagined? What did the Magistrate know? Would everyone betray him?

"I won't stop you from leaving," Crisdan said, tone distant. "Trillia wants you to escape. You must leave the city now; chaos is coming. And then after that, peace."

"She makes him do terrible things." Calla's voice trembled with sadness and anger. "And she took my girls." She bent closer to the

High Investigator. "Where are my children!" she yelled. "Where have you taken them?"

Tears filled Crisdan's eyes, and a sob choked any reply as he looked away.

Zornan gently pulled Crisdan's chin up to force him to look at Calla. "Answer the question, Trillia. Where are the girls?"

"Safe," the High Investigator said, though the word barely escaped another sob. "I'm so sorry . . ."

"Who's sorry?" Calla screamed. "Crisdan or Trillia?"

"They are safe," Crisdan replied. "She took them to keep them safe."

"Safe from whom?" Zornan demanded. "Were the Dundraz going to take them? And where is Zandia?"

"Safe from you," Calla said when Crisdan did not reply. "The children are safe from you. You have changed them, just like you have changed me."

Zornan turned to her. "What are you talking about? I haven't changed anyone."

"You have, Zor, you just don't know it. Somehow, you've changed us. I know all this because of your blessing. I can see things." She looked down at Crisdan, then back up at him. "I saw you both coming. And I've seen the girls held by Trillia's cruel hand." She turned her head and closed her eyes.

"You both need to leave." Crisdan grunted, trying to stand but failing. "All can be explained, but you must get out of here. There's chaos in the city, but that might not stop Lanthia from coming for you."

Zornan turned back to the High Investigator. "I can't leave you under her control." Why was he so worried about the man who was trying to steal away Calla? He brushed aside his jealousy. Right was right.

"You must." Crisdan closed his eyes and winced. "My destiny is dark. Yours does not need to be."

Zornan smacked Crisdan's forehead with his staff, and the man fell backwards, unconscious.

"Zornan!" Calla cried.

"I can cure him," he said. "I took it away from Mairie. I can take it away from him. Isn't that what you want?"

Calla's gaze softened, her tone kind and sad. "Of course, but not how you think it. I want to be with you, Zornan. I still want to be with you."

"Do you love him?" Zornan asked, wishing he hadn't.

Calla paused, face crumpling. He hadn't even noticed her tattered dress, her thin frame. After witnessing the kiss, he hadn't really looked at her. She looked weak, frail, like she'd been through the depth of the Fire Moon, like he had on Doorie. And jealousy had kept him from really seeing her.

"I don't know how I feel about him," she admitted, her honesty piercing Zornan's soul. "But I want to be with you and the girls. I'm sorry."

He wanted to hug her, wanted to accept her apology, but couldn't bring himself to do it, couldn't bring himself to release the betrayal, release the anger.

Zornan turned back to Crisdan and, closing his eyes, fully embraced the second sight. The green wrapped around the High Investigator's mind pulsed and shifted. Like he had with Mairie, he reached for it with his own mind, but it resisted. He could sense the power of some other mind, probably Trillia's, and she pushed him away, the green remaining unmolested. So he pulled again, placing all his will against it, body and mind straining as if he stuggled to pull out a tree stump with his bare hands. He pulled with everything he had, yet the green weaves remained wrapped around Crisdan's mind.

And then it was gone. Zornan dropped to the ground, breath knocked from his body. The green surrounding Crisdan's brain was gone, leaving behind only orange and yellow.

"He's free," Zornan spoke though a heavy breath.

"How?"

"I don't know. I can do things now, things I don't understand." Had he really blessed the girls, blessed Calla? He drew in a deep breath. What exactly had he become? Could he dismiss his own power as he'd done to Crisdan? Could he be free from all this madness?

"We should go now," Calla said. "But we can't leave Crisdan. If the Dundraz find him, they'll kill him."

Zornan holstered his new hatari. Kneeling down next to the other man, he picked up the High Investigator and carried him from the house, surprised by how light the other man felt in his arms.

28

A NEW EMPEROR

In the early morning light, Mizcarnon watched the miotop eat a small bush. They'd landed the night before, had gotten a good night's sleep, and he had commanded the large lizard to remain in the forest, eating and staying out of sight. He hoped the simple creature could follow those simple instructions, because Mizcarnon knew the panic the miotop would cause if anyone saw it. Though Miotops were incredibly docile, a local villager would likely think 'monster' instead of 'over-grown cow'.

"We should go." Jayzca stood next to him as Jayzca.

Mizcarnon nodded, looking down at the girl; it felt strange to see her as a little girl again.

From the woods, they walked in the direction of a small town. Part of Mizcarnon wanted to take Jo's form again; the larger race could move so much faster with incredible endurance. But if a giant lizard might cause a panic, two Hol'Feel'Koo sprinting through the countryside would be even more alarming.

Jayzca walked beside him, the pace slower than he would have liked. She wore determination on her face and in her purposeful stride, but she also carried sadness and fatigue. How much more could Mizcarnon expect from her? Holding Hol'Feel'Koo form was exhausting, but he had the blessed endurance of a Peak Crosser; she had no such advantage. His original plan had been to walk all the way to the capital, but at their current pace, it might take them days, even though they only had ten miles to go. Landing any closer to Bristrinia would have been impossible, though. Too many eyes to avoid.

"We'll hire a carriage at the village," Mizcarnon said.

Jayzca looked up at him. "I'm walking too slowly?" He almost missed it, but a small smile had come and gone.

He offered a bigger smile in return. "No, I'm just too tired. And I'm guessing you're done with flying."

"For the rest of my life, if I can help it."

Later that morning, they reached a town just north of the forest. He'd almost forgotten about his black eyes and ill-fitting Peak Crosser clothing. What must the villagers think of the pair? Mizcarnon dressed as a Peak Crosser, in pants made for a smaller man, and Jayzca dressed in a strange tunic unlike any Imperial fashion, with a golden skin tone that was less noticeable in the bright sunlight yet still unheard of in the Empire. And they shared the same, unsettling, dark eyes. What might have been an oddity of a man and a young girl walking out of the forest and into the town became an absolute anomaly when combined with everything else.

Mizcarnon walked them into the Peak Crosser keep, a small building with a small yard behind it. The building itself was two rooms: the keeper's bedroom and a small room for interacting with the keeper. No giant flyers walked around the fenced-in yard.

"Welcome morning, keeper," Mizcarnon said as he entered. Jayzca stood close enough by his side that her arm seemed connected to his left leg.

"Welcome greeting," the keeper replied, eyes wide and searching.

"Where might someone get un-winged transportation to Bristrinia?"

The keeper looked them up and down before responding. "Kirum has a horse-drawn coach. You'll find him at the Lonely Mrakaro; it's our only common house." The man stood from a squeaky chair. "If you're a Peak Crosser, where's your giant flyer?" His tone had gone from incredulous to threatening.

Mizcarnon met the keeper's aggression with a cold stare of his own. "Died, on the coasts of Croxshine," he said. "I am Mizcarnon Peak Crosser of the Emperor's Blessed Army." He bowed his head slightly. "Welcome parting, keeper."

The man's eyes said he didn't believe Mizcarnon's explanation, but he stepped back. "Welcome parting," he replied, not adding a title he didn't believe Mizcarnon held.

Frustrated, Mizcarnon walked toward the town's center.

"They don't like us," Jayzca said, bouncing amongst everyone's worried stares.

"They're scared," Mizcarnon replied. "They've never seen anything like us. I was scared when I saw your eyes for the first time."

"Do you have money to hire a carriage?" she asked. "I assume folks in your Empire don't do favors like that for free."

Mizcarnon shook his head. He hadn't taken any Imperial coin to Croxshine, since he'd never imagined sneaking back into the Empire like this. "Being a member of the High Trades offers many advantages," Mizcarnon said, "including command of the low trades like a carriage driver."

"I don't think anyone's going to believe you." She looked his clothes up and down, then smiled broadly. "You need a better tailor."

"Yes," Mizcarnon replied. "I will hire a different one next time."

They found the carriage driver in a half-full common house, pulling him from a game of brithdal. At first, he resisted the command, until Mizcarnon showed him the special mark for military

High Tradesmen on his hatari. The driver offered a sincere, nervous apology and took them to his carriage, but he stared at their eyes, and Mizcarnon was sure the driver doubted the veracity of Mizcarnon's claim. No matter. As long as they arrived in Bristrinia, it wouldn't matter what this man thought.

They drove along the dirt road in silence, Jayzca on the right side, looking out on the ocean. Mizcarnon peered out the left side, lost in his worries. How much time did the Empire have before Nansartans popped up from the ground or rained down from the sky? Even with significant time, could the Empire ready itself against a superior force? Most of the Emperor's Army consisted of regular, unblessed men. During war, the Imperial Guard would be employed, with Enforcers conscripted, as well, but that only numbered in the hundreds. Thousands of Nansartan soldiers were blessed like Enforcers, and hundreds more as Destroyers. Regular men of the Emperor's Army would be slaughtered like hatchlings left undefended in their nest.

Mizcarnon took a deep breath, trying to calm himself. He could only deliver the news. He'd trust in the wisdom of men like Emperor Tothdarin and Mizcarnon's commander General Chandish to oversee preparations and defense.

Soon, the rolling countryside gave way to the walled city of Bristrinia.

Jayzca's eyes widened as they approached the massive, gleaming city. "That is your capital?"

Mizcarnon coated his reply with pride. "Yes, the city of Bristrinia, home of the Greatest Emperor of the Peaks, Tothdarin, son of Gathrizdel."

"And you know this Emperor?"

"Yes," he said, the mention of the man filling Mizcarnon with anticipation and confidence. "He is a good man and a great Emperor."

"He will help us destroy the Nansartans?"

"Yes, Jayzca, I believe he will."

As the carriage neared the palace, it slowed to a stop amid shouts and commotion, almost like a panicked market.

Leaning his head out, Mizcarnon called to the driver. "What's going on?"

"Looks like they've closed the road, Peak Crosser."

Mizcarnon hopped from the carriage. The golden accents of the palace ahead danced in the bright sunlight. Jayzca joined him as he waved to dismiss the driver and walked slowly along the cobbled street.

Armed, unblessed soldiers had formed a tight circle around the palace, pushing back a small crowd, both sides shouting at the other.

Mizcarnon bent down to look into Jayzca's eyes. "Go between worlds, Jayz, and follow me closely." He glanced around, but with all the commotion, no one had even noticed the pair. "Quickly now."

Jayzca nodded and disappeared.

Mizcarnon pushed through the crowd, initiating foul retorts, which he ignored. Finally, he reached the line of soldiers.

"What's going on?" he asked the soldier in front of him.

The soldier, a young man who looked overwhelmed, started when he met Mizcarnon's eyes. "Peak Crosser, sir, I'm not sure, really. Something has happened at the palace. One of the Imperial Guard said we needed to form a perimeter—"

"Shut your mouth, soldier." An older soldier, though still young, stood behind the younger soldier, glaring at Mizcarnon. "This is a military matter. Back away like everyone else, Peak Crosser."

Mizcarnon considered pulling rank, but with his too-small uniform and his strange eyes, he doubted they'd believe him any more than the keeper in the small seaside town had. He nodded respectfully, then pulled back into the confused crowd.

Panic welled. What could be happening at the palace to stir this kind of commotion? Had the Nansartans already arrived? Were they marching across the plains of Bristrinia, toward the capital? Was this an effort to protect the Emperor from the fate befallen King Dichnire of Croxshine?

Then, another thought slammed Mizcarnon: What if their tunnel went right into the palace or the city? The Nansartans did not have to follow the same flight plan as they had in Croxshine. The Kuthraz and the Dundraz had the Empire balanced on a windy peak, with the Emperor and those faithful to him trying to keep it from falling.

He had to get inside the palace, had to make sure Emperor Tothdarin was safe, that the Nansartans hadn't found a way to . . .

Mizcarnon looked around. Despite his dark eyes and strange clothes, the churning chaos provided him cover. The roiling crowd focused on the guards, and behind them, the marble walls of the palace. Mizcarnon was tall, and even without inhuman eyes, he stuck out in a crowd. But he could now go where no one would see him.

Mizcarnon closed his eyes and pushed himself between worlds.

When he opened his eyes again, the surrounding world seemed distant, bright colors muted, edges fuzzy as if his eyes wouldn't focus.

"No one seems to have seen you." Jayzca now stood beside him, large eyes scanning the crowd.

"We must get inside the palace." Mizcarnon looked past the guards, toward the great steps leading to the great doors.

"We'll have to pass through dozens of people. We try to avoid that."

"It can't be avoided. Follow me."

Mizcarnon dashed away, and he felt Jayzca follow. As they ran through the crowd, the strange feeling of passing through living beings rushed through him, and Mizcarnon caught a glimpse of one or two looking in his direction before their temporary vision dissipated. When he at last broke through the line of guards, he stopped, and a few moments later, Jayzca appeared, her form bright and focused, and weaving between the guards' legs.

"You must keep up," Mizcarnon huffed, more winded than he should have been. Maybe passing through people had worn him out?

"My legs are just as short walking between worlds as they are in our world. Move slower if you want me to keep up."

Had an unwavering dread not filled Mizcarnon, he might have smiled at her pouty response. Instead, he ascended the stairs, making sure Jayzca kept pace.

They strode through the solid doors, passing only four Imperial Guards standing watch. Usually, the great door had three or four times as many guards as this.

As they entered the entrance hall, Mizcarnon paused, frozen by a moment of indecision.

Jayzca looked up at the mural of the central range of the Infinite Mountains painted on the high ceiling. "Are there really that many mountains together in one place?"

Mizcarnon looked up. He'd hardly noticed the painting during his prior visits; he'd been so preoccupied on prior trips. Now, seeing those distant peaks swelled a longing to fly between them on the back of Sunset. "There are those and many more, stretching from ocean to ocean, from the south to the Ice Mountains in the north."

As they considered the mural together, Mizcarnon noticed how few people they'd passed once they'd entered the palace. It seemed nearly deserted, with silence replacing the din of courtiers and servants.

"Come," Mizcarnon said. "We'll start at the throne room."

Mizcarnon led Jayzca in a brisk walk. At first, he started to cross through walls, toward the palace's center, but he didn't know the back halls and passages and couldn't be sure they went in the right direction, so he returned to the main hallway and walked the path he knew.

They passed the occasional person — several servants running in the opposite direction — but he saw no soldiers, no guards. Part of him wanted to rejoin his world, question one of the fleeing servants, but instead, he remained between worlds. Whatever had happened here would reveal itself soon enough, and appearing out of nothing to a frightened servant was likely to instill only terror.

They turned the corner, where the massive doors to the throne room stood open, with no guards watching. Mizcarnon broke into a sprint, leaving Jayzca to follow behind.

The throne room was chaos; a dozen Imperial Guard were scattered across the floor, with several others lying in pools of blood. And there was a lot of blood — pools and smears across the tiled floor.

His eyes rested last on the throne, where Emperor Tothdarin lay on his back on the dais, a brastilia arrow having entered below his chin and exited through his scalp.

Mizcarnon ran to the Emperor's side and, kneeling next to him, entered his own world without consciously trying. He lifted the Emperor's head, hoping beyond reason for proof of life, but the Emperor's chest did not move, and his eyes were open in a deathly stare.

No! his mind screamed, and he pulled the Emperor's face to his chest as he began to cry. "No!" he screamed aloud. "How could the gods allow this?" Mizcarnon fixed his gaze heavenward. "He was your man! He was doing your work! How dare you abandon him!"

"Mizcarnon . . ." His name had come out as a hoarse whisper, a faint sound that, at first, he thought might have been Jayzca, or Jo, or the gentle upbraiding of the gods he cursed. But it was none of those things, and the voice came again: "Mizcarnon Peak Crosser . . ."

Mizcarnon turned to one of the Imperial Guards removing a broken helmet and struggling onto his side. Mizcarnon gently laid down Emperor Tothdarin's head and approached the wounded guard.

"Gahrshak," Mizcarnon said, kneeling next to his friend. The man's long, blond hair was tinted with blood.

"Mizcarnon, it is you." The young guardsmen coughed, face contorted in pain. "I thought I had fallen unconscious and was dreaming."

"Who did this?"

"Lanthia." The word had barely escaped Gahrshak's lips. "She manipulated everything."

Lanthia. The Emperor had been betrayed by a viper in his own nest. Mizcarnon's face twitched with anger.

"We need to get you help. I will—"

"No." The young man sat up with some effort. "I'll be all right. Zornan did not kill any of us; just disabled us."

"Zornan?" An image of the unassuming man he'd rescued came to his mind.

"Mairie, the Destroyer girl, she killed the Emperor, but at Lanthia's command."

"I don't understand . . ." Mizcarnon tried to grasp the facts, but grief pushed out reason, and anger boiled underneath.

"We'll discuss it on the way."

"On the way to where?"

Gahrshak looked into Mizcarnon's eyes, not flinching at their new color. "The Emperor had foreseen this. Not exactly this, but Lanthia's betrayal. He had a plan. We're to regroup at Cliff Face. We must get out of the city before Lanthia locks us in." Cliff Face was a small city in the northern foothills facing the Bristrinian Plains, home of the Peak Crosser Academy.

Mizcarnon thought of the circle of soldiers who had barred their entry. "It's already been started. Soldiers have surrounded the palace."

The young guard nodded, then looked back at Mizcarnon. "What happened to your eyes?" he asked, as if he'd just noticed them.

"We both have much to tell," Mizcarnon responded. "Can you stand and walk?"

"Not without help."

Mizcarnon lifted Gahrshak to his feet, and the man took one limping step.

"Help the others," ordered the High Captain.

Mizcarnon saw other guards stirring, and he hurried to help them to their feet. Three guards did not stir. After checking, he confirmed they were dead.

Gahrshak placed a hand on Mizcarnon's shoulder. "Come, Mizcarnon Peak Crosser. We must get to Cliff Face."

"All is lost," the Peak Crosser muttered, looking back at his fallen Emperor. As two of the remaining guards reverently lifted Tothdarin's body, tears threatened to mar Mizcarnon's visage again.

"No, all is not lost." Gahrshak's face had formed into a stony expression. "But we must move now. Lanthia knows of our loyalty to the Emperor, and we witnessed her betrayal and cowardice. If we wait much longer, we'll have to fight our way out." The High Captain looked down at the bodies of the fallen. "No more innocents need to die today."

Mizcarnon nodded, and although he didn't really understand, he would nevertheless follow Gahrshak. "What now?"

"We regroup behind his appointed heir and fight."

"His appointed heir?" The Emperor had sired no children, and Mizcarnon did not know the law of appointing an heir.

"Yes. He named an heir three years ago in a secret ceremony in front of us, the High Counselor, the High Magistrate, and several ministers. It has remained a secret, to be revealed upon his death."

"Who?"

"He named Mizcarnon Peak Crosser as his heir. You, my friend, are now the Emperor of the Peaks."

Gahrshak fell to one knee, as did the other Imperial Guards; all but the two holding Tothdarin took a knee. Mizcarnon stared at the Emperor's body, trying to make sense of what Gahrshak had said. How could he be Emperor? High Trade were not permitted to be emperors. His mind whirled, feeling like he might faint.

The blond Guard stood. "Come, Mizcarnon, we must move now."

Mizcarnon looked at the Imperial Guardsmen, all now standing, awaiting his command. If he was indeed the heir, then these men would follow him to the death.

"Let's move, then, Captain. And please tell me there's a way out of the palace, one Lanthia might not know."

Gahrshak smiled. "Our entrance is a secret, Greatest Emperor of the Peaks, Mizcarnon, heir of Tothdarin."

Mizcarnon flinched at the title. He'd never get used to that.

He looked back at Tothdarin's body. What would the wise, young ruler have done in this situation? The weight of the Emperor's calling threatened to break Mizcarnon's feeble resolve, but no, he would not break, could not break. The Empire of the Peaks would not crumble. Mizcarnon would not let it.

Jayzca knelt in the throne room in the Otherworld, struggling to maintain her distance from her homeworld and trying not to fall completely into despair. She'd betrayed her father, given up her home, forced Chage and Jo away from their people and their land, and for what? Mizcarnon's beloved Emperor should have been their salvation, and the magical armies of the Peaks should have been able to liberate her people.

But their Emperor lay dead on his throne, an arrow through his head. No salvation would come from him. Just as King Dichnire had died in his palace, surrounded by imagined security, so fell the Emperor of the Peaks. Nansart had conquered Boothdrinka and Croxshine, and now he would take the Peaks, as well. His gray form from her dreams haunted her at each turn. Even if they climbed back onto the Miotop and found another continent far away, there would be no escape from him. Nansartans claimed their leader was a new god, a god raised to replace the gods of ancient times, to replace the moons, the sun, and whatever other being one might worship. His rule would shine on the whole world, like the sun shined on all lands.

Jayzca placed her head on her thighs, curled into a tight ball, and sobbed.

Do not give up. Chage's deep baritone echoed in her mind. *We will find a way.*

How? she pleaded, looking up at his form standing next to her. *This was the way! We have nothing! And I've stranded you and Jo in a strange land.*

Come walk this part of our world with us. It's not as desolate as father led

227

us to believe. These plains are covered in snow, but we can see green mountains to the north. Perhaps there is more to this land than we knew.

Jayzca considered fleeing the space between worlds to join Chage in his. Maybe the world of the Hol'Feel'Koo was the only freedom from Nansart, since his evil tendrils did not stretch there yet; she and Mizcarnon could join their companions, live a pleasant life away from all the chaos of their world.

But could she abandon the Mazzdu and all Croxshine to a conquered fate? Since she could remember, Jayzca had believed that the White Goddess had blessed Jayzca to be the salvation of her people. She'd been taught that by Mother and Father. If the White Goddess had turned her back on Jayzca and her people, was it now fair for Jayzca to walk away, as well? She had been exiled; she was no longer welcome amid the Mazzdu or the Hol'Feel'Koo.

She turned her attention to Mizcarnon, who existed in surreal, wavering colors. He spoke with a guard, the other man's hand on Mizcarnon's shoulder. The young guard's blond hair was matted to his head through a combination of sweat and blood, and his expression shown with worry. Despite the blood, sweat and worry, he was as pretty a man as she'd seen during her short time in the Peaks, his pale skin not too distant from the golden tones of the Mazzdu. Despite her despair, the man's resolute expression worked to raise her waning spirits.

"All is lost." Mizcarnon's voice had come as a whisper between the worlds as he looked over at his fallen emperor, his gaze showing the same despondence that shadowed her own heart.

"No, all is not lost," answered the handsome guard, voice light and filled with hope. His next whispered words were lost as she took in a deep breath to ease the dread crushing her chest.

"His appointed heir?" Mizcarnon replied to something the guard had said.

"Yes," the man said. "He named an heir three years ago in a secret ceremony in front of us, the High Counselor, the High Magistrate and several ministers. It has remained a secret, but it was to be revealed upon his death."

"Who?"

"He named Mizcarnon Peak Crosser as his heir. He named you, Mizcarnon."

Jayzca stepped invisibly close to Mizcarnon, whose mouth stood open, expression as shocked as she felt. Mizcarnon had either been overly humble of his standing in his own land or this was truly an unprecedented surprise. The guards in the room all kneeled and bowed their heads.

The blond guard placed both hands onto Mizcarnon's shoulders. "Come, Mizcarnon, we must move now."

Mizcarnon, Emperor of the Peaks. She had pulled from death the heir to this magical land, had endowed him with even more power. Tears came again unbidden, but she let them come.

No, she thought back to Chage, *all is not lost. The White Goddess smiles on us still.*

"Let's move, then, Captain." Mizcaron's face again reflected his stone-like sense of purpose. "And please tell me there's a way out of the palace, one Lanthia might not know."

The guard smiled a set of brilliant white teeth. "Our entrance is a secret, Greatest Emperor of the Peaks, Mizcarnon, heir of Tothdarin."

The Peak Crosser looked back at the former Emperor's body, then back at the guard. They started to move, but Mizcarnon halted. "One moment," he said. "What you are about to see will be confusing, but please, trust me. I will be gone, but I will be right back."

And before the guard could object, Mizcarnon's form frayed, then became solid to hang between worlds as Jayzca's did.

"You've been crying." He gently touched her cheek. "We must go now. Follow us, but stay between worlds. We're not out of danger yet."

"Emperor Mizcarnon," she said, barely above a whisper.

Mizcarnon nodded, expression grave, deep lines furrowed along his forehead. "I'm afraid the life we had planned for us will no longer be possible. My people call; duty calls. We will prepare the Empire for the Nansartans, and I promise you, someday we will save the Mazzdu. The terrible shadow of Nansart will not stretch across the world."

Jayzca managed a thin smile. "Go back to our world. I will follow."

He smiled, then dissolved back into reality. Together, Mizcarnon and the blond guard moved toward the entrance, followed by a dozen guards all adorned in the magical armor common among the Nansartans. How many magically blessed men and women now obeyed Mizcarnon's command? Two men at the back carried in their arms the body of the former dead Emperor as gently as if they'd held a small child.

Jayzca ran to match their speed as Mizcarnon led the group out of the throne room and down a hallway. Although dread still pulled at her, Jayzca allowed hope to shine through and wipe away her doubts. The White Goddess had not abandoned her after all, and Jayzca vowed to never doubt her benevolence ever again.

29

ESCAPE

Calla watched as Zornan stepped from the house first, holding Crisdan as easily as Calla might hold Caldry when Caldry was sleeping. Her muscles tensed. The last time she'd stepped into apparent freedom, Lanthia had slammed that door shut. Calla knew she needed to be free, knew that more captivity might break her.

She stepped out of the house and into the sunlight, the brightness welcoming and hopeful. Moonie had landed in the street right in front of them, screeching as he did, and the playful call brought a smile to Calla's face. The gesture felt weird, the muscles strangely tense; she hadn't smiled much lately.

Calla had never really liked Silver, Zornan's first mrakaro, but she adored the playful Two Moons. His orange and blue colors looked like something off a painting, like it shouldn't be real; birds in Fallindra were not that colorful.

Zornan laid Crisdan onto Moonie's back, tying him down with some straps.

"Two Moons will fly Crisdan and guide us out of the city," Zornan said as distant shouts, panicked and wailing, reached them.

"What's happened?" she asked.

"The Emperor is dead," her husband replied, his voice mournful.

"How?"

Zornan finished tying Crisdan down, then stepped away from his mrakaro. "It's a long story." He looked at the ground, then up as Moonie launched into the air. "Mairie killed him, but she was under Lanthia's control."

"Compulsion? Like a Shindar?"

"I can't say for sure," he said, finally looking at her, though his eyes never really met hers, and his reticence was like a thousand pinpricks. "Something more subtle, maybe, and I took it out. The Kuthraz will be blamed for killing the Emperor, and the blame seems about right to me." Zornan's gaze grew angry, and he looked away. "Loothdram used us, Calla, used us to get to the Emperor. Mairie might have loosed the arrow, and Lanthia may have pushed her, but Loothdram had put a mrakaro and a prairie cat in the same room. The end results are his doing."

Frantic shouts grew louder in the distance. The Emperor was dead, and he had no heir, no children to receive his mantle. Her stomach knotted. These angry calls were just the beginning of a fierce storm rolling across the Empire.

"We must go," Zornan said, eyes still distant. "Two Moons says soldiers are beginning to fan out from the palace. We need to get out of the city before they find me. I'll be blamed just as much as the others."

As they wove through the streets, Calla followed closely behind Zornan. All movement of people, horses, and carriages seemed chaotic, not the pleasant order she'd imagined the capital would have.

Outside one house, a man and a woman commanded servants to load three large carriages. The servants moved quickly to load chests and barrels, their departure imminent.

In the more common part of the city were two flows of people, some moving toward the center, to the palace and the growing chaos. Many, including women with children, hurried away from the epicenter.

Zornan grabbed Calla's arm, waking her from her observations.

"This way," he said, and he pulled her away from where the people flowed. "Two Moons says there's a mob two streets over."

As they approached the city's edge, mountains looming on the horizon, the throng of people grew stronger. Calla saw a closed city gate ahead, where a mass of humanity pushed toward. Shouts came from the gate, though too many voices muddled everything to pick out any words cleanly.

"Moonie says all the gates he can see are like this one," Zornan said, "blocked by soldiers, gates closed. He said the docks are also filled with soldiers, and they've started setting fire to boats."

"This city is going to explode," Calla replied, feeling the desperation hanging in the air like a collective breath that would need to be released.

As if to confirm this, a well-dressed man pushed past them toward the crowd of mostly commoners.

"Out of the way!" he shouted. "Out of the way, you inbred commoners!"

A large commoner dressed in tattered brown clothes caked with grease and dirt stepped in front of the aristocrat. "What did you call me?"

"Move, man!" the prim man bellowed. "Know your place!"

"The Emperor's dead," the large man replied. "There's no heir. There's no commoner or aristocrat or low trade or High Trade anymore. We're all equal now, as I see it. The moons have done flattened the field."

The well-dressed man in his silks and jewelry seemed to notice for the first time he was outnumbered. A servant trailed him, carrying some ledgers, but his slight build and hesitant manner screamed "accountant" more than "bodyguard." A small circle of dirty, angry-faced commoners had formed behind their large friend.

"Rumors," the aristocrat said, though his voice had lost its commanding tone. "I'm sure the Emperor is alive, and this is some trick of the rebels to cause panic—"

"If he's alive," another commoner said, "then why are you fleeing the city?"

The aristocrat huffed, but his haughtiness had lost its vigor. "We have business in Nansath. We are on our way—"

"Then why didn't you hire a ship?" a third commoner asked. "Would have been faster, by the moons."

"I think those books contain all his holdings," the first man said, mouth curling in a sneer, eyes as wild as a prairie cat's. "Lands stolen from us. Wealth built on our backs. Circlarl be damned, I bet his clothes could feed us all for a bloody week." The crowd behind him cheered, matching his disgust and snarl.

"I'm one of you!" the servant shouted, quivering. "I've been his slave for years. He's a cruel and dishonest master."

"Shut your mouth, Cordan!" the well-dressed man commanded. "Or I'll—"

"Or you'll what?" the large man said, stepping right up to the aristocrat.

The servant dropped the books and melted into the crowd, which cheered wildly.

At this, Zornan stepped forward, his hatari out and ready. "Leave him alone." Calla couldn't decide if she should admire Zornan's bravery or scold his stupidity.

"Leave it to a High Tradesman to defend one of his slave masters," the second commoner said, a club in his hand. "We'll beat you and your rich friend to a pulp!" The crowd cheered again, fists raised, and soon, they grew, onlookers curious to see the source of the commotion at the end of the unmoving line.

Everyone parted and ducked as Moonie swooped down, screeching loudly and picking up the cudgel-wielding man in his massive feet, flinging him nearly a block. With several powerful wingbeats, Moonie regained altitude and circled overhead with more piercing cries. Most of the commoners turned their attention away from them and the aristocrat, back toward the front of the line. After several moments, even the most vocal of the group, including the large one who'd started it, melted back into the crowd.

"Thank you, Peak Crosser," the man said, color slowly returning to his face. "I can't believe what's come over this city. I mean—"

"Return to your home and stay there," Zornan ordered, and before the man could respond, Zornan took Calla by the arm and led her back into the city.

"Where are we going?" Calla asked.

"Mairie is coming, but we need to find a less-populated street. This way."

They walked several blocks onto a wide street, where one vendor stood on the corner, selling fruit from a bag strapped across her chest, but the few passersby ignored her entreaties.

"This will do," Zornan said.

Moonie appeared over the nearest building, skidding into the street, and another giant flyer appeared a moment later, also flying just above the rooftops: a bat-like cosow, colored as dark as midnight. It landed near Moonie, spreading its thin wings along the ground. Mairie jumped off in one fluid motion.

"Help me move the High Investigator to Nightgrip," Zornan said. Mairie nodded, and they worked together to move Crisdan to the cosow.

Calla looked around. The street had emptied; even the vendor had cleared out. The people flowed around them, moving down a block or two to avoid the giant flyers; they weren't used to the giant creatures, and Calla could not blame them as she stared at the cosow's twin fangs.

A third giant flyer landed, its talons scraping against the stone street. Its coloring was brown with a tinge of red, with a plume of white erupting from just under its chin.

Mairie stepped up to Calla, bowing her head, trying for a weak smile she couldn't quite pull off. "Greeting, Lady Calla. I am Mairie."

Calla embraced her, and after a short moment, the girl hugged her back, her body pulsing with soft sobs. "Welcome greeting," Calla whispered.

"Come." They parted at Zornan's word. He also tried for a weak smile. "The crowd is ignoring us, and the soldiers are too busy. That could change at any moment."

"I'm going to ride on one of these?" Calla questioned.

"You'll ride with me on Moonie," Zornan said. "Haven't you said you've always wanted to ride a mrakaro?"

"It's one of those things one says without really meaning it," Calla replied.

Zornan flashed her a broad grin, and for an instant, all seemed normal. But as quickly as that moment came, it went.

Zornan lifted Calla onto Moonie's back, and the mrakaro whinnied as Zornan tied Calla's legs onto the saddle with some leather straps. In one smooth jump, her husband hopped up next. Mairie mounted the red-brown feathered mrakaro, and the cosow leapt into the air, carrying the still-unconscious Crisdan.

"Wrap your arms around me," Zornan said, and Calla complied. "We're going to fly low."

"What if I get sick?" she asked.

"Try not to get sick on Moonie's wing," Zornan said. "He's not fond of that."

Calla tightened her grip and lay her head against his back. She yearned for this closeness, to regain Zornan's trust.

"Where are we going?" Calla asked.

"The Kuthraz are regrouping in Corbay," he said. "We'll meet them there."

"And then what?"

"I'm not sure. I want to leave this moon-cursed revolution behind, but I doubt there will be a corner of the Empire free from all this."

Before Calla could ask her next question, Moonie began trotting down the street, taking to the air. Calla closed her eyes as her stomach filled with a flickering sensation unlike anything she'd ever felt. It was akin to the anticipation of a festival day, mixed with the fear one felt late at night in the dark. When she finally opened her eyes, the rooftops moved smoothly below them, flashing by with incredible speed. Finally, the city walls came into view, and the three giant flyers drifted together over the high grass of the Bristrinian Plains.

30

A PRAYER

The three days of waiting for Mayfran and his friends to arrive felt more like a week. Zandia carefully carried Kisthana over a small hill from the house where they'd kept Zandia, to the small house where the Dundraz had stayed. The house had two small beds, a table, and plenty of food — cheese, bread, and dried meats. Despite the strength she drew from the brastilia ore embedded in the mountainside beneath her feet, she nearly ate herself sick that first afternoon.

Most of the time, Zandia listened for the Enforcers who might have been alerted by Nin'Kindo or may have become curious through a lack of communication. The rest of the time, she cared for Kisthana. She set the woman's broken arm and wrapped her fractured ribs with cloth cut from extra clothes from Zortranc's things. But the Priestess did not improve; she drank and ate a little, but each breath was labored, and sleep came in short bursts due to the intense pain. One of Zortranc's vicious kicks must have ruptured something inside.

With her second sight, Zandia could see the orange of the woman, varying in color throughout her body, though she did not know what the shading or the color changes meant. There was a dark red dot in her stomach, but Zandia didn't know if that was normal or not; she'd used the second sight to hunt and protect herself, not to diagnose the wounded.

During one of Kisthana's frequent sleeps, Zandia went to a nearby stream to wash out her own vile clothing and to clean the wound on the back of her head. She felt the congealed blood. A scar had already formed there, her blessed body working to erase the effects of Zortranc's blow. Unfortunately, Kisthana was not blessed with a body like Zandia's; the Priestess could not heal herself.

On the third night, Zandia sat in the darkness, her clothes finally dry and Kisthana asleep. In the last few hours, the Priestess had begun a sudden burning fever, her skin almost as ashen as Zandia's. Perspiration soaked through her clothes, and in the chilly mountain air, Zandia feared the woman might catch her death.

I need you here, Zandia thought toward Mayfran, having reconnected with him shortly after she'd killed her father.

A storm has slowed our ascent on the mountain road, he replied. *We'll be there by dawn.*

Zandia glanced through the window at the three moons. Circlarl waxed, Dithdee waned, and the Fire Moon hung nearly full. Judging by their places in the sky, it would be four to five hours before the sun rose over the mountains in the east.

She hadn't slept since the aborted ceremony; she couldn't afford to be taken unawares. Despite her new strength, Zandia did not like her chances against the small army they would likely send against her.

A small sound broke her thoughts. Three hours until sunrise, so it wasn't Mayfran or his friends. Someone was coming.

Zandia slipped from the small shepherd's house to crouch behind a small tree. Through the second sight, she saw three men approaching from behind the house, one armed with the green glow of a brastilia bow and brastilia arrows. The other two wielded hatrindi. The two sword-bearing Enforcers approached, while the archer circled the house, looking for a good place to provide cover.

Zandia circled farther around; she had to get the archer first. She walked along the stream, using her senses to guide her through the darkness. The second sight helped her track the moving archer, and her ears provided direction with the breeze breaking around trees. She caught the scent of the Enforcer, the smell of a man who hadn't bathed in weeks. Enforcers could be so sloppy.

Once she was behind him, he stopped, arrow drawn. He'd probably mindspoken with his associates, whose orange shapes approached the small house. She would need to do this quickly.

Her bare feet stepped lightly, silently on the soft ground as she came up behind the dark-clad Enforcer. She didn't need her hatnuthri, so she kept them sheathed. She gripped the Enforcer's head from behind and turned it with one swift motion. His neck snapped, and she caught him before he dropped to the ground. Zandia laid him down softly, picking up his bow and two arrows.

He had chosen a perfect spot to provide cover for his comrades or to kill them. Zandia took her up the bow and took aim.

She aimed with her second sight, sending an arrow through one man's chest; the green of the brastilia merged with, then stopped in the darker orange of his torso, and he fell a heartbeat later, dead or close to it. The second Enforcer made to move behind the house, but Zandia let a second arrow fly, which hit him in the shoulder.

Zandia pulled the bow over her chest and sprinted toward the wounded but still standing second Enforcer. She reached him, her eyes open to fight using the moonlight. He swung weakly, but she dodged, then kicked his knee. With a sharp crack, it buckled. She spun and kicked the other knee, getting similar results. The Enforcer slumped to the ground onto his side. Zandia hadn't even taken out her own weapons.

"Are there more of you?" Zandia growled.

"Rot on the Fire Moon," the Enforcer said.

She grabbed the arrow, twisted it, and the Enforcer cried out in pain. "How many more of you? I won't ask again."

"One more, he's a—"

Before he finished his sentence, Zandia heard an arrow loosed in the forest behind her. She moved to dodge, but too late, and she felt the metal's pierce before she saw it. The arrow had penetrated her shoulder, coming out the other side.

She ducked behind the house, putting it between her and where the arrow had come from. Again came the twang of the bow, and this time the arrow went through the forehead of the second Enforcer.

She looked down at the arrow sticking out through her shoulder: metal, not brastilia. She peered around the corner with her second sight, seeing nothing glowing green or orange in the forest beyond except for a couple of nocturnal animals, small and scurrying away. Whoever was out there was invisible to her second sight. Zandia had never heard of such a thing. Was whatever lurked in the woods hunting her, her attackers, or both?

The barely audible steps of her pursuer or pursuers broke softly from the woods. He was circling her, readying another shot. Zandia slipped into the house, closing the door behind her. Once inside, she broke off the arrow tip and pulled it back through her shoulder. Blood poured from her wound, but she ignored it.

That shot had almost killed her; had she not heard the arrow loosed and dodged, the aim would have found its mark: her throat. A shoulder wound was not great — it would make using her left hand in a fight that much harder — but she would live. She briefly checked on Kisthana, whose shallow breaths continued but had become less strained and less frequent. In the second sight, the red spot in her belly area had increased. Zandia shook her head; she assumed that was bad, though she couldn't know for sure.

For the next several hours, nothing happened. Zandia sat tensely, out of view of the windows, not giving the enemy archer a shot at her. She'd thought of pulling Kisthana down onto the floor with her, but the attacker hadn't taken a shot at the Priestess. Zandia could not risk leaving Kisthana alone, so she would wait it out, at least until sunrise.

We're close, came Mayfran's voice, and Zandia could not have been happier with the mental intrusion.

Be careful, she replied. *An archer was in the woods. Shot me clean through the shoulder. I'm all right, but he might still be out there. I think he's High Trade; made two unbelievable shots in the dark.*

We'll spread out and circle in toward you. If he's still out there, I'll stick him myself.

Zandia relaxed her muscles and her mind, even though the danger might not have been past. For weeks, she'd felt nothing but constant tension, and her body pled for relief. Even Baldra had their limits, and she feared she'd nearly reached hers.

We found no one, Mayfran said some time later, his voice breaking her meditative state. *Must be gone. I'm letting you know that two of us are coming into the house, so don't gut us.*

Zandia stood and stepped away from the door as Mayfran walked in, followed by an older woman.

Zandia did not hesitate, coming to him in an embrace.

You came for me, she said, continuing mindspeak.

"I told you I would," he spoke aloud. "How's the Priestess?"

Zandia pulled away. "Not good. Internal injuries, maybe. She took a severe beating from Zortranc."

"What happened to your father?" Mayfran asked.

Zandia hesitated. Would he think less of her if he knew she'd beheaded her own father? Would it prove her to be the monster so many feared? Unlike most of her kills, this one had neither been compelled nor necessary to defend her life or anyone else's.

"I killed him," she finally said, her voice lacking the confused, swirling emotions moving within her.

Mayfran nodded. His face lacked any judgment, and she felt none through their bond.

The older woman knelt next to Kisthana's cot and began to examine her. After a couple minutes, the woman stood and spoke to

Mayfran. "I don't think she'll make it. She's burning up, likely from an infection."

"It's in her stomach," Zandia said. "I could see something strange in her belly."

The woman looked at Zandia and nodded. "That makes sense. If her attacker struck hard enough, it might have ruptured an organ. There's little I can do for her. And we'd need to carry her through some tough country."

The woman healer's stark words pulled Zandia's stare to the Priestess. A layer of sweat covered Kisthana's forehead and drenched her hair to the point that it looked like she'd just taken a bath. But her face was peaceful, not contorted in pain as it had been the past few days.

If Kisthana died, Zandia's hope for someday rescuing Nin'Kindo would go with her.

"Thank you," Mayfran replied to the woman. "Leave us."

The woman nodded again, then stepped out into the early morning.

"I can't go back to the Kuthraz." Zandia knew the timing of the words wasn't right, but they'd formed anyway.

"I know." Mayfran frowned, face heavy with sadness. "Neither can I."

"What?" Zandia couldn't believe his words.

"I might have been right about some things regarding you," he said, a smile returning to his eyes, "but you were right about something else: Loothdram has lost sight of a great many things. He's using people, putting innocents in harm's way. The clean line I used to see between us, the Empire, and the Dundraz has blurred to the point that. . ." He paused, his eyes sad and his face drawn down. "I'm not sure what's best for the Peaks anymore. I'm not sure there's anyone who will do the right thing."

Kisthana's cough interrupted their conversation, and the woman's eyes opened, though her lids drooped as she fought unconsciousness.

"Zandia," she said, voice cracking with dryness and fatigue.

The Baldra knelt by her bed. "Yes, Priestess?"

"Watch over Mairie." Her voice cracked on her daughter's name, and she took several moments to calm herself before she spoke again. "The Empire, the Kuthraz — they would use her. Tell her that I love her. Tell her I'm sorry. Tell her . . ." Her voice faded, and her eyes shut. A few minutes later, her shallow breathing stopped.

"She sacrificed herself for me." Zandia stood, imprinting the memory of Kisthana's peaceful face into her mind. "Mairie deserved a mother, deserves a life."

"So do you." Mayfran spoke over her objection. "With Kisthana's final pleading, I know you think you need to watch over Mairie like a hen over a hatchling. But that is not your duty. Mairie is a grown woman, and she'll forge her own path."

Zandia lowered her head, praying silently that the gods would show Kisthana mercy, and that the Priestess would be taken into Circlarl on a chariot of light. She hadn't uttered a prayer in decades, but it felt right in that moment, and it brought a sliver of peace to her tortured soul.

"We should be going," Mayfran said. "They will likely have reinforcements."

"Where to?" Zandia asked. For the first time in nearly twenty years, the question would not end in compulsion or a desire to kill her father.

"Corbay," Mayfran said. "Your brother is taking his wife there. They freed Calla."

At the news, Zandia's heavy heart lifted some, but it fell just as quickly as she considered their daughters.

"Do they know about the girls?"

"I don't know," he said. "And I think we should be the ones to tell them."

"I could tell Zornan now; I could reach out to him."

"As you wish."

Zandia reached out, feeling for her brother's mind. *Zornan, I have something I need to tell you.*

I know. I know about the girls. Trillia took them. His reply stunned her. *How?*

I'll explain when we see each other. It's a complicated story.

I'm so sorry, Zor. I failed you. I failed the girls, I—

No. His strong response stopped her apology, his words like a storm off the ocean. *Trillia did this. I trusted her, told you to trust her. I wish you'd told me, but this is not your fault. But no more secrets, Zandia. You may be the only person left in this wind-blasted Empire I can trust.* Deep sadness seeped through the bond, deeper than anything she'd ever felt from her brother.

No more secrets, she repeated. She wanted to say more, though she didn't know what to say.

I love you, sister.

The words broke her, and she sobbed. Mayfran caught her before she slumped to her knees.

I love you, brother.

Mayfran held her as she cried.

"We should go," she said, wiping away tears and standing straight.

"We should have the healer—"

"I'm Baldra, Mayfran. Maybe no longer in purpose, but I am in form. I will heal. Trillia, when I find her . . . she won't heal from what I will inflict upon her."

"No," he said, "I don't think she will."

EPILOGUE

Dagger crouched on a city wall watching the sleeping capital of the Empire of the Peaks. It was technically a three-moon night, but the white moon was a small crescent, though its light still eclipsed its younger cousins. The strange natives of this land, like some of the Croxshinese she'd met, worshiped the moons. What a silly superstition. Those three cousins were dead gods, killed for treachery against their grandmother. Every child in Dagger's native Boothdrinka knew the tale. Why worship the discarded bodies of dead gods?

Dagger's current mission was simple: watch the movements of the soldiers patrolling Bristrinia and determine patterns. Trillia wanted to ensure that all eyes were pointed away toward the rebels across the plains and not toward the real threat. Chaos reigned in the Empire of the Peaks — all the better for Nansart and His believers.

Others might have been bored by this assignment, but not Dagger. She'd spent hours as a child, crouched much like she was now, weaving small baskets her family used to pick strawberries. Her extended family had worked those fields for generations, harvesting seven or eight crops a year. Those had been the happy times, before the elders had torn everything apart.

Any movement? Trillia's voice came into Dagger's mind, interrupting her memories.

None, Most Honored One. The garrison is quiet for the first night in weeks. And the patrols walk the walls and watch north. They suspect no threat from the ocean.

Good. Trillia's glee matched Dagger's own. The time was coming, just as it had in Boothdrinka, just as it had in Croxshine. Nansart was coming tonight if the will of the Grandmother saw fit to allow it.

You should meet us at the docks, Trillia continued. *You should witness our master arrive.*

Dagger fought down the urge to shout with joy. She'd not seen His first entry into her native Boothdrinka, and she'd been in the forward force in Croxshine, so she'd missed His first steps on that subjugated land as well. But tonight she'd witness history, witness the new God come to bring order to this corner of His world.

I am not worthy of such an honor, Dagger replied. *Nansart's feet and my own should never tread the same ground.*

Stop with the theatrics, Trillia chided. *Don't miss history because of overdeveloped awe.*

Dagger did not say so, but she wondered sometimes if Trillia had enough respect for Nansart. She often called Him "a god" and not "the God." The difference was significant. Didn't God require theatrics? How else did one honor God if not through showing his superiority to all others who walked the skin of the world? No, if anything, Dagger needed to revere him more.

I am coming, Trillia, fellow servant, second only to God.

Annoyance flowed from Trillia to Dagger through their mindspeak bond, but Dagger brushed the other woman's emotions away. Even those touched by Nansart's grace needed more seasoning.

She climbed down the city wall like a cat down a trellis. Her dark clothing made it unlikely that she'd be seen by the soldiers patrolling the city. Night patrols had become common since the unbelieving rebels had assassinated their unbelieving emperor. But dodging them was easier than skipping through a berry patch; the unbelievers all wore brastilia weapons, which Dagger could sense from a mile away, and they were all so noisy with clanking armor, loud breaths and stinky bodies. Dagger had not enjoyed her time in Croxshine, with the terrible food devoid of flavor and people who were too pleasant to be trusted. But at least the Croxshinese bathed each day. These unbelievers thought it proper to bathe just once a week. Yes, proper for a cow maybe, but not for a person.

Dagger tried to suppress her excitement as she wove through the city streets, but she could not. She'd met Him twice, yes, but both times had been too brief. First, she'd seen Him on her blessing day. She'd been blessed by another, but as she awoke, Dagger's eyes had fallen on her new God. Then, after the battle to take the Croxshinese capital of Jigraile, she'd received praise, by name, from His holy lips. He'd commended her efforts in assassinating the king and the entire royal bloodline. The euphoria of the moment still fueled her.

She wished she'd seen him take Boothdrinka, but she'd been a housewife then, weaving baskets for her idiot cousin, the marriage mandated by tradition after the death of her mother, father and brothers. Her husband had enlisted to serve the army of the elders, to defend Boothdrinka against Nansart. But they had been ants standing in front of a tidal flood, swept away by the new God. When the call had come to serve Him, Dagger knew she would go. What was left for her? The elders had destroyed everything, stolen everything. Whatever force had vanquished those villains deserved her allegiance.

The familiar scent of the ocean told her she was close. And then, in the moonlight, she saw Trillia standing out on a pier with two others, watching the dark ocean. Praise the Mother, Nansart came!

She stopped being as silent, walking normally down the dock to the three figures bathed in moonlight. Two dark figures flanked Trillia, both of their smells familiar to Dagger's senses. The first was Cradris, another servant of Nansart who refused to bathe regularly. Whenever she was around him, she had to fight to keep her face from scrunching in disgust. Everything about the man seemed greasy, as if he could never rid his skin, hair and soul of the dirt he apparently found more appealing than cleanliness.

The other was her fellow Destoyer, another woman, a Croxshinese. She wore similar clothes to Dagger: loose pants, a tight tunic, all dark, all designed to blend into the night. The other Destroyer's dark hair was long, cascading in curling waves around her shoulders. Even in the dark, Dagger could see the twin scars crossing her blessing-sister's face. Despite those scars, or maybe because of those scars, Dagger found Burn to be beautiful.

Welcome, blessing-sister, Burn spoke into Dagger's mind. *You are here for this glorious occasion. I am glad. I have missed you.*

I have missed you as well, Dagger said. *I am glad to share this with you. I wish we didn't have to share it with the stinky one.*

Burn's amusement flickered through their connection. Burn shared Dagger's disgust for the unwashed. *Nansart bathes. Maybe Cradris will learn that. If not, maybe you and I will have to take him to a river and do it ourselves.*

Dagger stifled a laugh as she sidled up next to Trillia. Dagger guarded her emotions closely. Cradris was a talented Investigator, and she did not need their mocking amusement to reach his sensitive emotional sense.

Trillia acknowledged Dagger with a glance and a nearly imperceptible nod.

If Nansart was God, what was Trillia? His messenger? His avenging angel? Nansart could bless others with great power, could use all the powers himself, and He could fight like no one Dagger had ever heard of. His efforts in Boothdrinka were already legend. A lone figure, fighting the thousand chosen, ripping them apart, and then killing all seventeen elders with his bare hands. Dagger had heard an account from a fellow servant who'd seen most of the battle with his own eyes. Nansart was power.

But Trillia could do nearly everything Nansart could do, only less so. She blessed, she used the magic, and Dagger had heard stories that she was one of the fiercest fighters the Grandmother had ever sired. So, if Nansart was God, did that make Trillia a god?

A distant sound reached Dagger's blessed ears — a boat cutting through the water, the rhythm of oars pushing it along. The sound soon matched an image of shadow, a small boat moving toward them. Though the vessel was not small, the god standing inside of it made it look so. His gray skin reflected the light of the three moons: white, orange and blue. He wore nothing but a loin cloth. Here He was, making His triumphant entry into His new land. The last kingdom of men, soon to become the home of God.

Praise the Grandmother, Nansart had come to the Empire of the Peaks!

* * *

Sign-up for Adam J. Mangum's mailing list to get updates and free stories!

ACKNOWLEDGMENTS

First and foremost, I must recognize my wife, Kathleen. Despite not breaking out as a big success, she continues to support my dream of being a writer. I can't thank her enough for that. Don't tell her, but she's my muse.

Second, I wanted to thank all the readers who took the time to provide valuable feedback on this series and this book in particular. So thank you Marise Borja, Tiffany Lewis, Jenny Reinsel, Alan Seawright, Melissa van der Werf and Catherine White.

A book is not really created solely by the author, as others play a key role in the process. I worked with two editors on this project, Kimberly Grenfell and EditorNancy/Fiverr.com. Both made the book better, not just in grammar and the like, but in the story and how I told it. The great illustrated book cover was designed by VividCovers.com.

Made in the USA
Middletown, DE
20 October 2022

13139138R00154